Mack Bolan wasn't a tool of U.S. international policy

He was driven by the need to protect the victims of corruption and terrorism. Husbands, fathers, brothers and sons were executed brutally, while wives, mothers, sisters and daughters were raped and mutilated by Janjaweed forces.

The Darfur crisis, and the Rwandan slaughter a decade before, were symptomatic of an international apathy in regard to Africa. Its jungles and deserts, once colonial prizes of European governments, were considered lost causes, realms where white people had no business interfering.

Skin color didn't enter into the Executioner's equation of justice. The Thunder Lions were about to make the Darfur crisis even worse, which elevated them to the top of Bolan's priority list—for a bullet.

Don Pendleton's Mack Bolan.

Plains of Fire

A GOLD EAGLE BOOK FROM

WORLDWIDE.

TORONTO • NEW YORK • LONDON
AMSTERDAM • PARIS • SYDNEY • HAMBURG
STOCKHOLM • ATHENS • TOKYO • MILAN
MADRID • WARSAW • BUDAPEST • AUCKLAND

First edition November 2008

ISBN-13: 978-0-373-61526-1
ISBN-10:   0-373-61526-4

Special thanks and acknowledgment to
Douglas P. Wojtowicz for his contribution to this work.

PLAINS OF FIRE

Printed in U.S.A.

Be sober, be vigilant; because your adversary
the devil, as a roaring lion, walketh about,
seeking whom he may devour.

—*1 Peter* 5:8

Human predators abound, preying on the weak, the
helpless. These lions do not need taming. They
need to be put down.

—Mack Bolan

To those who have made a stand and refuse to let the world ignore the horrors at work in Darfur.

CHAPTER ONE

Darfur, Sudan

General Thormun "Thor" Bitturumba watched with approval as his artillery crews screwed the canister warheads onto the 240 mm rockets. The fat tubes, nearly ten inches thick, each held a concentrated mixture of biological weaponry in an inert suspension. The suspension had a vaporization point that was well over fifty degrees Fahrenheit. In the blazing African afternoon, the carrier fluid would evaporate swiftly, assisted in its dispersal by a low-temperature, high-velocity explosion designed to hurl the weaponized microbes into the air.

The viruses had toughened cellular membranes, enabling them to survive as their long cilia spread out to catch air currents and ride the wind.

Bitturumba's satellite phone rang. He knew who it was.

"How goes the preparations, Thor?" Alonzo Cruz asked. Bitturumba smirked. Here he was, speaking with one of Spain's most prominent businessmen, on the eve of a biological weapons test, seemingly as a gigantic spit in the face to the world. Certainly, the general realized, the multimillionaire's sat phone had incredible encryption protection, much like his own phone. But the call, only hours before a preview of hell on Earth, would have been detected despite its indecipherable nature.

"They're going well, Lonzo," Bitturumba answered. "The hammer will fall at dawn."

"No need to be cryptic, brother," Cruz replied, the quality of the digital signal so clear and free of static that it was as if the man were right next to the African. "No one could break this call down."

"Never say never, Lonzo," Bitturumba admonished. "Just when we think that our keenest laid plans are going to go one way, reality takes over."

Cruz chuckled. "The cunning animal wisdom of a warrior."

Bitturumba sighed. "One does not rise to the rank of general without being absolutely prepared for the worst. Idi Amin was an optimist when it came to attempts on his life."

Bitturumba's hand absently dropped to the .50-caliber Desert Eagle on his hip. Though most experts declined to recommend the massive Israeli-designed hand-howitzer for self-defense due to its need for perfectly tailored ammunition, Bitturumba was careful in his feeding of the Desert Eagle. Its reliability and power had protected the general's life on numerous occasions, tearing through the body armor of assassins and even shattering the thick, armored skull of an enraged bull charging at him. In no instance had the thunder pistol ever failed him. Given that his half brother, Cruz, always called him Thor, after the Norse god of thunder, the big .50 was a welcome companion.

Bitturumba had been deemed the African god of war by many in the press, and his army had been given the nickname "Thunder Lions." The roar of launching rockets and the thunder of 105 mm shells were his militia's heralds on the field of battle.

"Just remember not to get caught downwind of your barrage," Cruz warned. "I'd hate to lose blood just to run a quick test."

"Fear not, little brother. We are prepared," Bitturumba replied.

The phone call ended and Bitturumba raised the binoculars to his eyes once more, scanning the refugee camp in the distance. It had been established and was currently under the protection of members of the Ethiopian Expeditionary Force, a trained army of African veterans who had been subjected to enough of the horror stories emanating from Sudan. They had come in hard and fast, putting the Janjaweed forces on the defensive. Only Bitturumba's army had been unfazed by the Ethiopian interference, but that was because Bitturumba had the same intensive military education that the EEF's leader possessed. Both men were students of war, and theirs wasn't a brutal slugfest as much as a show of jabs and feints as both armies looked for weaknesses in each other's defenses.

Bitturumba's wide lips turned up in a cruel smile. This would be the first shot that he'd launched that would bring the Ethiopian forces to their senses.

THE DISTANT SOUND of launching rockets sounded like a warthog clearing its nostrils, at least to Lieutenant Alem Tanku of the Ethiopian Expeditionary Force. The Avtomat Kalashnikov rifle that had been resting across his knees was instantly in his hands, and he jerked to his feet. On the horizon he could see the white yarns of exhaust smoke trailing from the thrust nozzles of a half-dozen rockets and he stuck his fingers into the corners of his mouth to amplify his whistle.

The shrill bleat woke the other sleepy Ethiopian troops on his side of the camp, and they began rushing along the shanty homes, rapping doors or rickety walls to awaken Sudanese refugees.

Tanku squinted as the contrails of the artillery rockets snaked across the sky. He didn't put it past the Thunder Lions to launch a quick reconnaissance by fire with a long-distance salvo. He was halfway to the communications shed when the rockets reached the apex of their climb. Losing power, they began their descent, gravity proving stronger than burned-out chemical motors. The contrails bent sharply as the remnants of their fuel gave out, smearing flat black streaks across the graying dawn.

"Artillery launch from Thunder Lions' recon force," Tanku shouted as he reached the entrance of the communication shed.

The comm operator, Lieutenant Jolu Okuba, nodded, already rattling off the information.

"Launch coordinates?" Okuba relayed from headquarters.

"Six miles out," Tanku said, eyeballing the end of the puffy dissipating arch of smoke. "Northwest, call it heading 310."

Okuba barked the information to the Ethiopian Expeditionary Force command. He glanced nervously back toward Tanku. "The evacuation?"

"We're rousing the civilians. Luckily, they're early

risers," Tanku said. "This section of the camp is already filing out through the fence."

Okuba nodded. Tanku could tell that his fellow soldier wanted to bolt from his position, but his duty kept him on station. It wouldn't be much of a consolation when nearly ten inches of enemy warhead dropped out of the sky, delivering the punch of dozens of kilograms of high explosives. The lieutenant looked toward the descending rockets when he saw one burst into a blossom of smoky tentacles that stretched across the sky over the refugee camp.

"Gas attack!" Tanku bellowed at the top of his lungs. "Gas masks!"

Okuba whirled back to the microphone, updating the EEF's officers about the changing nature of the rocket assault. Other rockets began detonating as they dropped within a certain height, splitting the air with sharp cracks that were unnervingly devoid of the light of flame.

That was the surest indication on Tanku's part that they were dealing with some form of chemical assault. The Ethiopian's face twisted into a rictus of anger as he glanced toward Okuba.

"Put your gas mask on!" Tanku snapped.

"You don't have one!" Okuba replied. "They don't have masks outside!"

"Just do it!" Tanku ordered.

Okuba did so. His gas mask was in the bottom drawer of his desk.

Tanku cursed himself for not bringing his mask with him, but he knew that none of the refugees would have more than a wet towel to protect their lungs from whichever chemical scourge Bitturumba's Thunder Lions were dropping on their heads.

With the introduction of weapons of mass destruction, Tanku idly wondered if there was a possibility that the United States would take a more urgent role in the Sudanese conflict. After all, it was the fear of Muslims with chemical weaponry that started the Iraq war, and that had been spurned by far less spurious evidence than an actual chemical attack such as here.

Tanku steeled himself, waiting for the first symptoms of poison or nerve agent to appear. There wasn't even the scent of burned almonds, indicative of cyanide gas, in the air. He knew that nerve agents were odorless and flavorless, but once they touched him, he would begin twitching uncontrollably, frothing at the mouth as he felt his insides liquefy. Unfortunately, a quick glance to Okuba reminded him that the gas masks the Ethiopians wore were thin, almost useless protection against the horrors of weapons like Sarin or Tabur.

He waited for a full minute, breathing shallowly, as if the lowered respiration would somehow protect him from the ravages of chemical weapons that could be absorbed through the skin. He looked at his deep dark forearms, imagining the colorful globules of nerve agent molecules drifting and wafting down to his skin, turning his nearly black forearms gray and diseased as they landed, penetrating living flesh to invade his bloodstream.

"Alem?" Okuba asked, his voice muffled by the gas mask.

"Keep it on," Tanku grated. His shoulders were knotted so tight that he thought that his tensed muscles would snap his clavicle like a twig.

"I don't think anything was released into the air," Okuba stated. "There isn't any reaction anywhere in the camp."

Tanku glanced around. His fellow Ethiopian soldiers were radioing in and he could hear their voices over Okuba's radio. They were reporting a complete lack of casualties.

"I don't even see any harm from shrapnel released by the air-bursting rockets," one EEF trooper announced.

Tanku's shoulders loosened and he took a deep breath, releasing it in a sigh of relief.

"Maybe they wanted to show us that they had the means to release bio or chem agents into the air," Okuba noted, pulling off his mask. "To let us know that we don't have anything to stop them."

"You think they'd really bring down the ire of the Americans?" Tanku asked. "Saddam had a chemical weapons program, at least before he shipped it off to Syria before the invasion."

Okuba shook his head. "Iraq is full of oil. This is the Sudan. What would the Americans care about here?"

"So Bitturumba isn't the least bit concerned that he's opened a can of worms," Tanku grumbled.

"We're on our own. I can't think of a single white man who would come over here, roll up his sleeves and fight for us," Okuba growled.

ALEM TANKU DIDN'T FEEL a thing. He remained healthy and unaffected, even as every one of his breaths sucked down dozens of airborne viral spores, parachuting gently to ground level on their long, slender cilia. The viral organisms rode the wind and found a welcome home in the bronchial sacs lining the Ethiopian's lungs. Billions of their brethren were finding root in the respiratory systems of hundreds of EEF soldiers and Sudanese refugees.

Once the instantaneous effects of poison gas and

nerve agents seemed missing from the aerial bombardment equation, the sighs of relief only served to make it easier for the Ebola mutations to ride currents into warm places where they could latch on to permeable cells and begin to feed. Within an hour, fully gorged on genetic material, the virus spores began to propagate, multiplying. One cell became two, which then became four. Some of the newly birthed spores spread their cilia and were blown out, exhaled into the world. Normally, the hemorrhagic fever spores would have been in the bloodstream and sputum of a larger organism, such as a tick, mosquito or the mammals they fed upon. These spores, however, had been redesigned. Their viral cellular membranes were thicker, allowing them to survive outside a liquid suspension. They no longer required transfer via the mixing of bodily fluids, as when a lesser animal would bite a human.

They could take to the air, riding the exhalations of the hosts where they first bred.

That's how Tanku infected Okuba as they clinked their metal coffee cups in a toast to surviving a supposedly inept assault by Bitturumba.

It was only after Tanku began running a fever that the sighs of relief were suspected to be death sentences. His stomach felt as if a brick had been laid inside of it, and any thought of lunch and dinner repulsed him. Half of the refugee camp had assembled for lunch, but only a few people were willing to sit for dinner, possessing an appetite. Tanku's limbs and muscles were knotted again, but this time involuntarily. Aches ripped through his frame.

An hour after sunset, when Alem Tanku was convulsing and trembling, tears of blood rolling down his cheeks, rivulets of crimson mixed in with the mucus pouring from his nose, the first of the EEF medics developed a fever. Those who hadn't worn simple paper masks when dealing with the victims of the hemorrhagic fever outbreak were coming down with symptoms their patients had reported much earlier. Those medical personnel who operated under infectious disease precautions were unharmed.

At dawn, the viral spores had turned Tanku's lesser blood vessels, the fine, slender capillaries, into sieves. His tears and his sweat were crimson, filled with ruptured red cells, no longer capable of transporting oxygen to the rest of his body.

By noon, Tanku was the first to die from what the Ethiopian Expeditionary Force had named Ebola Thunder, in honor of the madman who had unleashed it upon the world.

Unfortunately he wasn't the last, as in the next second a dozen refugees vomited the bloody slush that used to be their lungs and expired, as well.

By evening, thirteen hundred corpses were being shoveled into the bottom of a grave dug up by bulldozers. The World Health Organization resources sent to respond to an unprecedented outbreak of a new form of Ebola arrived just in time to see all but a handful of bodies turned to ash by concentrated streams of burning gasoline.

It was a preview of hell, Tanya Marshall thought. She took pictures of the carnage, documenting the destruction of the infected victim bodies in the pit.

CHAPTER TWO

Alexandria, Egypt

The three men moved quietly across the Egyptian docks, night enveloping them in a cloak of darkness that aided their stealthy approach. Rumor and gossip had brought the trio to this outlet on the Mediterranean Sea, clad in combat blacksuits and armed to the teeth.

When Mack Bolan contacted Stony Man Farm for help, the men of Phoenix Force usually stepped forward. But in this case only Rafael Encizo and Calvin James answered the call. David McCarter, Gary Manning and T.J. Hawkins had sustained various gunshot wounds, pulled muscles and ankle fractures that kept them anchored in the Blue Ridge Mountain headquarters.

James and Encizo had lost sight of Bolan, but they had no worries about the man known as the Executioner. Though more than six feet tall and carrying two hundred pounds of lean, well-honed muscle, Bolan was one of the stealthiest human beings on the planet. Moving with the sure-footed stride of a stalking panther, the

Executioner was the embodiment of a ghost, flitting between shadows in the blink of an eye while creating no more sound than an errant breeze.

This night's probe was tracing a cache of Cold War–era biological delivery systems—germ warfare shells—to Alexandria. The shells were being delivered by the Russian *mafiya,* and all indications from Bolan's investigation led him to believe that they were earmarked for use in the Darfur ethnic cleansing sessions. Bolan had been intending to make his presence known in the region, to bring down the horde of madmen who engaged in wanton murder and almost ritualistic rape to destroy the non-Muslim population sharing western Sudan. The State Department across multiple presidential administrations had been handicapped by a desire not to offend Islamic governments by interfering with the Sudanese government.

Mack Bolan, however, wasn't a tool of U.S. international policy. He was driven by the need to protect the victims of corruption and terrorism. Husbands, fathers, brothers and sons were executed brutally, while wives, mothers, sisters and daughters were raped and mutilated by the Janjaweed forces. The Darfur crisis, and the Rwandan slaughter a decade before, were symptomatic of an international apathy in regard to Africa. The jungles and deserts of the continent, once Colonial prizes of the European governments, were considered lost causes, a realm where white people had no business interfering. Bolan's brow furrowed at the thought.

Skin color didn't enter into the Executioner's equations of justice. What did come to mind was the fact that Europeans had run roughshod across Africa, creating a powder keg. After stripping whatever resources they

could, they left disenfranchised millions behind without a workable governmental infrastructure. The jackals who did move in took their lesson plans from their
predecessors and fostered a culture of corruption and tribal retribution that helped them keep their wallets fat
and their enemies cowering in fear. As long as ancient
tribal feuds raged, no one would be able to accumulate
enough power to unseat their corrupt rulership.

It would require an outside force to even the odds,
and the Executioner and his allies were that outside
interference. The fact that the Thunder Lions were the
militia acquiring the lethal weapon systems put the Darfur crisis right at the top of Bolan's priorities.

Mack Bolan was just one man and he did what he
could. And when he set his mind to a task, few things
could deter him. However, a sentry on patrol was about
to notice that his partners, Encizo and James, were preparing to slip into the water from the end of the dock.
The guard was a hardened warrior, moving with precision, his mind focused on systematic scanning of the
pier. It would only be a matter of moments before he
saw the Phoenix pair as they took to the water on their
mission of sabotage.

Bolan stalked the Russian ex-special forces man
walking patrol. He recognized the man's Spetznaz pedi-
gree, having encountered hundreds of them before. His
disciplined military bearing, Slavic features and the
scent of cheap Turkish tobacco that the Russian commandos seemed addicted to were unmistakable in combination. Add in the fact that the black-market weapons
were on a Russian ship, owned by the *mafiya,* and it was
plain to Bolan that the man was a trained commando.
The muzzle of his rifle was held at waist level, finger

off the trigger, but resting against the guard, ready to snap down and rip off a burst of autofire with a reflexive action.

The Executioner knew that it would only be a moment before the ex-military mob enforcer noticed the presence of his partners, or feel that Bolan was on his trail. Without a moment's hesitation, the Executioner rose from the shadows. One of his hands clamped over the Russian's mouth, while the other speared a hard-knuckled fist deep into the base of his adversary's skull. The punch connected with the knot of neurons where the spine met the brain, causing an overload that paralyzed the patrolling sentry. With a savage jerk, Bolan yanked his insensate opponent back into the shadows, his arm snaking under the stunned Russian's chin. He flexed both of his arms, and with the power of a full-grown python, he broke the unconscious man's neck. The moment the sentry would have recovered a fraction of his senses, he would have mustered the strength to pull the trigger on his rifle, alerting the rest of his allies. Given that the guard was ex-military and working for organized crime, Bolan could live with the fact that he most likely had sent a murderer to justice.

A quick glance around the dock told him that the rest of the Russians on the outlaw freighter hadn't noticed their guard disappear. Moving swiftly, Bolan peeled the corpse out of its jacket, then the red-and-white-striped sailor shirt, pulling them both on. He'd used a small utility knife to cut slashes in the side of the dead man's T-shirt to allow himself access to his battle harness and shoulder-holstered Beretta, while still concealing his blacksuit and war load from casual inspection. He tucked the Russian's cell phone and hand radio into his jacket pocket.

"Took out the snooper, continuing his patrol pattern," Bolan said softly into his throat mike as he stepped out onto the dock.

There was the sound of two clicks, Encizo and James responding nonverbally to his transmission. The two men were underwater now and wouldn't have seen Bolan take down the sentry and appropriate his clothing. They pressed the transmit buttons on their radios, the only way they could communicate with him while just below the waves, breathing through snorkels. Secure in the knowledge that his allies wouldn't mistakenly target him, Bolan followed the guard's regularly scheduled route.

"Guys," a voice called over the radio in Russian. "Pull back in. We have the headlight signal."

"Affirmative," Bolan grunted in Russian, keeping his voice low. The Executioner made an about-face and returned to the freighter. Riflemen were posted on the railing, but their attention was on the burning pairs of headlights rolling down the back streets. In the shadowy light of the dock, neither of the sentries would have been able to see each other, which was an advantage. The men on the pier would be hard to target by any incoming force. The lack of light was no disadvantage to a Spetznaz commando.

Bolan could see the shadowy outline of the other Russian who had been patrolling the pier. He bracketed the other side of the gangplank, his eyes fixed on the newcomers.

"Anatoly," the man whispered, "I heard that the stupid bastards used some of our shells last night."

Bolan shrugged.

"I don't like it," the guard continued. "If we get

caught with the rest of their shipment in our hold, we'll bring down a shit storm."

Bolan nodded.

The Thunder Lion convoy rolled to a halt, its headlights off. Bolan counted six vehicles, four of them SUVs, two of them two-and-a-half-ton trucks, which were workhorses and more than capable of carting off enough bioartillery to render Central Africa a lifeless wasteland. The members of the Thunder Lion crew were all tall, strong men with black skin and grim expressions. They assembled in front of their vehicles, all of them packing high-tech French FAMAS rifles.

One man stepped forward. If the clusters of medals on his left breast hadn't set him apart from the rest of his crew, the broad smile on his lips did. Bolan searched his mental mug book, comparing the African to known members of the Thunder Lion hierarchy, finally deciding that the commander was Major Antoine Bashir. The major had a particularly notorious reputation, having started his career as the chief muscle for a Corsican arms dealer.

That explained the presence of French rifles and sidearms. A quick examination of the SUVs in the darkness reinforced the link between the Thunder Lions and the Union Corse. The four off-road vehicles were top-of-the-line Peugeot designs. They sat low on their wheelbases, betraying their armored status, meaning they'd "fallen off a shipment" meant for the French military.

"Cheer up, lads," Bashir said, clapping Bolan on the shoulder. "You'll be back floating to the Baltic, rotting your guts out on vodka before dawn."

Bolan held his tongue, keeping an eye on the militiamen spread out in front of him. All it would take

would be a step back and he'd fall off the pier and into
the waters next to the ship, taking him out of harm's way
for a moment. He had no doubt, though, that the rifle
fire from the railing would punch through the old docks
and into the water after him. The AK-107 in his hands
was a modern update of the highly successful AK-47,
right down to the powerful 7.62 mm ComBloc round.
The only changes were synthetics replacing wood, and
modern metallurgy increasing the old design's already
rock-solid durability and reliability. The other Russian
smugglers were similarly armed.

Enciso and James were only carrying pistol-caliber
machine pistols. This was supposed to be a stealth infiltration, meant for sabotage. The addition of a platoon
of militiamen to the mix was unexpected.

"Hull ripper charges set," Enciso's voice said through
Bolan's earpiece. "Give the word."

Bolan looked at Bashir strolling up the gangplank.
The militia officer would provide the Executioner with
a wealth of information. However, plucking him from
between his own armed soldiers and the paranoid Russian gangsters would require a major distraction.

"Fire 'em up," Bolan said out loud. He whirled and
charged up the gangplank toward Bashir.

The Thunder Lion riflemen jerked in reaction to
Bolan's sudden movement, their FAMAS rifles rising
after a second of hesitation. On the railing, the Russian
smugglers, already on edge, simply had to pull the triggers on their own rifles, spraying the militiamen.

The freighter shook violently as spiderweb-shaped
charges, strung along her hull, erupted. Detonating high-
explosive cord cut through the sea-weathered steel at
high velocity, shearing half a dozen five-foot breaches

in her belly. The sudden influx of hundreds of gallons of water disturbed the balance of the freighter.

The gangplank bent deeply, buckling as the weight of the old steamer shoved on it. Finally the wooden walkway splintered, but not before Bolan snaked an arm around Bashir's neck and yanked him over the guide rope. The Executioner and his captive hurtled through the darkness toward the rapidly fluxing gap between the ship and the pier.

Bashir grunted in response to the sudden capture attempt as the two of them sliced through the air, dropping past the guillotine formed by the freighter, and the pier snapped shut. Planks splintered under the impact of thousands of tons of upset steel, the jolt knocking both Russian and African gunmen off balance. Their weapons chattered, but the jarring lurch of the ship against the dock kept either side from maintaining any semblance of accuracy.

Under the churning surface stirred up by the suddenly sinking ship, Bashir thrashed wildly in Bolan's grasp. While the Executioner had been ready for the daredevil dive, filling his lungs on the way down, the African militiaman was not so prepared, aspirating water. Bolan kicked along, trying to escape the currents formed as six holes in the belly of the ship provided a direction for the water to go. If he didn't keep pushing toward the surface, he'd be yanked into the ruptured hull and trapped.

Bashir's hand lashed out, clawing at Bolan's face. The Thunder Lion's thumb raked across the Executioner's eyelid, the nail scratching skin. Bolan grimaced, and tightened his grip on Bashir's throat, the choke hold jolting his captive. Instead of going after his adversary's face, Bashir struggled with the arm snaked under his chin.

It would have to be enough, Bolan thought as he used all the power in his legs and his free arm to drag himself and his captive toward the surface. Rushing water pushed in the opposite direction, but the Executioner was a strong swimmer. Years of warfare had given him the physical prowess necessary for him to breach the waves and fill his lungs with a lifesaving gasp of air.

Then it was Bashir's turn, Bolan rolling on his back and shoving his face up into the air. The militia commander gurgled, vomiting up a lungful of water and sucking down a fresh breath before Bolan folded his body, knifing into the depths again. On the surface, the big American had heard the chatter of automatic weapons as the Russians and Africans engaged in a firefight. He was certain that James and Encizo were batting cleanup, making sure that neither side received an advantage. Their suppressed MP-5s enabled them to snipe with impunity, as autoweapons produced flash and noise. Invisible amid the roar of enemy rifles and the burning flares at their muzzles, the Phoenix Force warriors could fire from cover and concealment. It would make up for the reduced range and power of their machine pistols.

Bolan's powerful limbs pulled him under the water, and he swam with his captive until they reached a jetty twenty yards from the stern of the lurching craft. He reached up and anchored himself on the low-slung dock.

Bashir had recovered enough of his senses to break loose, hammering Bolan in the stomach. The African had intended to knock the wind out of the Executioner, but his fist's power was blunted by rock-hard abdominal muscles. Instead of catching Bolan while both of his hands were occupied and he was off balance, Bashir only elicited a sudden surge, Bolan snapping the African's forehead against the hard edge of the jetty. The water-worn wood met Bashir's skull with a stunning impact, splitting the skin on the man's forehead.

Stunned, blood pouring down his head and stinging his eyes, Bashir was a docile charge that Bolan heaved up onto the planks. With a kick, and the power of both of his arms, Bolan launched out of the water and knelt next to his stunned captive.

Bashir wiped his eyes free of the blinding blood and began to sit up when he noticed the massive .44 Magnum Desert Eagle leveled at his nose.

"Don't move," Bolan ordered. He planted his knee into Bashir's chest, then looked toward the gunfight between the smugglers and the Thunder Lions. Broken planks and dented hull were fused together, and the Russian and African factions had ceased their mutually destructive battle to escape being sucked under the water by the sinking ship. The Peugeots and the transport trucks lurched and slid off the dock, creating fountaining splashes as they hit the water.

Bolan looked back down to Bashir. "Roll over and place your hands at the small of your back."

"Don't kill me," Bashir begged, his face a glistening mask of blood.

"Do as I say, and you'll live at least another day," the Executioner promised.

Bashir glanced at the carnage, watching men scrambling across railings and broken piers and splashing helplessly in the dock waters. In the space of a few seconds, his captor had turned a major arms deal into pure mayhem. He rolled onto his stomach and assumed the position of surrender.

CHAPTER THREE

Calvin James gunned the engine on the Fiat, swinging it around to rendezvous with Bolan.

The Executioner strode forward. He had Major Antoine Bashir by the collar, his hands bound behind him, the omnipresent Desert Eagle screwed against the prisoner's ear.

"That's a hell of a souvenir," James said, pulling up to the end of the boardwalk. Rafael Encizo sat in the shotgun seat, MP-5 at the ready, scanning for the opposition. The Russians and the Africans were still busy escaping the destruction of a multiton freighter grinding down on a pier, but all it would take would be two or three men with rifles to turn their Fiat into a sieve with a blast of automatic rifle fire.

"Take him to the safe house," Bolan told James. "I'm not finished yet."

James glanced back at the carnage that he and Encizo had inflicted with their sabotage efforts. "You're going to slip in among the Russians?"

Bolan nodded. "It will take them a few moments before they realize that a third party caused all this ruckus. Hopefully, Bashir's second in command will take in the surviving Russians."

Bolan gave Bashir's collar a sharp tug as the African militiaman's eyes grew wide at the sound of his own name. "Yes. I know your name. And I know that Captain Aflaq is your aide and principal bodyguard."

"Want me to talk to him?" James asked, pantomiming an injection. With Encizo's aid, the Phoenix Force medic would undoubtedly strip Bashir's defenses and whatever intelligence he carried with him via a shot of scopolamine. The drug was a powerful inhibitor, making people more susceptible to questions and suggestion, and James was skilled enough to administer the drug without causing undue cardiac stress.

"Do it," Bolan said. "I'll see if I can get anything on the Russians and the Thunder Lions, then get some wheels and meet you back at the safe house."

Encizo helped Bolan push Bashir into the backseat of the Fiat. Bolan's statement of getting his own wheels wasn't lost on the Cuban. "Bring me back something nice and shiny."

Bolan glanced around. "In this neighborhood?"

Encizo chuckled. "Take care, Striker."

The Executioner whirled and disappeared into the shadows.

BOLAN FLIPPED OPEN Anatoly's cell phone and went through the programmed numbers. His limited knowledge of Russian Cyrillic symbols helped him to decipher the dead sentry's phone book, and he had the name of the man who was likely Anatoly's field supervisor, a Russian midlevel crime boss named Grigorei. He hit

Send, then stuffed a pair of disposable earplugs up his nostrils to add to his planned ruse.

The phone rang, and Grigorei answered on the third ring.

"Anatoly?" Grigorei asked.

"Where is everybody?" Bolan asked, his words slurred and distorted by the earplugs blocking his exhalations. It was a simple means of disguising his voice.

"Anatoly?" Grigorei asked again. Bolan waited a moment.

"It's me," Bolan answered. "I got smacked in the face with a plank. I think my nose is broken."

"Sounds like it," Grigorei said. "What the hell happened on the gangplank?"

"I saw a flash of metal in the distance," Bolan responded. "I thought they were going after the African."

Bolan heard Grigorei's voice, muffled by a hand. "Anatoly is confirming that there were third-party snipers."

"That sounds possible," Aflaq said. "Neither of our groups had pistol-caliber submachine guns, and yet I have wounds on several of my men matching low-powered carbine hits."

"Same here," Grigorei concurred. The Russian's voice grew clearer as he removed his hand. "Anatoly, where are you?"

"Hard to tell, all these docks look the same," Bolan lied. "Especially since all I have is one eye working."

"Where is Bashir?" Aflaq's voice was audible over the speakerphone function of Grigorei's set.

"I lost track of him. We got separated. I tried to hold on to him, but he fought too much." It was a partial truth. Bolan simply omitted the fact that when he became separated from Bashir, it was on dry land and into the custody of Calvin James and Rafael Encizo.

"Sadly, the major is a poor swimmer," Aflaq said.

"I'm sorry," Bolan returned.

"I'm sure you are," Aflaq responded.

Bolan tensed. He could detect the skepticism in the African militiaman's voice.

"We'll send someone for you," Grigorei explained. "Head to the nearest access road."

"Sure," Bolan replied. He snapped the cell phone closed and glanced around. He still retained the AK-47 he'd taken from Anatoly, but the assault rifle would make far too much noise. He knelt and dismantled the Beretta 93-R and the Heckler & Koch MP-5. Both the 9 mm handgun and the machine pistol had suppressors mounted on them, and he had to make certain their mechanisms were in good condition. A quick examination confirmed that they were ready for the upcoming fight. The quiet guns would be his advantage. The AK-47's dunking wouldn't have proved a problem even if Bolan had swum through sewage thick enough to stand a fork in. The Desert Eagle would require a more intensive inspection, but he didn't have time for the detail stripping necessary to restore his confidence in the massive handgun.

He wrapped a length of cloth around his head, covering one eye to give himself as much of a cushion of uncertainty on the part of his enemy as possible. The AK hung in full view, loose on its lanyard. Bolan limped to a corner to maintain his ruse as the battered Anatoly.

If the voices of Aflaq and Grigorei together hadn't convinced Bolan that the two factions had reunited in the wake of the freighter's destruction, then the sight of a jeepload of white and black men sitting side by side and armed to the teeth with assault rifles would have clinched it. Fortunately, the Executioner was fully aware that the surviving gunmen from the covert meeting had banded together. He swept the shadows in alleys, looking for the betraying signs of a jeep heading down a parallel road to flank him.

Bolan's hand radio hissed to life through the universal earplug he'd locked into it.

"We see him," came a Russian voice. Bolan was glad that when he'd looked through Anatoly's cell phone, he'd found the emergency alternate frequency for the Russian gangsters' communication. Sure enough, they doubted the Executioner's identity as one of their own, because they were speaking over the channel that Anatoly had put into a memo note on his cell phone. As the jeep rolled closer, Bolan bided his time, knowing that his ruse was crumbling rapidly.

"Is he reacting to you?" Grigorei's voice asked. "Try to take him alive. We could get some information out of him."

"Right, sir," the gangster in the jeep said.

That was all the Executioner needed to hear. He whirled, bringing up the silenced MP-5 like a handgun, his other hand tugging his fake bandage aside, then unleathering the Beretta in his shoulder holster. Bolan's initial salvo of suppressed slugs chugged out of the end of the blunt canister. Since the suppressor only captured the muzzle gases without retarding the velocity of the 9 mm rounds in the magazine, he had opted for extra-heavyweight, subsonic 9 mm rounds—squat, fat barrels of lead with a flat, ugly nose meant for contacting as much enemy flesh as possible, all wrapped around an overweight core of dense tungsten. The Parabellum slugs erupted out of the suppressor at a speed of 1000 feet per second, just slow enough to avoid producing a supersonic crack, but the bullets weighed in at a full 180-grains, more than sufficient to produce the kind of momentum and penetration that made up for the subsonic velocity.

The jeep's windshield disintegrated, shattered glass and deformed blobs of lead and tungsten vaulting into the face and chest of the African militiaman at the wheel. The broken windshield carved only minor slashes on the Thunder Lion's face, but the quiet and deadly bullets smashed through the driver's rib cage, shattering bone into splinters and tumbling petals of flattened lead whirling like the blades of a lawn mower to slash brutally through lung tissue. The coalition jeep lurched violently as one slug stopped cold in the thick and heavy muscle of the African's heart, dying reflex causing him to jerk the steering wheel violently to the right. The dead man's companions scrambled to bring up their assault rifles and return fire, but their formerly steady platform was now out of control, forcing them to pay more attention to hanging on for dear life than opening fire on the Executioner.

Bolan had his Beretta up and firing, punching bullets into the head of the gunman in the shotgun seat. They cracked open the skull of the Russian mobster sitting beside the slain driver and burrowed through his brain to turn his central nervous system into whipped froth. The jeep rocketed along, an African militiaman in the back of the vehicle lunging wildly to grab at the steering wheel.

No amount of turning could have saved the three men in the back as the driver's heavy, dead foot was jammed into the gas pedal, speeding them into a confrontation with the back wall of a warehouse. The hood crumpled violently, and the Thunder Lion who had striven to reach the steering wheel was launched headfirst through the remnants of the windshield, his face torn free by the jagged wrinkles of the collapsed nose of the jeep. Fortunately for the mutilated gunman, his suffering at the loss of his face was measured in nanoseconds. The top of his skull met the stone wall of the warehouse, and his vertebrae burst and collapsed. A spear of bone shoved deep into the socket of the man's brain, killing him before his neurons could even register the pain of his nose and cheeks torn from his facial structure.

"He's onto us!" a voice yelled over Anatoly's radio. Bolan heard the echo of the Russian's voice emanating from an alley off to his right, informing him that the flanking maneuver he'd anticipated was in motion. Had they tried it against any other man, they might have had a chance, but the Executioner's years of experience and his ability to improvise had given him a killing edge. Bolan rushed toward the crushed jeep, the two surviving gunmen crawling out of its backseat, oblivious to his presence. He spared the briefest of moments, his boot lashing out to render the survivors insensate with well-placed kicks. They were both unarmed, the force of the crash ripping the rifles out of their hands, and the onset of shock helped the remaining Russian to forget about the handgun in his hip holster. Rather than slaughter helpless opponents, Bolan put them out of commission, preferring to save his ammo for the alternate force coming up behind him.

The strike team arrived only a second after Bolan's

estimate, which was to the warrior's advantage. He had the drop on the enemy force, and had put the wreckage of the jeep between himself and their rifles. Firing from a position of cover and knowing his enemy's angle of approach, Bolan had put all the cards in his favor. He gave the members of the African and Russian team time to expose themselves as they exited the alley, then triggered the MP-5 and Beretta. The suppressors on the weapons swallowed the muzzle-flash and bark, which would have betrayed the Executioner's position, while the rear frame of the jeep provided him with a solid rest position to assist him in controlling the two weapons he fired simultaneously.

The Russian *mafiya* leader screamed as a stream of bullets from the MP-5 drilled into his heart, multiple tungsten-cored slugs burrowing through the tough muscle and smashing his spine on the way out. An African militiaman to his left vomited blood as a Beretta round crushed his windpipe.

With two of their number down in a heartbeat, the remaining quartet of smugglers and troopers panicked, their rifles spitting out wild streams, fanning the shadows. The jeep's wreckage shook as bullets were stopped by its massive bulk, protecting the Executioner.

"Any movement?" one of the African militiamen asked as Bolan listened on the Russians' party line.

"Negative," a smuggler responded. "Step out and have a look."

"Fuck you," the Thunder Lion responded. "He'd just shoot me while playing possum."

The Russian chuckled. "But then we'd know where he was."

Bolan held back a sigh that would have lamented his

opponents' lack of radio discipline. Rather, he hauled the corpse of the Russian in the shotgun seat to the ground, then triggered a burst of AK fire from the dead man's rifle.

That brought a salvo of concentrated autofire down on the front seat of the jeep. The corpse of the driver jerked violently under the combined storm of lead that hammered him. Bolan shouted, approximating the Russian's voice, to stop shooting. He grabbed the dead mobster by the back of the neck and pushed his head above the jeep, using his other hand to wave the corpse's arm.

"It's me!" Bolan shouted.

"Fuck. Boris! I could have killed you!" one of the Russians called. "What happened?"

"I was hit pretty hard when we crashed. Where is everybody?"

The quartet of gunmen broke from cover, moving low and quickly toward the jeep. Their intent was to hook up with their surviving ally, as he was behind some of the best cover on the street.

Instead, Bolan tossed the dead man aside and fired his AK across the front seat. The Russian at the front of the pack screamed as his belly burst open under the onslaught of rifle bullets. Intestines boiled from his savaged abdomen, thick loops of entrails sagging down to his knees. Somehow, the gangster had the strength to continue standing as the rifle rounds zipped through his ruined guts and out his back, tearing into the trio behind him.

One of the Thunder Lions whipped around in a circle as the high-velocity devastators pulverized his pelvis. As his finger was on the trigger as he was hit, his

FAMAS rifle spoke, snarling a violent death song in response to his crippling. Rather than hit Bolan, his muzzle had swung around and jammed into the groin of his fellow African. The front sight snagged on the pants of his partner, holding the barrel there as thirteen rounds burned away the rifleman's crotch and upper thighs. In blind anger and rage, the wounded victim stuffed his own rifle under the crippled Thunder Lion's chin and pulled the trigger, bullets pulling trails of brain out of his murderer's skull in a volcano of gooey tissue. Both African militiamen flopped to the street, one with his brains blown out, the other rapidly bleeding to death as his femoral arteries jetted streams of thick crimson onto the concrete.

The last of the Russian smugglers whirled and ran as Bolan's borrowed AK cycled dry. The Executioner let the empty rifle fall to the ground as he vaulted past the dead driver and the dying remnants of the flanking force. The mobster's fighting discipline had disappeared at the sight of his allies chopped to ribbons by one man. The way he ran, clutching one uselessly dangling arm, had also indicated that the Russian had taken a bullet.

Bolan knew that the gangster's first instinct would be to get back to his closest allies.

Settling into a ground-eating pace and sticking to the shadows, the Executioner tailed his quarry, knowing that he'd have a chance to finish off the last of the mobsters who'd thrown in their lot with the Thunder Lions.

It was a simple message, Bolan mused.

Seek profit from helping in the Sudanese slaughter, and your only wages will be the wrath of the Executioner's cleansing flame.

CAPTAIN AFLAQ LISTENED to the rattle of distant gunfire and dying screams, then glanced over to Yuri Grigorei, his brow furrowed in disdain.

"I thought the *mafiya* had the services of Russia's finest warriors." Venom dripped from Aflaq's every word.

Grigorei sneered at the African militiaman. "What would a scumbag like you know about anything Russian?"

Aflaq's nose wrinkled, but he shook off the insult. "Now is not the time for us to be at each other's throats. Someone stumbled onto us, and they have done an excellent job at turning this deal to shit."

"Your enemies?" Grigorei asked.

Aflaq shook his head. "The goat-fucking primitives and their Ethiopian defenders don't have enough brain cells combined to even spell Alexandria, let alone send a covert operations team here."

"Setting off a bomb in an Egyptian harbor isn't the style of the CIA," Grigorei noted. "And there isn't another crime organization with the kind of reach to touch us here."

The Russian's eyes narrowed as he saw a shadow in the distance. "That idiot."

Aflaq followed the Russian's line of sight and saw a man running down the street toward their position. His arm hung uselessly at his side and his pale features were twisted into a mask of terror and pain.

"He's leading the enemy to us!" Grigorei snapped. "Everyone! Harden up!"

Aflaq's hand tightened around the pistol grip of his rifle. "You'll frighten off our adversaries, yelling like that."

Grigorei glared at the African. "If we do, then we'll live another day."

Aflaq shook his head in disbelief at such a naked display of cowardice on the Russian's part. Still, there was the evidence of nine men shredded into lifeless sacks of meat in the length of a minute. It was possible that it could have only been three-to-one odds, but none of his men had survived long enough to estimate the size of the force that had killed them.

Could it have been one man, utilizing psychology and stealth to strike at the forces who outnumbered him when they were at their weakest and most underprepared?

If so, then Aflaq counted the men around him. Adding in Grigorei and himself, he had twelve gunmen total. Thirteen if the bewildered, wounded fool jogging frantically toward their position recovered his wits long enough to utilize the handgun he wore on his belt. For someone who'd snuffed out nine men in under sixty seconds, it wouldn't be much of a challenge.

"Flashlights!" Aflaq ordered. "Get some lights on the shadows! A herd of elephants could walk by in this murk!"

He received a nod of approval from the surviving leader of the Russian smugglers. Cones of light splayed out, slicking apart the darkness, seeking out the lone opponent who'd turned their arms deal into a wash of carnage.

Yuri Grigorei swung his rifle, following the diameter of light thrown off by one of his men. He wanted to be on the spot to take out the bane of this evening.

Aflaq watched in disbelief as three explosions erupted on the side of Grigorei's head, geysers of gore vomiting out and spraying his face as he looked at the Russian's dying shudders. More bullets flew, striking only at the Russians, all except for the wounded, terrified man who simply folded into a fetal position when he saw his friends shriek and die under a hail of silent, brutal death.

Aflaq's own Thunder Lions were untouched.

"Captain Aflaq," a voice said from Grigorei's radio.

Aflaq looked down at the corpse, the small electronic device speaking his name.

Bolan's voice cut over the airwaves. "Pick up his radio. He won't have any use for it."

Aflaq picked up the radio. "Hello?"

"Captain. I'm giving you a courtesy call. Tell General Bitturumba that if he was trying to seek my disapproval, he found it," Bolan said. "The predatory scum among you who call yourselves Muslim militiamen know who I am. I am God's wrath for your twisting of the path he laid out for you. Surrender and retirement will save your life, once you send my message to Bitturumba."

"He would surely kill me," Aflaq answered.

"Then phone him. And hide," Bolan retorted.

Aflaq looked around. "Are you…?"

A bullet smacked violently into Grigorei's slack face, the round exploding through flesh and bone.

"Small talk is over. You have my message," Bolan said.

Aflaq listened to the static on the other end of the line, feeling the darkness of the dock grow deeper and colder as he waited for another act of wrath.

But the Executioner had moved on.

There were other matters to attend to before the sun rose.

CHAPTER FOUR

Alexandria, Egypt

The Executioner had let his guns remain silent, but he was far from through with the Thunder Lion contingent of survivors. The men gathered into two vehicles, seven men stuffed into the jeeps that hadn't been hurled into Alexandria harbor by the sinking Russian smuggling ship. Aflaq had taken a moment to put two bullets into each of the other pair of SUVs to cripple them.

Too bad for Aflaq that the bullets went into the radiators of the jeeps. Bolan was able to affect repairs on one of the jeeps by jury-rigging a patch with swatches of duct tape and a flat plate of metal that he'd kicked off a rusted section of fender. With the improvised patch in place, sealing the radiator's leak, all Bolan required was a discarded soda bottle and water from the harbor to refill the radiator. Aflaq had been in too much of a hurry to efficiently cripple the abandoned vehicles. He'd seen them as nails, and his gun as the only hammer. Had it been Bolan, he'd have manually gone through the engines, slicing apart hoses and tearing out the alternator generator, hurling it into the bay.

Bolan was taking his time, allowing his quarry to move along toward their destination. He spent the time grabbing spare jerricans of gasoline off the second crippled jeep, and removing its battery, loading it into the back of his repaired ride. With the gas and battery, Bolan would be able to devise some high-intensity improvised explosive devices to even the odds when he paid a visit to the Thunder Lions' safe haven in Alexandria. Satisfied that his preparations were complete, he flipped open his satellite phone. He was connected to Stony Man Farm immediately.

"They have a two-minute lead, Striker," Aaron Kurtzman said. "They're moving slow, though. I think they're trying to make sure no one's on their tail."

"Too bad for them that they're being tailed by eyes five thousand miles above them," Bolan countered. "I gave Aflaq a real shot of terror and he will keep an eye on his six. He needs to think that there's no leash. He sees my headlights in his rearview, I won't have a chance to visit the rest of the militia's presence in Alexandria."

"We're not lying down on the job here, Striker," Kurtzman said. "I've got his path downloaded to your PDA."

Bolan nodded, patting the pocket where the compact personal digital assistant was tucked away. "Any data processed from Cal's interrogation of Bashir?"

"Nothing so far. He's got the camera and mike set up, but he's still running the interrogation baseline," Kurtzman replied. Bolan understood the difficulty of a proper chemical interrogation. Baseline truth or false reactions had to be recorded to ensure the veracity of subsequent answers. Bashir would be hooked up to a polygraph machine to not only register unconscious reflexive responses to lying, but to monitor Bashir's cardiological responses to the scopolamine. If the militia commander was under too much stress from the addition of the "truth serum" to his bloodstream, the stress would show on the polygraph and James would be able to head off a heart attack.

"Bashir must have had some medical difficulty for Cal to take so long in preparation," Bolan noted. "He probably lost too much blood from his head knock and his pressure was low."

"I've learned not to doubt your deductive skills, Striker. I'll keep you updated on Aflaq."

"You're a lifesaver, Bear."

Bolan slid behind the wheel and took off, driving parallel to the Thunder Lions' path. It took little effort to catch up to and shadow the African militia survivors as they limped toward their safe haven in Alexandria. The Executioner let his quarry have their lead, knowing that once they had settled in, their nerves would be less tightly wound. Right now, the Thunder Lions were on edge, and would be alert to his presence. Bolan rarely tried to go against a full-alert security force, preferring to use stealth and surprise as his force multiplier. Thanks to his interference at the arms deal, however, the militiamen would be prepared for any assault. A direct intervention right now would be a steel trap snapping down on the Executioner's neck.

The Thunder Lions pulled into an abandoned hotel and Bolan stayed back five hundred yards. He picked an apartment building and scurried up the fire escape, crawling all the way to the rooftop. From there, he had a clear vantage point over the militia safe house. He pulled out a monocle, a compact unit that not only had low-light amplification, but was a full ten power magnification. Even from five hundred yards away, Bolan was able to see the faces of grim, edgy militiamen, their eyes sharp and alert for intruders in the area. Following one sentry on patrol, Bolan received a guided tour of the Thunder Lions' security setup for the evening. All the information that he gathered would be supplemented by downward-looking radar and infrared scans of the hotel, the powerful eyes in the sky Stony Man Farm "borrowed" from the National Reconnaissance Office.

Satisfied with his telescopic intel gathering, Bolan took his sputtering SUV back to the warehouse that he'd set up as his base. The duct tape patch was loosening on the radiator, but the engine wasn't being stressed by off-road travel or high-speed pursuit. Normal street traffic was still enough to start wisps of steam and smoke to dribble from under the hood. Bolan kept his speed low, nurturing the vehicle until he pulled into the loading dock. The engine finally seized up, overheated.

"This is my nice shiny new ride?" Encizo asked from the doorway. He scanned the road behind Bolan out of ingrained habit. Though the Cuban's partners in Phoenix Force and the Executioner were all skilled in the art of evading pursuit and tails, complacency was a mindset that would get him killed. Bolan knew that Encizo's Heckler & Koch USP pistol was supplemented by an AK-47 propped behind the loading-bay door. Had someone proved stealthy enough to avoid Bolan's attention, Encizo's belt-and-suspenders approach to security would have picked them up, and the Phoenix warrior would be ready for battle.

"If you wash it, it'll shine," Bolan noted. "But you might want to fix the radiator first."

Encizo chuckled.

"Got anything interesting from Bashir yet?" Bolan asked.

"We're taking a short break. Bear let us know you were coming back to us," Encizo stated. "As it is, we're held up on Bashir. He's not healthy enough to handle a full-court press."

"I figured that Cal might have to shore him up from blood loss."

"If I didn't know that you had spoken to Aaron a half hour ago, I'd swear you were psychic."

Bolan shrugged. "Bashir seemed stabilized when I left him with you."

"We had to aggravate the cut you put on his forehead," Encizo noted. "Don't forget, we're not the Executioner. People's bowels don't turn to ice water when we glare at them."

Bolan patted his friend on the shoulder, chuckling. "You two can do things I can't. That's why I have you on my side. C'mon, let's go put a little scare into Bashir."

The pair secured the loading dock, then went to the interrogation room as Calvin James gave Major Bashir a refresher dose of scopolamine. Bashir's eyes widened at the sight of the Executioner. Bolan's lips turned up in a humorless grin.

"Please," Bashir sputtered. "I'm talking as fast as I can."

"Just keep talking," Bolan told him, his voice as cold and hard as a gravestone. "I'm happy to listen."

Bashir sang, desperate to please the Executioner.

Darfur, Sudan

BITTURUMBA KNEW IT WAS early, but he poured himself a tumblerful of brandy, his eyes tracking across the desk to glare at Kedzi Kartennian.

"So we lost the second shipment of canister shells?" Bitturumba asked.

Kartennian nodded.

The general sloshed the brandy around, not caring that he was bruising the body of the liquor. He took a deep swig and grimaced. "To whom?"

"Aflaq called in and said that it was an American. The Russians described him, as well, as someone they feared," Kartennian stated.

Bitturumba looked over the olive-skinned Turk. "You're kidding, right?"

Kartennian shook his head. "One man, they said."

"I sent twenty-four fully armed men!"

"And only seven, including Aflaq, survived."

"Where's Bashir?" Bitturumba asked.

"Aflaq said he's at the bottom of the harbor," Kartennian said.

Bitturumba sneered. "Where did he get that information from?"

"From the lone crusader," Kartennian stated. "Who'd disguised himself as one of the Russian smugglers."

"So Bashir is alive," Bitturumba mumbled.

"What?"

"Bashir's alive. I don't know how well he is, but he's

in enemy hands," the Thunder Lion chief stated. He took another swig, looking at the big machete lying on his desk. It was a well-worn blade, its edge gleaming and slender from multiple sharpenings, the thick spine displaying a slight curve from countless impacts as it sheared through bone and heavy muscle. He reached out and flicked a speck of flesh from a small crack in the spine.

"Any chance of recovering him?" Kartennian asked.

Bitturumba shook his head. "No worries. Bashir knows where our bases are in the Sudan, but he doesn't know the actual plan. He's expendable."

"And the others?" Kartennian pressed.

"Have them go on soft alert. I'm pretty certain that Aflaq was followed back to the fallback," Bitturumba stated. "This American's going to close in on him, and I want to provide a delaying action. Perhaps even expend some of this mysterious warrior's resources."

"The American has always been said to fight alone," Kartennian noted.

Bitturumba smirked. "If he even exists. It's a psychological ploy. He has backup, and he has resources. We lay a trap for him. Call your friends in the Muslim Brotherhood. We won't let Aflaq know that he has backup. I want a ring of fire and steel ready to collapse on the American and his allies when he goes after the backup base."

"Why would he go there?" Kartennian asked. "He knows that we'll be ready for him, and that we might even call in additional support for our people."

"I've heard this man's legend. He is nothing if not thorough," Bitturumba stated. "He will visit flame and death upon our organization. He will destroy our forces in Alexandria, leaving their corpses as a signpost to our inability to maintain our security."

"To send a message to us," Kartennian mused.

Bitturumba nodded. "He'll wait a while, so we have time to marshal a force to bolster the remaining men. Let Aflaq know that this is to be a scorched-earth defense. No amount of sacrifice is too much."

"He told me that you'd say something like that," Kartennian relayed. "He told me that he was willing to die for the cause. We will cleanse our lands of the unbelieving scum, praise God."

Bitturumba looked at Kartennian, then mechanically muttered, "Praise be unto him."

The burly militia commander paid lip service to the Muslim Turk's utterance. While he'd been raised by a moderate Islamic mother, Bitturumba had no real stake in any organized religious faith. He put on the facade of one of the faithful, however, only because those fanatics threw their support behind him. Bitturumba used their blind insanity to bolster his climb to power, creating one of the most powerful militias in Africa. The Prophet, however, held no sway over Bitturumba's decision-making, no more than the Christian Messiah held any sway over his half brother Alonzo Cruz.

There was only one god that Bitturumba surrendered himself to, and that was himself. As the Thunder Lions grew in power, so did he. Many in the militia had transferred their worship from the Prophet to the African thunder god who wielded a hammer that would rock the entire world. His half brother, a European sorcerer who had forged an even more powerful thunderbolt for him to wield, was the Loki to his Thor. It was only fair that the two gods would unite to begin their own pantheon. Bitturumba was the embodiment of war, Cruz the master of misery and suffering. Together, their intellects and resources combined were far more powerful than they were alone. Bitturumba didn't mind. He loved his sibling, and knew that the sum was greater than the parts, power growing exponentially from their united effort.

Kartennian was one of Cruz's gifts to Bitturumba. The Turkish rebel had branched out, bringing about the hardcore Wahabite teachings of radical, extreme Islam to the rest of the world. Bitturumba was familiar enough with the Koran and the Hadritha to walk rings around the Turk in a theological debate if he wanted to. The only thing that the Prophet had accomplished that impressed the African warrior was the sheer terror he'd inflicted on the Middle East, decapitating thousands of enemies, and enjoying the lamentations of their women and children.

"Praise be unto him," Bitturumba repeated.

Kartennian looked at the brandy remaining in Bitturumba's glass. "You really should not drink."

Bitturumba looked down. "I am a warrior, embarking upon a battle that will shake the world. Did not the Prophet allow for true believers to partake of hashish in order to gird their will?"

"But…"

"Did he not?" Bitturumba asked. "And yet, where is your gift to me, the warrior who will bring God's will to this continent?"

"Alcohol is the devil's tool," Kartennian mentioned.

Bitturumba tapped the glass. "Then Satan's swizzle is pretty damn transparent."

Kartennian managed a laugh.

"My mind and heart are clear. Satan has placed no words in my mouth," Bitturumba told him. He wrapped his beefy paw around the glass bottle. "I hold the wick of the devil and control it."

"Peace be with you," Kartennian stated with a nod. "I shall speak with our Egyptian brothers."

Bitturumba dismissed the Turk with a smile. Naturally, Kartennian's communications would be monitored.

One did not become a god of thunder and war without keeping an eye on even those who'd claimed to be allies. If Kartennian betrayed him, his head would be mailed back to his family with a grenade jammed in the neck hole.

"Praise be unto that, you idiot fanatic." Bitturumba spit, tossed back another swig of brandy, then planted the glass upside down on the table next to his machete.

Stony Man Farm, Virginia

AARON KURTZMAN SAW the flagged communication pop up on his monitor. There was no secret that Unit 777 of the Egyptian military kept a close eye on the Muslim Brotherhood. The elite counterterrorist organization gathered its own intel on the renegade extremists who threatened the cold peace between Egypt and Israel. Stony Man Farm and the Executioner had allied with the highly trained commandos in the past, so tapping their information was hardly an intrusion.

In this instance, Bolan had informed Kurtzman to keep an eye on the rogue Egyptians. If the Thunder Lions were going to seek backup in Alexandria, it was going to come from the Brotherhood. Kurtzman opened the communication socket and took a close look at the conversation captured by Unit 777's electronic intel.

"Our brothers in the Lions require assistance in Alexandria," a Turkish-accented voice said. Brognola took the recorded snippet, copied it and fed it into the known voice database of international terrorists for identification. As each voice had its own unique signature and frequency, the match would be a definitive means of finding out who was assisting Bitturumba.

"How much assistance?" a Muslim Brotherhood named Zambron asked.

"As much as possible. The one we dare not name has arrived in Alexandria," the Turk said.

There was an audible gulp. Kurtzman allowed himself a grin. Even though Mack Bolan, the Executioner, was officially dead, a myth that was supposed to have faded into antiquity, the terrorist world was fully aware that a superpredator stalked the shadowy alleys of the world, hunting down insurgents and criminals. It wasn't the same as when Bolan was still officially alive, hunting the *mafiya* in his one-man crusade against organized crime, mainly because various terrorist organizations had different names for the Executioner, but the legend still existed. It was just another tool in the warrior's arsenal, a means of cowing the thugs.

"I have four score men assembled," Zambron replied. "Where to?"

"Our hotel," the Turk stated.

"How many allies can we count on?" Zambron inquired.

"There are twenty left among our soldiers," the Turk explained. "He has given us a terrible rout."

"Undoubtedly." Zambron sighed. "I'll have them ready. When?"

"We believe he will strike tonight," the Turk said.

"Count on our assistance," Zambron promised.

Kurtzman made another copy of the conversation, forwarding it to Bolan, Encizo and James. The three of them would have to change their plan of action, but the Stony Man cyberwizard remembered the Executioner's order of battle. Drawing out the enemy while making them think he was the victim of their trap was one of Bolan's most successful tactics.

"Thanks for the heads-up," came a quick e-mail response from the Executioner.

It was an efficient, almost flippant response to the knowledge that a terrorist army was waiting in the wings to pounce on him.

Kurtzman smiled.

Now he was positive that the Executioner was counting on extra backup for the Thunder Lions, and wasn't slightly concerned.

Kurtzman felt a pang of guilt for the doomed terrorists who thought they had their prey dead to rights.

CHAPTER FIVE

Alexandria, Egypt

The cliché "forewarned is forearmed" was a vital part of Mack Bolan's arsenal. Clichés endured because of their veracity. With the Executioner, every bit of knowledge was a tool to be used. Now that he was aware that the Thunder Lions' compound was a trap, the raid had the potential to double its rewards. Bolan had crossed swords with the Egyptian terrorist organization known as the Muslim Brotherhood before, and the opportunity to strike a blow against their membership was irresistible.

"I'd rather be on the ground backing your play, Striker," Calvin James said over the hands-free radio.

"Yeah, you're the best sniper of the three of us," Rafael Encizo added. "We're the close-quarters types."

"Cal's an excellent long-distance marksman," Bolan countered. "He's been Gary's backup sniper on hundreds of occasions, taking out sentries simultaneously with him. And the both of you are Phoenix's designated grenadiers. I need you two to be my force multiplication. The Brotherhood will bring everything they can, and the two of you can plant a 40 mm shell into their lap accurately and quickly."

Bolan couldn't help the feeling of gratitude that the two Phoenix Force commandos were willing to take his place directly in the line of fire. They stopped their complaints, seeing the wisdom of Bolan's strategy. James and Encizo were skilled and capable and the Executioner couldn't have asked for better backup, save the aforementioned Gary Manning, Phoenix Force's sniper and a long-distance rifleman who rivaled Bolan's own skills.

"We've got your back," James said. "Put some boot to ass."

Bolan remained silent. He was in the strike zone and had a sentry in his sights. Not literally, because right now Bolan had only a knife with a black phosphate blade in his hand, and the suppressed MP-5 machine pistol cinched over his shoulder. He was prepared for close-quarters combat, falling into the profile that his prey were told to expect. As long as he was only going against the Thunder Lion militia, James and Encizo were to hold their fire. Their guns were reserved for shattering the spine of the Muslim Brotherhood ambush.

Bolan lunged at the Thunder Lion sentry, his black-bladed Cold Steel Recon Bowie knife driving deep into the guard's sternum, piercing the abdominal wall and spearing into his heart. The African's dying cry of pain was strangled and trapped in his throat, cut off by Bolan's forearm crushing into his windpipe. The kill was over in the space of a heartbeat, completed with no more noise than the rustle of a bird's wings as it took flight. Bolan hauled the corpse into a set of decorative flower bushes, stowing him out of sight. He took the dead man's rifle and his bandolier of ammunition to bolster his firepower for the coming battle.

There was a feeling in the air, and a more superstitious man would have attributed the eerie prickling at the back of his neck to some supernatural sense. The Executioner, however, was far more practical and realistic. It wasn't a psychic awareness that he was being watched, but his subconscious mind picking up sensory data that his higher functions weren't focused on. Bolan's danger sense was an acute awareness of subliminal sensory data—a shadow in his peripheral vision, the silence of normally active rodents in their alley, or the whiff of hashish smoke still clinging to a Muslim Brotherhood warrior. Bolan's subconscious mind processed all of this information with an uncanny ease, and the warrior's experience and intellect were honed to pick up on these subliminal signals. The result was the Executioner's almost omniscient understanding of any battlefield he found himself in, able to anticipate his enemy's action even before they took it.

Forewarned was forearmed, he mentally repeated. That truly was the case for Bolan, and his arsenal of forewarning provided him with the firepower to obliterate twenty-to-one odds. He unslung the MP-5, then rushed to complete the sentry's patrol path. Catching up to the dead African's schedule, as observed from the night before, Bolan turned the corner and came face-to-face with a second Thunder Lion guard. Bolan expected the sentry, but the militiaman was thrown off balance by his partner's replacement. Before the guard could react, Bolan fired a single suppressed round between his eyes, dropping the African in his tracks.

Two down and still eighteen Thunder Lions left to go, thanks to Kurtzman's satellite reconnaissance of the hotel compound. That wasn't counting the contingent of Muslim Brotherhood gunmen who'd been called in by Bitturumba. Bolan took the magazines of FAMAS ammo off the second corpse, adding it to his reservoir as he looped the bandolier of 25-round magazines over his neck and shoulder. He approached the back of the hotel compound, closing in on the service entrance. Bolan knew from the previous night's recon that there were two Thunder Lions on post there, but as many as six could be on hand with a single cry of alarm. The soldier paused long enough to scoop up a rock and then hurled it with all his strength at the wrought-iron gate, raising a loud clang.

The heavy stone had accomplished its task, drawing the attention of one of the militiamen. The sentinel poked his head out around the corner, his face an easy target as he leaned off balance on the gate. Bolan fired a short burst of suppressed SMG fire, bullets tearing through the militiaman's face. The second guard posted at the back let out a loud cry to alert the rest of the militia troopers as his partner convulsed, then collapsed in death, hanging halfway over the fence.

Everything was going according to Bolan's plan, and the soldier turned and circled back around the way he'd come. While the Thunder Lions focused their attention on the service entrance, ready to repel the one-man assault, Bolan leaped up and grabbed the top of the eight-foot privacy wall. He powered himself to the top of the barrier and crouched. From his vantage point, he saw that a clot of six Africans were braced at the service entrance. Three of the militiamen were out of breath from racing to join their comrades in defending their post. He heard the scuff of boots in the distance as more of the African gunmen mobilized. Bolan pulled the stock of his MP-5 to his shoulder and triggered it.

Bolan's nighttime camouflage made him into a barely visible ghost in the Thunder Lions' peripheral vision, and their attention was directed forward, not to their flanks. The mighty warriors named for lions were more like sitting ducks as heavyweight 9 mm rounds ripped through the flank of braced gunmen, drilling tunnels through vital organs. Two of the riflemen dropped immediately, another staggering as his thighs were shredded by the salvo that had been slowed by the corpses of his partners. As the wounded guard had dropped his weapon, Bolan focused on the ones still standing as they reacted to the sudden deaths and injuries among their number. They whirled to face the Executioner, but he stepped off the privacy wall, dropping eight feet to the ground and landing in crouch. The move had dropped him beneath their focus as the riflemen fired, spearing 5.56 mm bullets through the air that Bolan had occupied a heartbeat earlier. The sudden drop had bought the big American an additional second of confusion among his foes, and he took full advantage of it by hosing down the last three Thunder Lions.

The trio convulsed as bullets punched into their faces and chests, bodies trembling under the onslaught as they tumbled dead to the ground. The injured gunman reached out for his fallen FAMAS rifle. It was a mistake, but not an immediately fatal one. Bolan triggered a burst of 9 mm bullets that forced the man to hastily withdraw his hand.

"You'll want to bandage that," Bolan said, gesturing to the man's bloody thighs.

The gunman looked up at the Executioner, his eyes wide. He glanced to the FAMAS.

"I wouldn't," Bolan warned.

The guard lunged anyway, tugging the butt of his rifle to his left shoulder. Bolan was ready for the resulting firestorm, taking one step to the side to avoid the initial trigger pull. The FAMAS was a sturdy, reliable assault rifle, and its bullpup configuration kept the black weapon compact by placing the trigger guard and handle well forward of the firing mechanism. This way, a twenty-inch barrel could be put on a weapon that was only slightly longer than thirty inches, maintaining full power while improving maneuverability. Unfortunately for the African rifleman, the FAMAS was an older generation bullpup, which meant that the ejector port threw blistering-hot empty casings out of a breech right at the face of the shooter if he used it in the wrong hand.

While the FAMAS was great for a right-handed gunman, spitting its shells out over his shoulder, when the rifle was fired from a left-hander's stance, as the guard tried to now, his head was right in the path of a stream of superheated cartridges. The brass tore at the rifleman's left eye and cheek, slicing flesh. The guard screamed and dropped his rifle. Blinded and lacerated, the sentry curled up into a ball, harmless and whimpering in agony. Bolan reversed his MP-5 and slammed the steel stock into the side of the wounded man's head, knocking him out cold.

"Told you," Bolan said. He tucked the MP-5 behind his back and transferred to the fully loaded FAMAS he'd taken from his first victim. The scuff of boots announced that two more Thunder Lion militiamen were rushing toward his position. As they turned the corner, almost as if they were on a preset schedule, Bolan had his rifle ready for their anticipated approach. The FAMAS snarled two rapid bursts, bullets punching through the militiamen's chests.

A loud crack filled the air, the passage of a supersonic bullet across several rooftops. Waves of air displaced by the high-caliber sniper round bounced off nearby surfaces. It was James's warning to Bolan that the Muslim Brotherhood was making its move. James's first shot from his Israeli M-89-SR, a silenced 7.62 mm sniper rifle, had the power to obliterate a human skull in a fountain of bone fragments and vaporized brain tissue, even at five hundred yards. There were cries of dismay as Egyptian terrorists watched their friend's head explode. The semiauto rifle had launched two more rounds in the time it took for the first bullet to reach the renegade Egyptian. Multiple shouts of alarm, warnings against a sniper attack, were suddenly cut off as James's subsequent shots struck their targets.

Thumps filled the air as 40 mm grenades landed two hundred yards from the wall. Bolan knew full well that Encizo's grenade launcher had a 350-meter maximum effective range, so he could guess that the stocky Cuban was firing on Muslim Brotherhood forces who were staging closer to their sniper's roost. Encizo's salvo of grenades spit up columns of smoke and debris that Bolan could see over the service-entrance gate, the first shot landing in a street. Bolan also caught a glimpse of a rooftop erupting, bodies backlit by an explosion, the length of a mangled machine gun twisting in front of the blossoming fireball.

The Brotherhood had its own sniper roosts spread throughout the surrounding rooftops, but the Cuban disrupted them with 40 mm packets of steel and fire. He had a second M-89-SR to back up James, but for now he was relying on the effective Russian RG-6 revolver-style grenade launcher to pour devastation on the heads of the carefully laid ambush.

"Enemy force engaged," Encizo announced over Bolan's earpiece. "I have movement heading for the wall you just scaled. No clean shot. Be advised."

"On it," the Executioner replied. He grabbed a second FAMAS rifle in his off hand and tucked himself behind a low planter wall filled with decorative ferns. As the wall itself was made of thick stone and filled with densely packed dirt, it shielded the Executioner as the Brotherhood blew open the wall with a pair of RPG-7 rocket grenades. Exploding masonry bounced all around Bolan as he braced himself against the dynamic entry. He fired the FAMAS in his left hand as if it were a pistol, keeping the ejector port well away from his face to avoid an injury similar to the one suffered by the unconscious African lying next to him. He emptied the French rifle's 25-round magazine through the breach, eliciting howls of agony. The thump of two corpses sprawling across the bottom of the blasted hole in the wall let the Executioner know that his suppressive fire was more effective than he'd counted on.

In response to Bolan's salvo, the Muslim Brotherhood cut loose with their AKs. Wild autofire slashed through the night, proving ineffective in dislodging the Executioner from behind the low wall. The sheer volume of autofire was deafening, informing Bolan that his opposition had been thrown off its game.

Bolan's next trick was going to put it into sudden death. He reached into his thigh pouch and pulled a fragmentation grenade. Knowing the distance and the angle he needed to make the shot, he sailed the orb through the hole in the wall, right into the knot of Brotherhood gunmen on the outside the hotel compound. Six-and-a-half ounces of plastic explosive detonated, hurling splinters of razor-sharp wire at high velocity through vulnerable flesh, inducing crippling lacerations that tore apart skin, muscles and internal organs. It was a brutal, devastating maneuver, as likely to produce painful, slowly lethal injuries as it was instant death. The Executioner couldn't spare time or mercy for the mangled and mortally wounded. He was outnumbered and living in the space between the hammer and the anvil.

The Executioner whirled and drove deeper into the Thunder Lions' headquarters, drawing the Brotherhood forces after him into the compound. This night was going to be a message heard across the underworld of radical fanatics.

The message was that extremist groups had someone to fear.

"MACK'S INSIDE," Rafael Encizo told Calvin James as the Phoenix Force medic triggered his silenced sniper rifle.

James's shot hit another of the Brotherhood's fighters who had noticed their position. The Egyptian was on the parapet of a roof and was in the process of turning his RPK light machine gun when James punched a 7.62 mm NATO bullet through the bridge of the gunner's nose.

"The troops are paying too much attention to us now to do more than spot for him," James said. "All the rooftops are crowded with snipers and machine-gun nests. This is almost as bad as when the Russians came after us at Gary's place in Montana."

"There were twice as many of those guys," Encizo reminded his friend. "And we were all deployed in one general fortification because we only had to defend one approach. This time, we've got them surrounded."

James glanced over his shoulder, then swung his rifle around, popping a suppressed bullet into the chest of another rooftop gunman. "You think?"

"Well, we're fighting them on two fronts, instead of just one," Encizo corrected. He punctuated his argument by triggering his reloaded RG-6, lancing a clot of armed Egyptians coming up the street with a 40 mm fragmentation shell. Bodies scattered as the round detonated, hurling heads and limbs from torn torsos in a grisly testimony to the launcher's fearsome power. Encizo scanned for more targets, then caught the sound of boots and bodies rattling the ladder of the fire escape that had brought them to the roof. "Company's coming."

The Cuban set down the RG-6 next to James, trading it in for his Heckler & Koch USP. The 9 mm pistol didn't have quite the same devastating ability as the other weapons, but Encizo wanted to err on the side of weapon retention. It was easier to hang on to a handgun in close-quarters combat than it was to retain a long arm, which provided an attacker with more leverage. An angry face topped the ladder and Encizo aimed and fired in a split second. Two rounds from the 9 mm H & K struck the Brotherhood assailant within an inch of each other, one coring an eye socket into a smear of punctured cornea, the other cracking against the forehead, the wide mouth of his hollowpoint round snagging the bone and breaking it, but not penetrating to the brain beneath. The bullet through the eye, however, took care of the right hemisphere of the Egyptian's brain, and his head snapped back, fountaining gore.

Encizo rushed to the top of the ladder now that the Brotherhood attacker's brainless corpse surrendered to the embrace of gravity, pulling it out of the way between him and the rest of the climbers. Egyptian faces looked up in a mixture of anger, fear, determination and resignation. Encizo shouted an order in Arabic. "Turn back or die!"

A handgun barked from lower on the ladder, but the climber had to shoot one-handed and off balance on a rung while aiming around a higher climber. The topmost Egyptian hugged the side of the ladder, giving Encizo a clean shot at the Muslim Brotherhood aggressor. The Phoenix Force commando took it, drilling the feisty terrorist through the top of his head. The 9 mm slug fractured the bone at the top of the Egyptian's head, cracking down between his right and left lobes to peel him off the ladder and dump his lifeless corpse to the floor of the alley, thirty feet below.

Three of the other Egyptians had slid back down the fire escape as fast as they could, realizing that they were sitting ducks for the Cuban warrior on the roof. A rifleman who was at the base of the ladder opened up, trying to tag Encizo at the edge of the roof. The Brotherhood trooper who had elected to sit out the fight on a ladder rung screamed in pain as two AK-47 bullets slashed through his right leg.

Encizo pulled a fragmentation grenade from his harness and dumped it over the side. Screams of dismay filled the alley as the terrorists recognized the egg-shaped envelope of death spiraling down into their midst. The rifle salvo ended as the terrorist chose to run,

rather than be blown to smithereens. It was too late.
Thunder boomed, grounded gunmen smashed into
greasy pulps of crushed flesh and bone, destroyed by the
high-powered blast. Encizo reached down to the injured
Egyptian and took his hand. There was a moment of
doubt on the Brotherhood prisoner's part, but he let the
Cuban haul him onto the roof. Encizo's powerful upper
body strength made lifting the slender Arab as easy as
hoisting a child.

"They shot me," the man whimpered in broken English, voice trembling from a mixture of pain and betrayal.

"Cal, we have wounded!" Encizo called out.

"Busy!" James responded. The Phoenix Force medic
had transferred to his Beretta and was in the process of
stitching a line of 9 mm rounds into a gunman on the
next rooftop over. The M-89-SR lay at James's feet, action locked open, the magazine well empty.

Encizo caught movement on another rooftop and
whirled, spotting three gunmen rushing up in James's
blind spot. He snapped up the USP and let them have it
with a salvo of rapid-fire rounds, drilling two of the terrorists when he heard the crack of another pistol firing.
The Egyptian he'd rescued emptied half the magazine
of his 9 mm Helwan into the third attacker.

"They shot me," the ex-Brotherhood gunman growled,
having shaken off his moment of shock. Betrayal still
burned in his eyes as he reloaded the Egyptian Beretta
copy. "I don't owe those traitorous dogs more than goat
shit and death."

Encizo gave him a friendly smirk. "That's the spirit."
He went back to searching for more rooftop ene-

mies, but the Phoenix Force pair and their newfound ally had depleted their ranks.

"Clear for now," James said, rushing over with his first-aid kit. "I'll look after our buddy's leg. Rafe…"

"I've got Striker's back," Encizo replied. He scooped up the sniper rifle and fed it a fresh magazine. "Take good care of him. Hearts and minds."

"You know it," James responded.

The Cuban warrior nestled behind the sniper rifle and set to work thinning out the crowd of Muslim Brotherhood soldiers who were trying to rush the rear of the hotel's compound. There was still work to be done.

CHAPTER SIX

Captain Fial Aflaq had been prepared for the coming of the nameless crusader for a full day. It was common knowledge among even African militiamen trained by the radical Islamic clerics of the Middle East that there was an American commando who stalked those who fought for the cause of converting the world to their ways. This one man, almost mythic in strength, prowess and the sheer number of kills attributed to him, was unknown, other than for the effects he had left behind him.

Aflaq jolted as he heard the rattle of a lone FAMAS preceding the rolling thunder of a multigrenade barrage. Shock gripped the Thunder Lion leader.

"Only ten men are reporting in," Lieutenant Anid told him, looking up from his radio.

Ten men? Aflaq's stomach churned as he processed his nephew's words. He realized that his fighting force had been halved in a matter of seconds. He was about to give the evacuation order when a powerful concussion shook the small hotel. Aflaq looked out the window and saw a column of smoke billowing upward from a corner of the compound. Rifles exchanged blistering salvos through the breach in the hotel grounds before the firefight was terminated by the bellow of a hand grenade.

"He's in here with us," Aflaq said, stunned.

Anid's eyes were wide with horror. "He told us not to side with Bitturumba any longer."

Aflaq's lips drew into a tight, bloodless scar across his face. "Run."

"But, Uncle—" Anid began to protest.

Aflaq gave the young man a hard push. "I ordered you to run!"

Anid nodded and spun, racing into the hallway. Even as Aflaq's door swung open, the Thunder Lion officer heard the blazing chatter of French FAMAS rifles, snarling in a vicious two-way cross fire. Anid whirled in the doorway, his shoulder blown into a bloody mess by a snap shot from down the hallway. Aflaq leaped across the office and pulled his nephew back to cover behind his desk. Was it too late for his sister's son?

"Fall back! Fall back!" Aflaq bellowed into Anid's walkie-talkie. "It's not worth dying for! Retreat!"

"Listen to your boss," Bolan's chilling voice agreed over the radio. The Executioner's Arabic was thickly accented, and by no means fluent, but where his words were slightly halting, the tone of voice conveyed a message easily understood. "The Thunder Lions will be extinct inside of a week. Why join Bitturumba all the way to the bitter end?"

"God," Aflaq prayed.

"No," Bolan responded, returning to his native English. "Not God. Just your judgment, Captain. It takes a lot more to earn my forgiveness."

Aflaq looked down to Anid, who was clutching his

wounded limb. "I have a wounded boy in here with me. Spare him. I ordered him to stay with me here."

Bolan strode into view, his tall frame filling the doorway. Clad all in black, bristling with weaponry, the grim figure of the Executioner turned Aflaq's bowels to ice water with his fearsome visage.

"No!" Anid shouted, almost deliriously. Somehow the eager youngster had twisted his left hand around and had pried his South African Vektor pistol from his hip holster. The sleek black Beretta clone filled his fist as Anid rose to confront the ferocious wraith looking across the desk.

Aflaq lunged and crashed into the wounded lad, knocking the pistol from his grasp. Its metal frame clattered on the floor of the office.

Bolan glared at Aflaq, who was certain that he had doomed himself.

Then the wraith spoke. "Make sure the kid behaves."

Aflaq kicked the weapon across the floor to Bolan. "I will."

"Good call." Bolan glanced out into the hallway. "Keep behind the desk. It's going to get a hell of a lot hairier in here."

Bolan fired three swift bursts down the hall, tagging targets in the distance. Satisfied that he'd bought himself a few moments, the Executioner reached into his battle harness, opening a pouch and taking out a small packet. He turned and lobbed it to Aflaq. "It's something to make the blood clot. Pour it on his shoulder wound, and it'll stop the bleeding."

Aflaq tore open the packet. "Peace be unto you, soldier."

Bolan was taken aback by the militiaman's gratitude. "Let's hope not too soon. I've got some aggression to extinguish."

The Executioner turned and fired another long burst from his FAMAS, targeting enemy gunmen making another approach to the office. He disappeared from Aflaq's sight, and the former militiaman did his best to be a healer.

THE THUNDER LION RESISTANCE had been shattered to pieces in almost record time. It didn't hurt that Bolan had destroyed half their fighting force in the space of ten seconds, but the conversion of Fial Aflaq and his nephew was an unexpected bonus. Now the Executioner was free to focus on the Muslim Brotherhood contingent who had foolishly dealt themselves into this battle. He keyed his throat mike. "Pushed back a fire team from the Egyptians. Any other advancement on my position?"

"Movement around the lobby at the front of the hotel," Encizo explained. "I don't have the range on my launcher and no straight shot with my rifle. Can't help you with them."

"Approximate numbers?" Bolan inquired.

"Eight to ten," Encizo answered. "I'm holding off another group, but they're retreating to try another approach."

"Let them through and just concentrate on your side of the hotel. They've only got one path to get to me, and if I know my back's covered, I can deal with their pressure," Bolan returned. "I've got my battlefield set up, and they're just being funneled into a slaughterhouse."

"Cattle don't usually bring AK-47s and RPGs into a slaughterhouse, Striker," James admonished.

Bolan plucked a fragmentation grenade from his thigh-mounted pouch and bowled the minibomb down the hallway heading toward the lobby. As the fragger's momentum petered out, the tip of the first Muslim Brotherhood assault team lurched into view. Bolan could see three sets of eyes widen with horror as they looked down at the smooth-skinned green egg of damnation that skittered toward them at head level as they rushed to the top of the steps. A moment later the grenade detonated and the three terrorists disappeared behind a cloud of flame, smoke and dust, their death cries swallowed in the throaty roar of the explosion.

The wall of fragmented razor wire wrapped around the grenade's explosive core didn't have the velocity to reach back to the Executioner as he crouched in a doorway twenty-five yards from ground zero. On the other hand, the renegade Egyptians were well within the ten-meter total kill radius of the rocketing, flesh-shredding shrapnel. Meat and skin were pulled from the Brotherhood's skulls, ripped away as the high-powered sheet of concussive energy struck them like an invisible guillotine blade, shearing through neck bones and ripping the dead men's heads clean off.

Killed twice over, the mutilated masses of flesh toppled backward onto their overpressure-stunned compatriots, throwing the Brotherhood's charge even further off balance. Bolan knew he'd only given himself a small window of opportunity against the Egyptian militia, so he charged to the end of the hallway as fast as he could. He fed the FAMAS a full kill-load while he was still on the run, charging a live round into the chamber as he put on the brakes. Bolan's momentum glided him across the smooth tile floor as if he were ice skating, slowing to a halt at the grenade-crumpled top step. He looked down the stairway and into the dazed opposition as they struggled to free themselves from beneath the tangled limbs of their three decapitated comrades.

Bolan opened fire with the FAMAS. At a range of less than three yards, the French rifle's full-powered 5.56 mm NATO rounds, launched from a full-length twenty inch barrel, had no difficulty in tunneling through the mass of jumbled bodies between him and the still stunned enemy. Searing along at 3200 feet per second, the bullets shredded through lifeless meat and bone as if they were made of tissue paper. Ugly craters dented the torsos of the terrorists jammed beneath the deadweight of their friends.

It was a brutal, merciless slaughter, one in which his opposition had very little chance, but Bolan knew that if he had been a mere two seconds slower, the Egyptian renegades would have pulled themselves free from their jumbled mass, grabbed their weapons and launched a hail of lead against him. The difference between two different one-way slaughters was the breadth of three or four heartbeats, and the Executioner's ruthless efficiency had kept him alive through thousands of such encounters.

"More movement on your side, Striker," James warned over the radio. "Rafe was right, that group swung back to try a different approach."

Bolan saw the mob of Muslim Brotherhood gunmen approach the lobby door. His FAMAS had been locked empty, and he let it drop on its sling, transferring to the mighty .44 Magnum Desert Eagle on his hip. When the Egyptians made their move, the need for his stealthy 9 mm weapons had ended, and the suppressed weapons didn't have the same reach and power as the Israeli-designed hand cannon. In a lightning quick movement, he leveled the .44 at the lobby doors, waiting for the right moment.

The first Egyptian through the door stopped cold, as if he'd struck an invisible brick wall, 240-grains of lead smashing violently through his forehead. The heavy-weight slug punched out of the back of the dead man's neck and speared into a gunman behind him, the poor guy screaming as the deformed hollowpoint round lanced into his groin, shredding through muscle to cut his femoral artery. It was a two-for-one shot that Bolan sometimes encountered when firing high-powered weapons at his enemies. It was the kind of bonus that Bolan didn't want to count on in the field. A jet of arterial blood hosed onto the other gunmen beside him, jolting them in surprise. The Executioner adjusted his aim and triggered two more rounds into the third and fourth terrorists who were trying to charge through the entrance.

The doorway suddenly became an unnavigable mass of bodies as four corpses blocked the way, bodies piled high enough to force anyone behind them to climb up and over the dead. This gave Bolan an opening to draw another fragmentation grenade. He popped the cotter pin and launched the munition past the pile of lifeless Egyptians. It bounced off a corpse's back and landed at the feet of a clutch of stacked up Brotherhood gunmen. The terrorists weren't able to go forward because the bodies of their Magnum-mutilated comrades were too high to easily step over, and the men at the back of the group were shoving too hard against them to allow them to haul the bodies out of the way. When the jammed up gunmen saw the lethal grenade arc into their midst, panic seized the group and they tried to force their way back against the crush of gunmen at the rear of their group. The riflemen at the back were unaware of the impending detonation at their feet until it came through.

The M-26 fragmentation grenade disintegrated, unleashing an umbrella of cutting force through the legs of the snarled terrorists, carving through thighs, knees and shins with enough force to rip them from their owners' bodies. Shrapnel sliced into vulnerable bellies, ripping open abdominal muscles and crushing intestines and lower spines. Bolan took the opportunity to slam a fresh magazine into the FAMAS and clean up the horrific mess caused by his grenade, firing head shots to end the suffering of those who still lived despite their brutal grenade-mauling.

"The Brotherhood's in full retreat," Encizo announced. "Ambush broken."

"Watch yourselves," Bolan warned. "The Brotherhood might not be too happy with you guys and take a parting shot."

"They tried to get us before," James stated. "They'd come up on the roof with us, but we put them back down."

"Let the survivors run," Bolan said. "The Brotherhood knows who they came after, that's why we had nearly a hundred of them show up to fight. By now, they've learned their lesson, in spades."

"The faster these creeps learn that they're no longer the top of the food chain, the better," James stated. "These screwheads need to be more scared."

"Trust me, I'm getting through to some of them," Bolan replied. "At least one of the Thunder Lions had a significant change of heart."

"We had a convert up here, too," James answered. "He won't be walking too well, but he's no longer interested in helping out violent insurgency anymore."

"Wish the ratio of slaughtered to converted was the other way around," Bolan said. "More good people are always welcome in the War Everlasting."

"Better than none redeemed," Encizo interjected.

Bolan returned to Aflaq's office. The former militia-man looked up from his first-aid efforts on his nephew.

"How's the shoulder?" Bolan asked.

"You'll never cow a true warrior for the Prophet," Anid snarled.

"Is that so?" Bolan returned. "The Egyptians abandoned close to fifty of their dead brothers after we were done with them. Let's call it sixty true warriors for the Prophet, bleeding their guts out, and forty or so survivors running away through the shadows, all defeated by three men. Three men including me."

Anid swallowed.

"My quarrel's not with the followers of Islam, only the jackals who use the Koran's teachings as a license to engage in rape and murder," Bolan said. "Tell me how gang-raping children and mass executions bring enlightenment to the people?"

Anid remained silent, his eyes cast down at the wound in his shoulder.

"Search your soul. Who is the truly merciful one here? Who destroyed an overwhelmingly superior force and crushed the fight out of it, then stopped long enough to assist in the healing of your wounds?" Bolan asked.

"You did," Anid admitted.

"Your uncle saved your life," Bolan told him. "Pick the right path in your beliefs and actions. The one that the Thunder Lions have chosen only brings them defeat and suffering at my hands."

Aflaq gave his nephew's hand a squeeze.

"I'm not telling you two to turn your back on God. I'm telling you that there are ways to be true to your faith that don't involve murder and pain. As your uncle said, peace be unto you."

Anid looked up and met Bolan's eyes.

"Understand?" Bolan asked.

"I do," Anid answered.

Bolan nodded and left the office.

Cartegena, Spain

SHAVED BALD, YET STILL wearing a thick beard, Igor Sharpova looked uncomfortable as he sidled up to Alonzo Cruz's table at the café. The midsummer sun raised a sheen of sweat on the Russian's forehead as Cruz watched the man's eyes flick nervously behind his sunglasses. The bulk of Sharpova's chest was further thickened by a concealed bulletproof vest.

"I ordered some iced tea for you, amigo," Cruz said.

Sharpova sat heavily. He snatched up a napkin and mopped at his wet brow. "I'm used to cooler climes. You do realize that this city comes under considerable scrutiny from NATO, the CIA and Interpol, do you not?"

Cruz chuckled. "Which is why we are talking here. This is a major port, the largest in Spain. Intrigue drips from the walls. Besides, you're a Russian. Yesterday's news. It's the Islamicists that the West fears."

Sharpova sighed. "So we're secure."

"Not if you keep acting so antsy and suspicious," Cruz replied. "Relax."

"What happened to the shipment?" Sharpova asked.

"What's the worst possible thing that could happen to you, Igor?" Cruz responded.

Sharpova grimaced. "You mean that we've been found out."

"I mean that your bogeyman has emerged from the shadows. And he's become very interested in the Darfur tests," Cruz told him. "Does he know what truly is going on? Unlikely."

Sharpova frowned, his jowls hanging, which increased his resemblance to a bulldog. "You don't understand. This man has derailed countless plots of ours around the world. He is the living doom to any who dare oppose him."

"Poetic," Cruz commented with a nod. "This time, however, we have knowledge on our side."

"Knowledge. Ninjas. Nerve gas. Nanotechnology. Nuclear weapons," Sharpova rattled off. "Nothing we've ever employed has been above his ability. You call him a man, but he is not human. No mortal could be so unerring and infallible."

Cruz smiled. "Yes, he is a terrifying opponent. Don't forget, you're allied with Thor and me."

"And the two of you actually possess the powers of gods?" Sharpova asked.

"Yes, we do," Cruz answered. He spread his hands, his fingertips tracing a globe in the air. "The two of us can halve the population of an entire continent at a whim. A continent full of teeming resources that would be lost or destroyed by any other means. Diamonds, oil, precious metals and nuclear materials litter Africa. Such a prize is beyond anyone's dreams."

Sharpova swallowed.

"You look very tense for a man who can tame the wild renegades of the Commonwealth of Independent States and open up a whole new frontier of limitless resources," Cruz noted.

Sharpova took another sip, shifting to get comfortable in his body armor. "But the devil is stalking us like a hungry lion."

"My brother knows how to deal with lions, and is himself a devil, my friend," Cruz said.

Sharpova grimaced. "I have some men on hand. Highly trained commandos. A small army at your beckoning if you need them."

Cruz nodded, acknowledging the Russian's generosity. "And I have my own highly trained security force. Throw in Thor's militia and the allies coming to him as we speak, and we can sweep away any minor irritant."

"Do not see this devil as one man, Alonzo. He is a force of nature, and he is simply not to be underestimated. We have done that in the past, and suffered greatly for it," Sharpova warned.

Cruz sighed. "I'm not stupid, Igor."

Sharpova looked around nervously. "Others have said that. They aren't around anymore. Keep that in mind."

The Russian excused himself and left.

Stony Man Farm, Virginia

HAL BROGNOLA LOOKED at the data the Executioner and his two Phoenix Force allies had gathered over the course of their operations in Alexandria. The men were sitting in front of their laptop in a video conference, grim-faced as they were displayed, twice normal size, on the video monitor wall. Brognola could tell why the trio was unhappy. The implications of their discovery left the big Fed's gut knotted as he saw the potential for tragedy. Mixing black-market military weaponry, a murderous plague and the ethnically charged slaughter occurring in the Darfur region meant a death toll that could easily top six figures in the space of a few days. The presence of Bitturumba's Thunder Lion militia was a disturbing note.

"Weaponized Ebola in the hands of a violent, radical Islamic group," Brognola said out loud, looking at Barbara Price, the Stony Man mission controller. She'd been infected with an artificially manufactured version of Ebola and would have died had not a treatment been developed by the CDC's researchers thanks to intel gathered by Kurtzman and his cyberteam.

Price cleared her throat, remembering her near brush with death. "We need to see if this current variant is vulnerable to the same treatments that helped me out. Regular Ebola Zaire has proved resistant to any vaccines or countermeasures developed off the designer variant utilized on me. This version might be based off the same DNA blueprint, or even have been recovered from a stockpile used by the Imam."

"I knew something wasn't kosher when the Russians loaded up an arms shipment for Alexandria," Bolan said. "Otherwise, I wouldn't have called in Cal and Rafe. This situation is about as bad as it gets. If the Thunder Lions succeed at their goals in the Sudan, we can see a lot more of viral outbreaks like the one at the refugee camp."

"We'd be talking global nightmares," Price agreed. "The only saving graces are that you have almost a one-in-two chance of surviving infection, and once the virus has been dispersed and settles, it goes inert and is no longer infectious. It's only contagious in human respiration, and it either kills or fades out after twenty-four hours. Those who aren't killed aren't infectious, but they look like they've been run over by a truck."

"It's no longer infectious, or just dormant?" Bolan asked. "Who knows how long this brand of virus can remain valid in soil or groundwater."

"So far, the WHO hasn't found any residual virus in soil samples. The microbe breaks down quickly. So far, we don't have a viable, living virus to test anything against," Price noted.

"We'll head in," Bolan announced. "Our USAM-RIID backgrounds are already with the World Health Organization, right? Cal can lend us credibility as a medical emergency investigation team."

Brognola bristled. "You'll be right at ground zero for an epidemic."

"Trouble is, Hal, we have what looks like an artificially manufactured virus out in the Sudan. If it's manufactured, then that means there is a strong possibility that there will be a form of treatment or a vaccine to grant immunity. Even if there isn't, we can intercept the means of dispersal and destroy them before they claim any more victims," Bolan countered. "We've encountered designer diseases enough times in the past, and the scientists who bred them leave a back door to treatment, if only for their own personal safety. The fabricators of these diseases aren't suicidal, no matter who they give this particular loaded gun to."

"Some things are just plain incurable," Brognola mentioned. "Remember the incident in Utah?"

"I do," Bolan answered. "But what should we do in that case? I'm not going to hide my head in the sand and hope the disease goes away. I'm going in, and if I can't help locate a cure, then I'll at least bring down every member of Bitturumba's murderous militia. However, I am going to make sure that I can slam the lid on this box before any more demons escape. It's a few countries over, and Darfur has been on my to-do list for too damn long."

"Good luck, Striker," Brognola said. "The WHO has your package and they're vetting you. Bear's set it up, as always. You'll be bought hook, line and sinker unless you start acting like the professional ass-kicker you are."

"I hope we're not there long enough for them to look at us that closely," Bolan replied. "But once we get there, I have a feeling that we'll have the time to attract more attention than the Thunder Lions and their disease."

CHAPTER SEVEN

Darfur, Sudan

Elee Aslin wasn't keen on leaving Tanya Marshall's side, not when she was pushing herself to the edge of a breakdown as she sought a solution to the origin of the latest viral outbreak. Unfortunately, Aslin's job description was transport pilot, not Marshall's personal morale coach. She had a job to do, and she did it, picking up the three American USAMRIID operatives. The trio was being sent by the Army's Medical Institute of Infectious Diseases to assist in the current crisis, as their focus was the use of diseases as biological weapons. As she leaned against her helicopter, an old workhorse UH-1 Huey, she spotted them. The highest-ranking officer in the group wasn't a doctor. The only doctor in the group was Calvin Farrow, and he was accompanied by two vaguely described assistants. Aslin kept her suspicions silent, but she was aware that this could just be a cover for a covert operation to investigate the source behind the bioweapon releases in Darfur. She remembered her compatriots from the Nairobi branch of the WHO talking about the apocalyptic assault on their headquarters.

A three-man team of commandos had come in and prevented the theft of multiple contagion samples, which would have begun a worldwide pandemic. The trio had come to the rescue with a U.S. Ranger contingent, supposedly, but one of the rescued staff members felt that the trio had been much more than mere Army personnel. However, the three men who approached the helicopter didn't match the descriptions. All of those men had been white, of average height, and one had a marked British accent.

Calvin Farrow was an African-American, tall and lanky. The men with him were another tall, powerfully built man with jet-black hair and cold blue eyes and a stocky, handsome Hispanic man with an pleasant, somewhat flirtatious smile for her.

"This is Colonel Brandon Stone and Captain Rafael Ruiz," James introduced as Aslin stood to greet them. The ground crew was still refueling and inspecting the Huey for its journey back to the refugee camp and the village.

"Should I call you major or doctor?" Aslin asked. She noted that the men weren't wearing uniforms, nor insignias, though their BDU shirts gave them a military bearing.

James shrugged. "Major. I'm here to kill."

Aslin raised an eyebrow. "The virus dies fast enough."

"I've read that. It just doesn't die quickly enough for my tastes," James answered. "I'm here to help in the effort. Engage in preventative extermination. Kill it before it takes any more victims."

Encizo inclined his head. "You can call me Rafe."

Aslin looked away from James and gave the Cuban a beaming smile. "Elee."

"Charmed," Encizo answered.

Aslin glanced toward Bolan, who had the demeanor of a hungry lion, eyes and ears peeled to the horizon, looking for signs of marauding hyenas poised to swoop down on the pride he defended. "Colonel?"

"Brandon is fine," Bolan answered distractedly. Aslin turned to see what he was looking for.

"I haven't seen anything to worry about yet," Bolan informed her, giving her a reassuring smile. "But it's my job to be on the alert."

"Security seems a petty job for a colonel," Aslin mused.

Bolan shrugged off her suggestion. "I tend to lead from the front. My friends still call me Sarge."

"As in sergeant?" Aslin asked.

Bolan nodded.

"Hell of a promotion," Aslin commented.

"Consider it earned the hardest way possible," Bolan said. The suddenness and finality of the statement informed Aslin that he'd told her all he ever intended to about his background, yet still left the air clear of any hostility or secrecy.

"Usually the USAMRIID brings in a larger contingent," Aslin probed. She could read on the colonel's face that he was being given the preliminary inquiry about his cover story here.

"We're the advanced party," James explained. "We were in the area when we learned of the outbreak. I heard that there was a second anomaly."

"Anomaly. That's a fine word for it," Aslin muttered. "If you can limit calling the bloody, gruesome deaths of three hundred women and children just an anomaly. You have ice for blood, Farrow?"

"I'm referring to how the virus showed up, not its effects," James countered calmly. "You might not think us colored folk from the U.S. care about the folks in the old country, but people are people, Elee. If I seem detached, it's because I'm a scientist, trying to use logic to solve a problem before it claims more innocent lives."

Aslin took a deep breath. "Sorry, Major. I've just seen a lot of ugly death over the past couple of days."

"Call me Cal," James offered.

"Has anyone gathered any new data on the virus so far?" Bolan asked. "Stuff that isn't eight hours old?"

Aslin turned to Bolan. "No. We have a diminished team at the village gathering up data. The others are still tending to the survivors in the refugee camp."

"We'd like to check the village first," James said. "If the enemy has found a dispersal vector that doesn't involve artillery shells, finding it is our topmost priority."

"I have a friend there who agrees with you, Cal," Aslin told him. "My bird's almost ready to go. I'm going to go grab some coffee for the flight back."

She started to walk off when she caught a glimpse of Bolan whispering to Encizo before the swarthy, handsome Cuban jogged to catch up with her.

"I don't need a babysitter," Aslin said.

"He just thought I could help cart coffee back to the ship," Encizo replied. "With brass this high, us captains are little more than gofers."

"I thought he worked for a living," Aslin asked.

"Worked as in scraping his knuckles and getting his hair singed," Encizo informed her. "But when it comes to getting shit from the cafeteria, he likes to be waited on like the next colonel."

"That's a pretty good cover story," Aslin noted.

The Cuban's smile was almost warm enough to disarm her suspicions. "We are here to help, Elee."

"I know. I just think we're better served by a medical team, not secret agents," Aslin replied.

"Cal is a great doctor," Encizo noted. "And we'll also serve."

Aslin nodded. She realized that if the Thunder Lion militia was truly behind the outbreak, the Darfur region would need the kind of muscle these men would bring to the table.

This was a menace that required bullets as well as pills.

KARTENNIAN SHOOK HIS HEAD, looking at the after-action report sent by the commander of the Alexandrian Muslim Brotherhood. With seventy of their eighty-man force dead or missing, the Egyptian terrorist organization had suffered a crippling blow. Bodies were strewed across the abandoned hotel and surrounding streets. Frustratingly, none of the corpses had belonged to any non-Egyptians, and none were identified as members of Egyptian law enforcement or intelligence. Aflaq had described the lone warrior who had menaced him on the docks as a white man who'd blended in with the Russians. No such corpse turned up, and even Aflaq and his nephew were both missing.

It was doubtful that a Western special operations team would leave behind one of their own, even if he had been killed. What got into Kartennian's head was that the pitiful few survivors of the Muslim Brotherhood ambush force reported encountering only one or two men at the most. Descriptions, vague from the fog of battle, narrowed it down to three distinct enemies. Two were tall, one of average height. Of the tall men, one was Caucasian, but his face and hands had been smeared with black greasepaint, making him a nearly invisible wraith in the darkness. The other man appeared to be African and the short one was swarthy.

Three men against eighty Muslim Brotherhood warriors and twenty highly trained Thunder Lion militiamen. Thirty-three-to-one odds and the Islamicist fighters were routed completely.

"You seem a man with much on his mind." Bitturumba's booming voice cut into his thoughts. The Turk looked up from his intelligence reports. Kartennian knew his eyes were bloodshot, bags drooping heavily beneath them.

"I am reading a horror story, Thor," Kartennian replied. "I am reading of a terrible explosion of violence in Alexandria that left our brothers in arms devastated, but with no benefit shown for the action."

"No benefit?" Bitturumba asked.

"Seventy corpses in and around the hotel, and at least a dozen more missing. And yet, the attacker and his allies appear to have gone through unharmed."

"How many allies?" Bitturumba inquired.

"Three. Maybe as many as five," Kartennian responded. "No confirmed kills, nor sign of injury on their behalf."

Bitturumba nodded. "One trap failed. We will need another."

"Such as what? A stampede of elephants?"

Bitturumba chuckled. "I was thinking of a different force of nature. Where overwhelming force failed, subtlety will carry our standard."

Kartennian's stress faded and he allowed himself a sigh of relief. "Ebola Thunder."

"We shall have to make our bait especially tasty," Bitturumba noted. "If we make the trap too easy, it will foil the whole plan. We have to force the warrior to work his way to the conclusion, testing him both mentally and physically, so that when he walks into the jaws of death, he will succumb."

"Which means we will have to lose many more resources," Kartennian replied, his mood darkening.

Bitturumba smirked. "We have many allies around us. All of them are interested in joining my team now that I have demonstrated a level of power they have never seen before. They will lend me the cream of their fighting forces in exchange for a place at the king's table."

"Even if it's a blatant sacrifice to an unstoppable enemy?" Kartennian was incredulous at the thought.

Bitturumba stifled his next chuckle. "This is Africa, where men are forged against a continent intent on murdering humans. From the smallest microbes to the greatest pachyderms, from volcanic lakes capping a cloud of village-killing gases to heat that will crack skin to dust, man must either be the prey or the predator. Our newly recruited allies don't care about an individual life, and will see that thorn in our side as a challenge truly worthy of their might. They will strive to destroy him. If they fail, they lead him into our clutches. And if they succeed, we will triumph."

BOLAN COULDN'T HAVE examined the village more in-depth with a fine-tooth comb, applying his own considerable senses to determining how the population had been exposed to a lethal dose of airborne microbes. While it wasn't staging a one-man assault on a heavily defended enemy fortification, seeking clues was as vital a part of the Executioner's War Everlasting as aiming and pulling the trigger. His ability to collate and analyze data enabled him to track down subversive groups, underground terrorist cells and criminal conspiracies. That same skill helped him see the weak points of his enemies, enabling him to strike crippling, murderous blows against superior odds with a minimum of risk and effort. Bolan was a tireless hunter, following leads wherever he found them.

"Any luck?" Encizo asked.

Bolan shook his head. "So far no shrapnel or parachutes. I didn't see any indication of ground-based dispensers, like an aerosol container packed in the earth. The lack of evidence of any dispersal device seems to point in only one direction."

"Crop duster," Encizo stated, remembering the dissection of potential infection vectors. The Stony Man trio had brainstormed potential means of releasing the microbes on the flight down from Egypt to Sudan. "Or a helicopter. But the problem with that is the flight crew would end up infected. The pilots would be useless after one flight, even if they survived the initial exposure."

"Not if the ground crew was inoculated or otherwise provided with protective measures," Bolan said. "Since this appears to be a manufactured virus, my bet is on inoculation."

Encizo's brow furrowed. "We'll have to perform a recon of nearby airports and airfields. I've been going over the map, and with Bear's help I narrowed down some isolated strips. The Thunder Lions obviously would avoid using one of their own."

"That would require vaccination of all the militia and their support crews," Bolan agreed. "With that many doses of vaccine, there's a potential threat that a sample could fall into the hands of investigators, rendering their weapon useless. We're talking about a small, self-contained team. And they won't be near any indigenous population to limit the potential of a containment failure putting up a neon sign leading us right to viral samples."

"If we go in after the team, we'll need to capture at least two prisoners to get enough blood samples so that the WHO can reverse engineer a vaccination or even a form of emergency treatment," Encizo suggested.

"No one ever said our job would be easy, but at least we know where to look for a solution." Bolan frowned, thoughts turning over in his head. "I wish we'd been able to tap Jack for this operation."

Encizo knew that the Executioner was referring to ace Stony Man pilot Jack Grimaldi. "What about Elee?"

"I've got Aaron vetting her," Bolan replied. "If she turns out to be on the Thunder Lions' payroll, our recon is going to be short, messy and deadly."

"If there's something rotten about Elee, you or I would have picked up on it. Still, if there's something compromising her, Bear's team would find it. And if she is working for the bad guys…" Encizo paused, weighing the distasteful thought for a moment. "If she is a bad guy, then we can always ask her a few questions."

"But, if we get rough on her, we'll burn bridges with the WHO investigators," Bolan noted.

Encizo shrugged. "Then let's hope she comes up clean."

Cartagena, Spain

ALONZO CRUZ TOOK A PUFF on his cigarette, looking over the Gulfstream private jet as the team loaded its gear into the cargo compartment. Heinz Baldr walked toward Cruz, satisfied that his mercenary strike force was performing its preflight preparation with efficiency. Baldr was an Austrian who had been part of the elite COBRA antiterrorism initiative. Baldr's counterterrorism career had been cut short when it was learned that he was training Saudi Arabian security teams to the same standard as the Austrian government forces.

"So the Russians are freaked out by this guy?" Baldr asked.

"He's a nightmare, apparently," Cruz explained. "And from what went down in Alexandria, he's more than just a scary bedtime story to tell the little mobsters. The Muslim Brotherhood cell in the city was almost exterminated when they sprung their trap."

Baldr raised an eyebrow. "How many?"

"Eighty Brotherhood and twenty of Thor's boys against three to five opponents," Cruz answered. "You think you can handle him? Thor thinks he has the upper hand with his coalition in Darfur. He says he has a plan, but he thought he had that in Alexandria."

"I'll work with him," Baldr stated. "Your brother's not dim. You don't claw your way to the top of the food chain in Africa without being brutally cunning."

Cruz dragged in a deep breath. "You're right. I'm not on the ground with him over there. Just make sure this doesn't track back to me."

Baldr tilted his head. "All those bodies I've put in the

ground for you, and you're still worried that I'll make a mistake?"

Cruz smiled, disarming Baldr's offense. "I believe in the belt-and-suspenders approach. That's why you're going to Africa, and it's why I don't take your immaculate past performance for granted. I've never been disappointed by you, but there is always a first time, especially if you grow complacent."

Baldr nodded. "Fair enough. I'll take this bogey out, and no one will know you had a hand in it."

Cruz shook Baldr's hand. "Now, if you'll excuse me, I have a press conference to attend."

"One would think that you loved raking your brother over the coals," Baldr said.

Cruz chuckled. "I speak, and Europeans feel good about themselves that we're speaking out against the crisis in Sudan. Thor gets all the attention he wants and free publicity. Then he goes on African TV and gives his speeches against me, and Africa loves him for pissing in the white man's eye. The two of us are playing entire continents like violins."

CHAPTER EIGHT

Elee Aslin stormed into the tent where Calvin James rested, exhausted from hours of research.

"Wake up!" she snarled.

James blinked at her wearily. "What's wrong now?"

"Where's that bastard, Stone?" Aslin snapped. "Where do you people get off running background checks on me?"

James knuckled some sleep out of the corner of his eye. "Isn't it obvious that we don't have our normal pilot crew, and you're working with the military? We need someone we can trust. That he did a check on you shows how much trust you've earned already."

"What?" Aslin stiffened in indignation. "He trusts me, so he starts a background check?"

"If he didn't trust you, he wouldn't be jumping through the hoops necessary to get our command to approve you being brought onto the case," James explained as he stifled a yawn. "In fact, if Stone was working alone, without me or Ruiz, he'd have just bucked the normal OPSEC and just asked you to fly him around."

"OPSEC?" Aslin asked.

"Operational security," James told her. "It's been a long day, Elee, and I'm burned out. I need to get back to sleep."

"Stone trusts me," Aslin mused softly.

James nodded. "It's for the sake of the more paranoid people back home that we're subjecting you to this."

The Phoenix Force medic turned over on his cot, wrapped his arm around a pillow and was back to sleep in moments. Aslin left the man to his slumber, stepping out of the tent. She spotted Stone and Ruiz as they walked with a purpose toward her. Stone had a gun belt draped over his shoulder in addition to his own regular holstered weapons.

"I apologize for intruding upon your privacy," Bolan said. He handed her the pistol belt. "You might want to strap this on if you're going to be traveling with us."

Aslin wrapped the belt around her slender waist. The nylon harness and holster hung comfortably on her hips. She withdrew the pistol in the holster and looked it over. The slide read Smith & Wesson Military and Police 9 mm. She kept her finger clear of the trigger guard as she confirmed that there was a round in the chamber. "Loaded already?"

"Defensive firearms are useless with an empty chamber," Bolan explained. "Plus, that gun is a simple and safe design. It won't fire unless you touch the trigger. No complicated safeties or decockers, and it's as reliable as a fork. Of course, our background check has shown us you've been around firearms for all your life."

Aslin put the MP-9 back in its holster. "I'd have been good with a Glock or a Browning, but this is nice. Farrow explained about why you went into my records."

Bolan nodded. "I figured as much when you didn't even bat an eye and strapped the gun on without a fuss."

Aslin shrugged. "If we don't stop Bitturumba in Darfur, he'll be dropping Ebola shells on my home next. If that means I have to put a bullet into an ethnic cleansing sack of garbage, well, you've given me the ammo to do it."

Encizo grinned in approval. "I like her, Colonel. Can we keep her?"

Bolan winked. "It's not my decision, Rafe."

"I take it we're leaving right now?" Aslin asked.

Bolan nodded. "Rafe and I narrowed down some possible airfields that could have launched a crop duster or helicopter carrying the Ebola to the village in an aerosol suspension."

Aslin frowned. "So there might be a key to treatment if we find the airfield?"

"At least a vaccination," Encizo offered. "Not sure if the virus is treatable given how fast it attacks the cellular structure of its victims."

"Well, given its fifty-fifty lethality rate, it might just be treatable," Aslin noted.

"We'll cross that bridge when we get to it," Bolan said. "Right now, I'd like to get into the air to make the most of the night."

Aslin looked at the setting sun. "Then we'd best get moving."

BOLAN ADMIRED Elee Aslin's stoic restraint as she bore the burden of night-vision goggles hanging on her flight helmet. Flying a helicopter at night was a very vision-intensive activity, so the goggles were a necessity for Aslin, who had kept the chopper's running lights turned off. Bolan and his allies would be difficult to spot from the ground in darkness. Utilizing tree line cover and hills, Aslin was also able to minimize the sound profile of the helicopter. The woman had a natural skill for flying stealthily, and Bolan knew that she had learned such tactics and maneuvers from her father, a renowned bush pilot who had worked for the CIA in helping to cover various brushfire wars across the continent. Bolan sat in the role of copilot for Aslin, and was required to wear the heavy, awkwardly weighted helmet with the goggles, as well. The Executioner might not have had the same experience in flying helicopters as Aslin or Jack Grimaldi, but he'd spent enough hours at the stick of a UH-1 Huey to be able to take over in case Aslin suffered an injury or was otherwise incapacitated.

The thought of Aslin coming to harm weighed heavily on Bolan's mind. Sure, she had the gun on her hip and was wearing a protective helmet and Kevlar vest, but Bolan had seen far too many friends cut down, even behind the best of protective shields.

"I see a riverbed we can set down in," Aslin said. "If there's a force in the field, they won't have heard us. I can land, and you'll be able to sneak up on them."

"Good eyes," Bolan noted. He checked over his shoulder as Encizo readied their war bags for the upcoming assault. It was their third stop this night, but neither the Stony Man commandos nor their pilot were taking things for granted.

The helicopter's skids touched the bottom of the riverbed. Encizo handed Bolan his rifle. Both men were carrying VEPRs, American reconstructed versions of the world-famous AK-47 assault rifle.

The VEPR was a modern update, utilizing better

sights, a stronger receiver for improved accuracy and fiberglass furniture with Picatinny rails for needed attachments, such as the compact grenade launchers mounted underneath the stubby barrels of the assault weapons. The compact rifles were lengthened somewhat by the addition of flash suppressors to their muzzles. That, plus the low-flash high-grade military powder, would allow them to return fire against enemy soldiers without giving away their positions.

Bolan and Encizo pulled up their camouflage-pattern respirator masks to cover their noses and mouths. Plastic framed, with carbon fiber filters, the masks were tough and durable. All evidence from studies of the virus's progression showed that its infection vector was airborne, but not permeable through the skin or tear ducts. The masks would provide the two Stony Men warriors with at least some protection from Bitturumba's strain of Ebola if the abandoned hangar they saw was staffed with Thunder Lion forces. The likelihood of enemy gunners being present was uncertain as the trio hadn't found anything of worth on their previous two stops.

Bolan was glad to have left his helmet back at the helicopter, and his eyes quickly adjusted to the light thrown off by the reflective sliver of moon hanging in the night sky. He brought up his binoculars and swept the low blockhouse beside a graded, earthen airstrip. The setup was amenable to single-engine prop planes, but there was a flattened patch that looked as if it could serve as a helicopter landing pad. The curved barrel of a camouflaged, corrugated hangar shell was off to one side, but from his current position, he didn't have a clear view to see if there were any aircraft parked within.

Something else caught his attention. Grasses around the packed-dirt airstrip rustled unnaturally, moving when there was no breeze. Bolan looked back at Encizo, who nodded that he had also noticed the threat stalking through the long grass.

"It's not lions," Encizo said. "There's too much forest around. Leopards would be in the trees, not on the ground, and any of the big cats would have heard the helicopter and bolted. Their hearing would have picked up the bird's approach a lot better than mere human ears."

"There are Lions in the grass, but they're Bitturumba's pets," Bolan corrected. "He knew we'd eventually figure out how he was delivering the virus without use of artillery shells."

"How do we play it?" Encizo asked.

Bolan's answer was to slip a 40 mm fragmentation shell from his thigh pouch. Encizo grabbed one, as well, and stuffed it into the tube under the barrel of his rifle. The two pulled the triggers on their MP-203s, twin missiles searing in a gentle arc through the night to land amid the unnaturally rustling grass. They moved laterally, taking cover in a copse as the grenades landed, watching as their minibombs landed and detonated. Gunmen screamed in shock and agony under the shredding assault of the packed shrapnel rounds. Gunfire lanced toward the tree line, focusing on where the coughs of grenade launchers had been heard. Rifle slugs shredded grass and splintered tree trunks in impotent revenge for the explosive assault upon their force. None of the enemy gunmen had thought that their targets would have moved to flank them.

The enemy's rifles produced sharp muzzle-flashes, and their distinct chatter gave away the force's identity.

Bolan knew that the Thunder Lions loved their high-tech French FAMAS assault rifles, and the riflemen in the grass were shooting AKs. Bolan shouldered his own rifle and flicked the selector to semiauto, utilizing precision marksmanship to minimize his rifle's already low muzzle profile to begin thinning out the enemy. The maneuver allowed him to conserve ammunition as well as avoid enemy attention as he punched rounds into the sea of grass everywhere an enemy weapon flared.

Encizo kept his VEPR on full-auto, utilizing his weapon for suppressive fire against the massed enemy who were slowly aware that they were being attacked from their flank. Even though the Cuban's rifle was firing at its full cyclic rate, he wasn't wasting ammunition wantonly. He limited his bursts to three or four rounds, even as he raked groups of opposing soldiers.

"What's your estimate?" Bolan asked.

"I count forty," Encizo answered. "Once they get their act together, they'll surround us."

"Better surround them first," the Executioner responded. He popped off another burst to silence an enemy rifle. "Take that flank and pull some heat down after you. I'll check out the hangar."

Encizo nodded and scurried off, staying low. He encountered a clot of five militiamen, and from the start, he had proof that these gunmen weren't part of Bitturumba's cadre. Indoctrinated Thunder Lions were proud of their crisp, black uniforms and maroon berets. These soldiers were clad in rumpled khaki gear and the patches were as equally wrong as their personal weaponry. The Cuban processed this information in the quick glance he took before triggering his VEPR. His first shots smashed into one African at waist level, bullets pulverizing pelvic bone and breaking spine before tumbling on into the gut of a second man. The militia gunners scrambled, trying to escape the Phoenix Force fighter's fire, but one crashed to the ground with the additional weight of three bullets lodged in his heart. The African ground into the dirt, dragged down violently by gravity.

Encizo threw himself to the ground, just under the onslaught of the two remaining rifles. The enemy bullets cut the air over his head and the Cuban cut loose at ankle height. A burst of 7.62 mm rounds tore into the gunners' lower bodies, chewing up through thighs and bellies in a bowel-coring swathe of destruction. The brief firefight was over as suddenly as it had begin, but the damage was already done. Encizo's position had been given away and the airfield defenders turned their attention toward him.

The Executioner, who was swiftly circling to their left, lent a hand to his partner and fired off his reloaded MP-203 grenade launcher. The first grenade struck a standing rifleman between his shoulder blades as he rallied his men to fire on the Cuban. The high explosive split the African's torso into a spray of flesh petals, like a grisly rose, shrapnel shredding the gunmen around him. Bolan swiftly reloaded and fired a second shell into another group before triggering his VEPR on full-auto. The blasts ripped into the ranks of the enemy militiamen and pulled their attention off his teammate. The assault rifle added to the distraction with a slashing, sustained hose of 7.62 mm thunder that raked gunmen who were closing in on Encizo's position, buying him more time to lose himself in the fog of war.

He heard Encizo's rifle raking the exposed flank of

the defenders, chopping them apart. The Stony Man commando had formed the second half of the cross fire, and their use of cover and concealment had left the opposition completely surrounded, the two-axis assault providing no avenue of retreat for the militiamen.

It was a rout, and the survivors charged frantically to escape. Bolan didn't blame them for cutting and running. The murderous riflemen were used to unarmed victims, not trained fighting men, and they had assumed that they would just spring their ambush on enemies who didn't have the awareness or discipline to launch a concerted counterattack. Against the coolheaded and well-prepared Bolan and Encizo, the militiamen were simply outclassed. Outthought, outmaneuvered and outfought, the thugs were simply thrown off balance. Superior tactics had once again carried the battle.

"I'll move in on the hangar now," Encizo said.

"Wait," Bolan ordered. "The Thunder Lions laid out a trap for us, but I'm certain that those guys weren't the main event."

"It sure sounded that way," Aslin interjected. "I have an angle on the hangar from here, and through the binoculars, I can see a prop plane with an underwing canister setup."

Bolan's instincts were working overtime. He had maneuvered into position, but he didn't want to give voice to that information and give away his position. He brought his binoculars up and swept the interior of the hangar. "From where you are, you don't have enough resolution on your goggles. The plane has an underwing canister, but the ship doesn't have an engine. It's an old carcass."

"You sure?" Aslin asked.

"A prop plane needs propeller blades, doesn't it?" Bolan asked.

He could almost sense Aslin squinting across the terrain toward the hangar. "So what's in the canister?"

"A booby trap? Bait?" Bolan mused. Encizo reunited with the Executioner. Both men were aware that the Thunder Lions had earned their appellation by being masters of battlefield artillery. A hangar full of aerosol suspension biological weapons would be tempting bait, and the hangar itself was most likely already dialed in and targeted by various low-profile, high-mobility field pieces. All the two of them would have to do was get close enough to the hangar, and if the ring of shells didn't shatter their bodies or riddle them with a lethal rain of shrapnel, then a well-targeted round could have released the contents of the container. Be it Ebola Thunder in liquid suspension or a simple canister filled with napalm, Bolan and Encizo were well within a deadly fallout radius. There wasn't much worry that the two of them would inhale the airborne microbes with their masks on, but a concentrated artillery assault was still quite capable of making life a living hell for the two warriors.

"Of course, if we don't close in for inspection, we'll be leaving a biohazard threat unchecked and it could still fall into the wrong hands, or leak and infect a passerby later on," Encizo said.

"Follow me," Bolan ordered. The Cuban trekked back to the tree line, about four hundred fifty yards away from the hangar. Bolan shouldered the VEPR and set it to single shot. Encizo raised his binoculars as the Executioner adjusted his scope and sights for the extreme range.

"Rafe, get a thermite grenade ready for your launcher, just in case there's something inside the canister," Bolan suggested. Encizo swiftly did so.

Bolan concentrated on the long-range shot. Common wisdom kept the 7.62 mm ComBloc round at a maximum effective range of only three hundred fifty yards, but that was still dangerously close, especially with the potential for portable mortars and small field pieces camped out in the terrain around the airstrip.

Though Aslin had flown a circuit around the strip, assisting Bolan and Encizo in searching for potential artillery hides, there were still plenty of trees and depressions for mortars and jeep-portable field pieces to be placed, rolled out once the helicopter had completed its orbit and approach. Bolan held his aim high, compensating for the bullet drop across four hundred fifty yards of range. With a single press of the trigger, the round snapped into a curved parabolic arc.

Through the binoculars, Encizo could see the dust shake off the underwing canister as the bullet slammed into its thin metal skin. He lowered the glasses and glanced to Bolan. "No napalm or explosives inside."

"And no fluid leak?" Bolan asked.

Encizo checked the canister again. "Zilch. Just a hole in the lowest part of the canister. I presume you put the round down there to encourage drainage."

"If there was suspension fluid for the weaponized virus, I wanted it to spill in a small spot so you could follow up with the thermite grenade," Bolan stated. "Even though it would be as long a shot for you as it was for me."

"I'd have…" Encizo began, when there was a distant

crackle rolling across the terrain. "Guess they knew they missed their shot at us."

The rustle of mortar shells slicing in their own indirect arcs through the night sky rumbled hot on the heels of the mobile pieces reports.

Bolan was certain that the trap was defanged now as the impotent thunder of distant field pieces sounded. Artillery shells slammed, after their long journey, into the hangar, blowing it to splinters as other rounds peppered down into the grassy clearing. Hot white clouds burst in the sky, snarling maggots of flame twisting to the earth, white phosphorous setting the grass they landed upon ablaze in instants. As the detonating artillery fire walked closer to their positions, Encizo and Bolan raced back toward the helicopter and the riverbed.

Aslin had the engines firing up on the Huey as the pair scrambled aboard, hauling their war bags along with them. The earth shuddered under the vengeful wrath of the Thunder Lions, but the militia was too late to stop the Executioner and his allies as they took to the night sky.

CHAPTER NINE

"That was useless," Aslin muttered as the Huey rose, arcing away from the riverbed as mortar shells impotently slammed into the ground they'd only just occupied.

"Not completely," Bolan said. "We know that Bitturumba has expanded his authority to multiple militias. He's building a coalition with the strength of his bioweapon."

"That knowledge is worthless in terms of fighting Ebola Thunder," Aslin groused. "We were hoping to catch at least a live sample of the virus. Something we can utilize for a treatment."

Bolan took a calming breath. "I know. Don't think I'm not frustrated by the lack of results. I'm not looking at the world through rose-colored glasses."

"Sorry, Brandon," Aslin apologized. "So we head back to the refugee camp, or do we look for the real airstrip?"

Bolan kept his binoculars trained on the positions where the Thunder Lions had opened fire. "They're breaking down to return to their base. Swing around and get me ahead of them on the road."

Aslin raised a slender eyebrow. "You're kidding, right?"

"No. I'm going to try to infiltrate one of Bitturumba's bases to see if I can gather information from there," Bolan stated. "Keep a low profile so they don't hear us getting ahead of them."

"I didn't mean to embarrass you into risking your life for more concrete results," Aslin protested as she followed the course pointed out by the Executioner.

"You aren't," Bolan stated. "The Thunder Lions saw this helicopter leave, and they'll assume we are going back to base. I want them to keep thinking that, so I can catch them while they're unaware."

"What about me?" Encizo asked.

"Help bolster security back at the camp," Bolan said. "I'm certain that Bitturumba will make a move tonight, and you and Calvin are the best bet that the WHO and the Ethiopian guards have against any assault force moving in."

"And if they utilize air-burst shells to disperse the virus?" Encizo pressed.

"Make certain that anyone who hasn't been previously infected is equipped with a respirator. The survivors of the first infection have the bonus that they've developed antibodies against the disease," Bolan suggested.

"What we really have to worry about is their heavy field artillery landing in the camp," Aslin noted. "We came prepared for microbes, not submunitions."

"That's part of the reason I want to sneak back into Bitturumba's forward base," Bolan stated. "Their long-range guns could easily have turned that entire airstrip into a crater, but they only used the small stuff. I'm hedging my bets that the Thunder Lions are looking elsewhere to drop their big guns."

Aslin looked down at the woeful, lonely trail that had been worn by decades of hooves and tires, cutting a permanent scar in the grassland. "This is the place."

Bolan knew from his mental map that the hard-packed dirt road led back to Muslim-held territory. "Don't worry, Elee. I've done this hundreds of times before. Just ask Rafael."

Aslin glanced back to Encizo.

"He's not exaggerating," the Cuban noted.

Aslin hovered five feet above the road and Bolan hopped down to the dirt, landing in a crouch to cushion his knees and spine. The helicopter climbed higher into the night sky, racing back toward the refugee camp. The Executioner silently wished his allies well as he picked a spot to lie in wait for the Thunder Lions' convoy.

Bolan didn't have long to wait. Inside of a minute, he caught a flash of distant headlights and his blacksuit-clad frame slid into the long grass at the roadside, blending in with the shadows. He'd just finished burying a SLAM munition—a multipurpose, one-kilogram explosive device no larger than a package of cigarettes—in the dirt of the old trail. The device had been set to "motion detection land mine" mode, primed to detonate with the considerable vibration of a passing vehicle. He set up an ambush point, ready to open fire on the Thunder Lion convoy if they detected his presence. Bolan had a thermite grenade, as well as several 40 mm fragmentation shells on hand just in case he needed heavier firepower to equalize the odds against the African militia. One shot with the thermite grenade would be sufficient to cripple the militiamen's vehicles, but that wasn't Bolan's true goal.

The convoy drew close and as the lead SUV, a Mercedes 550 model, closed in on the SLAM, the mini-munition armed due to the vibrations created by the knobby tires on the hard-packed dirt. A heartbeat later, a focused cone of kinetic energy knifed up through the loosened soil and slashed through the 8-cylinder diesel engine as if it were butter. The eruption was powerful enough to punch through the belly of an armored personnel carrier and even the weaker points of a battle tank, so a simple "off the rack" four-wheel drive vehicle was helpless under the concentrated spear of thermobaric force erupting from the SLAM. The lead vehicle, not pulling an artillery piece, was split apart, its engine compartment carved into petals of ruined metal as if it were a soft-skinned fruit chopped by a machete. The driver and the rifleman riding shotgun with him died instantly, torn by shrapnel burning through their faces and chests as the dashboard erupted into a million fragments. A man sitting in the back of the 4WD clambered out, furious and smeared with blood. However, given his animated demeanor and the strength of his command bellows, the convoy commander was relatively unharmed, despite being soaked in the gore of his men.

Subsequent SUVs and technicals in the convoy pulled to a quick halt. The technicals were pickup trucks with mounted machine guns, and the crews riding in the back immediately opened fire, tracers scrawling arcs of yellow fire through the night, seeking out the ambushers who'd just taken out their commander's vehicle.

From Bolan's vantage point, only a few feet from a towed one-inch recoilless rifle, it was an impressive show of firepower, and had it been a military force that was planning a deadly assault, the swathes cut by .30- and .50-caliber machine guns would have carved up even the most hardened of attack teams. Bolan broke from the grass and leaped deftly on the hitch between the towed artillery piece and the Peugeot 4WD hauling the rifle back to base. The blood-splattered man's voice cut through the cacophony of machine guns, the call to cease-fire relayed by gunners all down the line. Bolan settled into place, braced out of sight of the driver of the Peugeot and the crew in the back. There wasn't a vehicle behind the Peugeot as the rear-guard, a Toyota, raced around just off road to tend to the commander and whatever other survivors would have remained in the Mercedes. One of the technicals orbited around the back of the convoy, plowing through the grass, but the driver and machine gunners were more interested in external threats than they were aware that a lone man might have secreted himself away on a vehicle hitch. Thus, they were unaware of the infiltrator in their ranks.

Once the convoy had convinced itself that it had dodged a bullet, the Thunder Lions shoved the destroyed Mercedes out of the way and barreled on, speeding along the road to make up for lost time. They were in a hurry to get back behind the secure lines of their firebase's perimeter.

The militiamen were oblivious to the one-man force of nature they were bringing home with them.

CALVIN JAMES HAD HIS VEPR ready and had climbed into a guard tower of the refugee camp. The WHO medics and their Ethiopian Expeditionary Force allies had added the two hundred survivors of the village outbreak to the camp's roster. The move had been made to improve safety and security, as well as to centralize medical treatment efforts for all the Ebola Thunder victims. It also facilitated the ability to quarantine the population in case of the virus suddenly benefiting from an ability to remain dormant among its forty-five percent of survivors. If those who had suffered became infectious carriers, then they'd all be in one place, and not out among the rest of the African populace.

The Ethiopian in the guard tower acknowledged James's presence with a quiet, respectful nod. James didn't worry too much about not appearing to be a U.S. Army officer because he was carrying an AK-based weapon. The modular format of the advanced VEPR's stock made it easy for the Phoenix Force medic to pass it off as a tarted-up M-4 assault rifle utilizing various furniture attachments. It would take an extremely sharp eye to note the steep curve of the banana magazine and the larger hole in the end of the rifle's barrel.

"We're in for some shit now, ah, brew?" the Ethiopian asked. From his accent, James guessed that the man had learned English from South Africans, and the appellation of "brew"—an Afrikaans-flavored variation on "bro" or "brother" were telling clues. The soldier sounded like death warmed over, and James recognized him as Okuba, one of the first outbreak's survivors.

"Not going to lie to you," James admitted. "How'd you guess?"

"Your rifle takes AK mags, looks like," Okuba replied. "Maybe you're Special Forces as well as an Army germ warfare doctor. Special Forces guy climbing a ladder and watching the horizon? Doesn't take a brain surgeon to figure that someone's gonna start a fight tonight."

James smiled. "I could just be up here checking on your symptoms."

"Took you a moment to recognize me, brew," Okuba answered.

"Well, how are you feeling?" James inquired. "I might just need some help tonight."

Okuba sighed. "I'm not gonna lie to you either, brew. I feel like I just fell off the top of a tall ladder. I ache like hell. Neck, back, shoulders, from the top of my head to the bottom of my balls. The WHO's been giving me ibuprofen and I'm drinking like a fish, but I still feel like someone's punching me in the kidneys."

"So you should be in bed," James noted. "But you've got a job to do."

"Yeah. You Special Forces, man," Okuba noted. "You don't think twice about doing it, even if you feel like shit."

"We're not in this for the fun. If I were, I'd be somewhere in the Caribbean with a cocoa-butter-smelling beauty in my lap and a cooler full of beer," James muttered. "The EEF isn't too keen on sticking close to the refugee camp."

"My brews who missed out on the first infection event, they're a bit nervous," Okuba said. "That means we do our duty as the walking wounded."

"How many aren't scared of catching the virus?" James asked, scanning the horizon with his binoculars.

"We've got a platoon of fresh lads, but the sickies outnumber the healthy about two to one," Okuba explained.

James lowered the glasses and offered Okuba a handshake, a symbol that he wasn't afraid of touching an infection survivor. The Ethiopian smiled and accepted the gesture. James grinned. "You never know. This might be a story you'll tell your grandchildren someday."

Okuba popped a pair of capsules and took a healthy swig of water. "I'd be happy just to have this ache clear up."

James double-checked the horizon. "My friends went looking for the Thunder Lions tonight. Maybe you saw the flashes in the distance?"

Okuba shook his head. "They might have gone pretty far afield. I didn't see anything. Were they trying to find out about what happened at the village?"

"Yeah," James answered. "There was a gunfight and Colonel Stone felt that Bitturumba might want to try something here at the camp. Anything from a full assault to just a disruption of our lab work. So I'm pulled off the microscope, and put back on the old holographic reflex scope."

Okuba chuckled, nodding to the rifle. "You Americans get all the cool toys."

"Too bad this is for killing, not playing. I'd agree it was a toy."

Okuba sighed. "They're out there. I can feel it."

Something flickered on the horizon, and both men turned, seeing the flashes of explosions. The rumble of distant explosions and small-arms fire rolled toward the camp.

"Shit," James snarled, bringing up his glasses. "Bitturumba's making his move against the main EEF garrison."

"It's probably a distraction," Okuba stated. "They make reconnaissance by force attempts pretty often. They throw sacrificial lambs at us to let us know they're still warriors."

James tracked his field binoculars around and spotted Elee Aslin's helicopter in the distance. He keyed his radio. "Rafe, it's Cal. Any bad news?"

"I've got good news, but not the best," Encizo replied.

"They're not bringing any mobile artillery this way," James responded. "But we do have company coming."

"Raise the alarm, amigo," Encizo said. "Looking at about twenty technicals and five trucks loaded with riflemen."

There was the rattle of weapons fire plinking against the helicopter hull, accompanied by Aslin's curses. "Taking fire," Encizo added. "But we're still flying."

James glanced over to Okuba. "Time to put out the call."

The Ethiopian scrambled down his ladder with remarkable speed and agility for a man recovering from severe influenza-style symptoms. James could hear his barks of alarm as he jogged to the communications tent. He didn't think there would be any good news on that front. The Thunder Lions were making their move against the EEF in force, preventing them from dispatching reinforcements for the camp's security.

"Rafe?" James called. "How does it look?"

"Bad," Encizo said. "The only saving grace I can see is that it's mostly small arms down there. They didn't even have an RPG to spare against the helicopter."

"A good portion of the guard force on hand is still on rubber knees from their bout with the virus," James said. "Many of the EEF are leery of being too close to the plague survivors. We're going to have our work cut out for us if that mobile force attacks."

"We can see the exchange between the Ethiopians and the militia from our vantage point," Encizo replied.

"They're giving as good as they can get, but it's enough to tie up the cavalry until the bad guys scalp all of us."

"No one ever said that our job was easy," James grumbled. "Just the fact that Striker called the both of us in to help him out was an indication of that. Too bad Elee's bird isn't strapped."

"I'll make do with what I've got from Striker's leftovers," Encizo commented.

Okuba scrambled up the ladder back to the guard-tower roost. "The garrison is too busy with Bitturumba's feint to send us anything. Any help we get is going to take a while getting here. We've got the platoon assigned to the perimeter pulling in."

"I've got some ranges," James countered. "Is the guard force commander open to some assistance from an American?"

"Given that I'm the ranking soldier here, fuck yes!" Okuba replied. "Got a plan?"

"It's not much, but I think we can arrange something," James responded.

The two sped down the ladder to confer with the rest of the Ethiopian soldiers.

MACK BOLAN MONITORED the news at the refugee camp over James and Encizo's "party line," but remained silent. The Phoenix Force pair were savvy veterans of countless battles. Together, they'd be able to make the difference between slaughter and victory for the refugees and their overwhelmed defenders. He couldn't expect them to do the impossible, but even if he had been on hand, there was little extra even his considerable skill and expertise could add. Right now, he had ditched his spot from the trailer hitch and fender of the last vehicle in the convoy. He'd disembarked from his stow-away position as the convoy slowed to enter the fortress.

He tumbled into the road, jarring his elbow, but as he rolled into the thick grass at the side of the dirt road, he knew it was preferable to sitting comfortably and catching a bullet in the head. Guards examined the convoy, inspecting vehicles and flashing mirrors beneath each chassis, looking precisely for infiltrators like him.

The Thunder Lion compound was well-lit and its perimeter was thoroughly patrolled. The chain-link fence was reinforced with two-by-fours at the base of the flexible metal mesh. Any way through the fence would be loud and clumsy enough to alert sentries in the blink of an eye. The fence was a dead end, and the tight gate security had kept him from riding in with the convoy. Bitturumba had created an impenetrable fortress, as secure from infiltration as it was from fully armed assault. The compound bristled with heavy machine guns, rocket launchers and short-range artillery, creating a ring of death that would chew apart even the mightiest army against its buttresses, even if the entire garrison of Ethiopians came at the encampment.

Bolan closed his eyes and inhaled deeply, using the smell of sewage as his guide. He opened his eyes and stalked around the perimeter of the camp, moving with a speed borne of urgency, but gliding through the grass like a native predator. His movements were efficient and low profile. He avoided the notice of tense and wary riflemen manning their posts diligently, alert for any anomalous movement. Luckily, the Executioner's stealth was more than up to the task, moving with the breeze, knifing between the tall blades of grass as his broad shoulders were angled to avoid disturbing them too much. He had to crack Bitturumba's security before he could do something about the allied militia assault on the refugee camp and on the Ethiopian forces.

That meant getting to the runoff sanitation canal. He reached the squared-off, brown sludgy pond, and swept the edges of it with his eyes, looking for the pipes that emptied into it.

The pipe's top was a third over the surface of the sanitation pool. Judging the opening visible above the thick, cloying sludge, it was large enough for Bolan to crawl through. Snaking down onto his stomach, he fished a small, flexible snorkel out of his load-bearing vest and clamped the bit between his teeth. This wasn't going to be the most pleasant or healthy of entrances, but he had to make it. Encizo and James were counting on him.

He crawled into the muck with barely a ripple, like an alligator slithering into a river to sneak up on its prey. This wasn't a clear, clean moving body of water, however; it was a stinking thick blob of sludge that would have made a less disciplined man gag and heave up vomit. The snorkel helped him breathe while keeping his head beneath the coagulated and curdled lumpy skin of the pond. The breathing tube was hard to see against the dark, murky background of the surface, and even if it had been seen, even the most paranoid of guards wouldn't have considered that there was a human being desperate enough to step in, let alone totally immerse himself, in the bowel contents of a militia contingent.

Bolan crawled through the mouth of the pipe, feeling his way through it until he came upon a metal grating. He pulled his knife and started to pry the mesh off the interior of the sewer. He concentrated on the lower half of the barrier, letting the thick liquid of the sewage smother the sound of twisting and bending metal. Bolan's shoulders swelled, arm muscles drawn tighter than steel cables as he fought against the grating's stiffness, ripping the moorings off the bottom of the pipe. The effort to leverage the freed bottom edge of the mesh pulled him to the bottom of the sewer pipe, his snorkel fully submerging with him, forcing him to hold his breath as he folded the barrier aside. Once the grating was bent far enough out of the way to allow him underneath, he stuck his head above the sludge and held his snorkel sideways to blow the scummy murk out of his breathing tube. Bolan scooped the sewage off his eyes and forehead as he broke the surface of the muck. He couldn't listen to the others on the radio, as the hands-free communicator's wires had been tucked back into their waterproof compartments on his load-bearing vest before he'd entered the runoff. He smeared slime off the face of his watch to see how much time had passed.

It had only been a few minutes, but it had felt like an eternity. Here in the reinforced concrete tunnel, even if he had the radio in his ear, he wouldn't have been able to receive a transmission from his fellow Stony Man warriors. All he could do was take a deep breath, ignore the stench swarming into his nose and mouth, and dive through the hole he'd made for himself. On the other side, he poked the snorkel's end tube up, and continued his crawl into the camp. The rest of the trip toward dry land was uneventful as the pipe he'd entered came up under a crawl space beneath one of the barracks.

Bolan pulled himself from the slime and used handfuls of dirt to scrub the mess off his blacksuit and battle harness to minimize the stench sticking to him. It wasn't a shower, which a small portion of his consciousness begged for, despite the admonitions of his enormous mental discipline. It would help, though, keeping him from being noticeable in close quarters. He pulled one of the compact SLAM munitions from the watertight pouch on his harness, and pressed it to a clot of small gas, fresh water and electrical pipes running under the barracks floorboards. He could see the bottom of a water heater, a vital necessity in the cold African nights, and the SLAM's kilogram of high-explosive power would combine with the gas pipes within to produce an earthshaking explosion. Bolan set the radio frequency on the detonator to a separate channel than the other munitions, in case he needed to use the barracks blast as a distraction. The loss of the building would throw enemy forces into disarray with one blast. He plugged in his earpiece and quietly requested an update from James and Encizo.

Silence. In the confines of the crawl space, Bolan didn't have the room to fiddle with wires on his communicator, but for now, he was effectively cut off from the rest of his team. His jaw clenched in concern for his allies. He dismissed the thought. The refugee camp was in the care of two members of Phoenix Force, and they couldn't be in better hands.

As Bolan crawled under the barracks, something fell through a gap, striking him in the forehead.

CHAPTER TEN

Elee Aslin glared in alarm over at Captain Rafael Ruiz the moment the first spray of Thunder Lions' small-arms fire raked the Huey. The heavier machine guns mounted on the technicals were not on flexible enough pintle mounts to allow the gunners to angle their fire against the aircraft. The technicals were meant to be utilized in an antipersonnel format, so they swiveled laterally, with only a slight bit of rise to deal with rooftop targets. Had one of those 12.7 mm weapons connected with the Huey, it would have been ripped from the air. The Cuban and his pilot would have been trapped in a flaming coffin forged from the blazing superstructure of the helicopter. Fortunately, the Cuban's aim was not so limited as he opened up with the VEPR rifle, raining the contents of a 30-round banana clip out the window. It was only a few seconds of autofire, but it gave the Huey some breathing room as truck-mounted militiamen ducked to avoid his return fire.

"Even against AKs or M-16s, this chopper isn't going to hold out for long," Aslin warned.

Encizo triggered his grenade launcher, an unused thermite grenade blossoming in a splash of fearsome liquid white. It struck the ground between two technicals, and the fluid heat swept over the vehicles' gunners. The burning men shrieked as the searing tongues of flame licked the flesh from their arms, shoulders and faces. One gunman, merely singed, leaped off the bed of his pickup, howling as he ran in blinded pain. His suffering came to an abrupt end as a racing SUV, trying to get an angle on the Huey, struck his smoldering form. The militiaman's skeleton, from the rib cage down, compressed violently, splintering under the thunderous impact of the speeding vehicle. His body's mass was enough to force the 4WD off course, fender violently grinding on the tailgate of another technical, metal twisting on metal in a squeal of sparks.

"I need some altitude," Encizo told Aslin, swiftly disassembling his VEPR.

She obliged, climbing into the night sky. The Phoenix Force warrior tossed the barrel of his assault rifle into the back of the helicopter and withdrew a longer, thicker barrel from his war bag.

"What are you doing?" Aslin asked, aghast that Rafe had taken apart the craft's most potent weapon.

"Heavy barrel. It'll hold up to the heat generated when I go cyclic," Encizo answered. He tightened the barrel into the receiver, then fished out a black metal snail-drum. The Cuban fed it into the magazine well of the assault rifle, then thumbed a 40 mm fragmentation shell into the breech of the underbarrel grenade launcher. Three more drums were visible in the war bag at Encizo's feet. They each held ninety rounds, but were too bulky and unwieldy to be utilized in close-quarters combat. From the helicopter, however, they'd prove to be the kind of weight he needed, enabling him to rake the enemy with prolonged sweeps of full-auto fire.

"We'll still need a miracle to keep the riflemen from chewing us up," Aslin stated.

"That'd be Calvin," Encizo responded. He didn't feel as confident as he sounded, though, knowing that the refugee camp was far from heavily fortified. "Let's go in hot."

"Stay back from the forward flank." James's voice cut over their radios. "The lads and I improvised a reception for the convoy."

"Why can't you soldier-types just say 'we're gonna shoot the hell out of the bastards'?" Aslin asked, adjusting her course, bringing the Huey into a strafing run at Encizo's and James's combined suggestions.

"Sorry, we're the wrong team for that," Encizo quipped. "We're the classy ones."

Aslin would have rolled her eyes. Instead, she rolled the Huey into a sideways slide, allowing the Phoenix Force gunner to rake a rapid series of bursts across the rear flank of the column of militiamen. It was only harassing fire, the 7.62 mm ComBloc rounds careening off cabs and side panels to keep the technicals and the truck-mounted militiamen harassed.

"Cal, Striker, they must be expecting artillery support, because we're not budging them."

"Yeah, they're hunkered down. We've got sharpshooters from the Ethiopians plugging away at them," James agreed. "I hope my next plan puts a little more pressure on them."

"What plan?" Encizo asked.

Suddenly, a flaming pillow-shaped object sailed from

the refugee camp, slicing five hundred yards across the grasslands surrounding its perimeter. It struck forty yards short of the enemy's front line, but when it burst, it vomited a cloud of flame that touched off the dry foliage, creating a wall of flame twenty yards wide and ten feet high. Militia antiaircraft fire paused at the sight of the eruption, seemingly from the bowels of hell. The Cuban didn't have to ask what had been launched. It was most likely a sack of flammable, nitrate-filled fertilizer, its combustible qualities enhanced by fuel, oil or even simple medical alcohol. How it had been hurled five hundred yards was a mystery, since its flaming trail wasn't the parabola of a catapult launched.

"Took the winches of a couple of SUVs, strong fence posts and a couple of loose inner tubes." James provided the explanation for Encizo's unasked question. "The WHO might not be soldiers, but they're pretty handy with tools."

A second flaming pillow landed, creating another barrier of blazing grass, this one twenty yards closer to the line of militiamen. Aslin swerved the Huey hard to avoid being blinded by a billowing wall of smoke that rose then collapsed into her flight path. The smoke screen spread across the night sky, and the militiamen hurriedly pulled masks over their noses and mouths to protect them from the choking cloud that James had created.

Encizo realized that he hadn't heard from Bolan in response to his last message. He burned off the rest of his first drum magazine on the VEPR in an effort to distract himself from the Executioner's condition. The assault rifle's full-auto onslaught roared out of the side of the Huey. The gun wanted to twist out of the Cuban's hands, forcing him to pay attention to the weapon and the targets on the other end. If Bolan had been found out, then he was most likely in for the fight of his life in the heart of the Thunder Lion artillery firebase. So far, there weren't any heavy shells slicing through the night, landing amid the helpless refugees, but that was cold consolation to the Phoenix Force commando. Sooner or later, the column of soldiers was going to be on the move, and even without high-explosive shells, the militia's firepower would tear ruthlessly through the Ethiopian defenders.

"We've used up a quarter of the ammo, and we haven't done anything to dent them," Aslin noted, giving voice to Encizo's fears. "How are we going to stop them when they go on the move?"

Encizo didn't answer. He didn't want to think of his lack of options when the Thunder Lions made their charge.

"HERE THEY COME," Okuba warned.

James's neck and shoulder muscles were already tight, pulled as taut as coil springs. The Phoenix Force medic hunkered down over the sights of his VEPR as he sighted the churning wall of smoke and flame that provided less protection than he would have liked. The truck-mounted militiamen and their heavily armed technical support would roll through breaks in the burning grasses, mechanized transports providing enough momentary protection from the grass fire to start their brutal charge. James had the Ethiopians focus their aim on the small corridor provided by the splayed impacts of the fertilizer sacks. Focused, coordinated fire on the three or four likely routes that the militia would take through the flames would slow up the opposing force, causing enough damage and casualties to break apart the assault.

It was an iffy plan, but James knew that the firepower assembled by the Ethiopians at the refugee camp might do enough. Aside from the standard EEF service rifle, the AK-47, they had the benefit of two light RPK machine guns, the same kind of firepower that Rafael Encizo had on Aslin's Huey. The linchpin of the defense, however, was the DShK Russian heavy machine gun. Though the design was from 1938, the big 12.7 mm cannon was as reliable a powerhouse as any fielded in the wars of the twentieth century, rivaling the excellent M-2 Browning of U.S. and NATO forces. Its big, fat rounds would tear through anything short of a tank with little difficulty, and the half-inch bullets would put down any mere human with unmatched authority.

James also had the half-dozen Ethiopian soldiers armed with the excellent G-3 battle rifles focusing their precision marksmanship through the flames, the extreme reach of the heavy NATO-caliber rifles allowing them to engage the hunkered-down enemy mechanized force even at nearly six hundred yards. The WHO staff had assisted in setting up the defenses, piling sandbags and sheets of wood to provide protection for the EEF's defensive positions. The doctors and nurses, however, didn't have weapons training. James had them pulled back to watch over the infirm refugees. It wouldn't be much protection for the noncombatants, not if the militia's own 12.7 mm machine guns and the Thunder Lion firebase decided to focus on the fifteen hundred easy targets behind the feeble skirmish line James and Okuba had desperately assembled.

"They'll be slowed down by the smoke and brush-fires we laid," James told his Ethiopian ally. "You sure you see them moving?"

Okuba had his binoculars held up with one hand, his other arm trembling under the weight of his AK-47. The man had burned through his few remaining reserves of strength in organizing this last-ditch defense against Bitturumba's assault. Still, he held his weapon, unwilling to surrender. A sheen of sweat glimmered on the Ethiopian's skin, and his shoulders shook. It was too soon for most of the infected survivors to be thrown into a pitched battle, but Okuba had pushed himself the hardest, for the sake of his men and the Darfur refugees, racing to keep up with James. Okuba was almost at the point of falling over.

"Kneel there and take a drink," James ordered. "You're getting dehydrated."

"Don't mother me, brew," Okuba grumbled, his big eyes flashing in indignation.

"Even if I'm not acting as your doctor, I'm ordering you to kneel there as your fucking tactical adviser. Take that firing position. The sandbags will stabilize your aim," James replied. "I don't need wasted ammo. I need rounds burning into those motherfuckers who're charging down our throats. Got that, soldier?"

Okuba let himself drop to a knee at the emplacement James had pointed out. His sweat-soaked face split into a sheepish grin. "Sorry. I got stubborn for a moment there."

"I've seen it before," James admitted, giving the brave Ethiopian a clap on his shoulder. James turned his attention to the horizon. The enemy vehicles were in motion, just as Okuba had warned, but they had been drastically hampered by the path they snaked to minimize their exposure to the grass fires he had orchestrated. A couple of WHO drivers and mechanics were manning the improvised arbalests that had fired the flaming bags of fertilizer. The concept was a millennium old, basically an oversize crossbow that, in ancient Europe, would have been utilized to fire logs through castle walls. Seeing the winches on the front fenders of several jeeps had given the Phoenix Force commando his idea. It helped that the concept of the crossbow was kept fresh in his mind by his Stony Man partners, David McCarter and Gary Manning. Where the two specialists had used a man-portable Barnett crossbow for quiet sentry removal, the winch-stretched inner tubes had given the refugee camp an improvised form of artillery.

James had his "gunners" swap out the fuel-soaked fertilizer bags for jerricans with grenades duct-taped to their metal skins. The grenades had their safety pins tied to a single wooden stick, which was hooked onto the ground. When the inner tube snapped free, the grenades would lose their pins and safety spoon levers, arming the miniature bombs. James wasn't certain if the fuses would last long enough to detonate in the midst of the enemy forces as they made their charge, but the spray of fuel ignited by the grenades would rain fire on their vehicles. The aforementioned Gary Manning, Phoenix Force's resident demolitions expert, trained his team in improvised explosives, just for desperate situations like these.

"Let them get closer!" James called. "Fire on my mark!"

The enemy militia's technicals appeared around the corner of a wall of flame, their heavy machine guns thundering. Powerful slugs punched into sandbags and wooden planks, tearing out massive gouts in the defensive positions. Ethiopians scrambled as their battlements were hammered by the high-intensity salvo. James couldn't afford to lose any of his troops, but right now the enemy was just outside the arcs of fire he'd arranged. The line of fire he'd etched into the Sudanese countryside was several yards outside the bulk of his team's maximum effectiveness.

That's when the rustle of 120 mm shells cut through the distant rumble of enemy machine guns. James felt his heart drop. The Thunder Lions' artillery barrage was started on time, supporting the assaulting force. High-explosive hell would wipe the beleaguered defenders from the face of the Earth.

"Let them have it!" James bellowed. The Phoenix Force warrior wasn't going to die holding his fire. He rose and cut loose with his VEPR, jerricans whistling past at lightning speed. The Ethiopians opened up in unison with him, knowing that the plan had been snarled by Bitturumba's big guns. None of the refugees' defenders was going to back down, even in the face of obliteration by 120 mm mortar shells.

Then a miracle occurred as the artillery barrage lanced not into the refugee camp, but into the heart of the advancing column of mechanized infantry.

The Executioner had come through, evening up the odds.

BOLAN RECOILED, his superb reflexes triggered by what looked like an arm flopping down through the shadows of the crawl space, but he relaxed when he felt the fabric of an empty sleeve brush his forehead. The momentary surprise, so soon after pulling himself from the total sensory deprivation of the sewage runoff, had given him some pause. As his eyes adjusted to the light, he saw that it was a jacket wedged into a gap in the floorboards. Underneath the sleeve was a small, tightly packed box. Bolan sliced it open and examined it by the light of his filtered torch. It was contraband, mostly: chocolate bars, cigarettes packed with either tobacco or hash, and various collections of pornography. The organization and the secrecy of the stash, as well as the roll of bills stuffed into the side told the Executioner that whoever had this section of crawl space was making a healthy business dealing goods to his fellow soldiers. He took the wad of money, intending to give it to the Sudanese refugees to make their life a little easier. The rest would be vaporized when he blew the barracks. As an afterthought, he tugged down the sleeve, pulling the field jacket through the gap in the floorboards. Wrapped tightly in an epaulet on one shoulder was a maroon beret, and Bolan slithered into the clothing. The uniform jacket and hat, along with his refreshed cosmetic greasepaint would provide him with a measure of anonymity inside the firebase's confines.

Looking out from under the crawl space, he could see artillery crews preparing their weapons on the tarmac. Crates of ammunition were piled up high and thick between sandbag walls. Soldiers were scurrying to carry out their tasks and the calls of an officer in Arabic gave Bolan a time line for the start of the artillery barrage. He didn't understand the whole of the man's orders, but he'd spent years in Middle Eastern countries, and he had been taught the basics of military commands by his old friend, linguist Yakov Katzenelenbogen. One of the things that Bolan had memorized completely was "I need this done in five minutes" in a dozen languages.

Thanks to the words of the Sudanese commander, Bolan knew he had five minutes to turn the Thunder Lions' artillery barrage to his own advantage. The guns were silent for now, meaning that whatever force that Bitturumba was throwing at the Ethiopian Expeditionary Force, it was doing so without the support of the heavy guns. Lighter artillery had either been sent to the trap for the Executioner or was perhaps brought to bear on the Ethiopians, keeping the strike force against the refugee camp light and fast.

The Executioner had a timetable to prevent the slaughter, but the moments he had to derail Bitturumba's forces were disappearing one by one. All he had on his side were a planted explosive in a barracks, a uniform that would only pass a cursory examination and the element of surprise. That would allow him at least a few minutes of stealthy freedom within the compound as unsuspecting artillery crews lined up their heavy guns on the refugee camp. He took a moment to make certain his night-black camouflage face paint left his skin looking right for the area, then walked into the open. He made certain to avoid light fixtures, concentrating on being a quick-moving shadow among shadows, just another soldier racing about his duties. Bolan reached one stockpile of artillery ammunition, a stack of 120 mm shells meant for an Egyptian-built D-30 howitzer.

He slipped one of the SLAM munitions in between a pair of crates, counting on the high-powered mini-bomb to detonate the pile. The stack of heavy firepower would go up with sufficient force to disrupt the crews surrounding the central piece. While it might not cripple the other guns, the concussive force and the need to rescue their friends would bring the whole line of howitzers to a standstill. He hadn't drawn any attention as he walked off, his role camouflage shielding him. The Executioner had toned himself down to be just another big black silhouette, indecipherable in the hectic activity of preparation.

Bolan walked along and scooped up a clipboard that an officer had laid down. He intended to use it to add to his disguise as another soldier, layering it atop the beret on his head and the oversize field jacket concealing his war harness. They combined enough flags of recognition to further obfuscate his presence, as a lone soldier with a clipboard was something that most artillery crews wanted to avoid. Bolan glanced at the top sheet, and his understanding of Arabic let him know that it was a list of communications frequencies. On the second page was a topographical map designed to help steer the artillery barrage. Unfortunately, using the clipboard to steer the gunnery crews wrong would only achieve a ruined disguise. Still, the information on the clipboard could be made useful later.

"Hey!" a voice called from behind him. Bolan turned and saw a militiaman jog after him, speaking in Arabic. Though Bolan didn't understand the whole phrase, he knew enough from the man's reactions to guess what was being said. "You took the wrong clipboard!"

Bolan's disguise was on a countdown to a messy, violent end. He reached into his pocket and wrapped his fingers around his radio detonator. He thumbed the firing stud and the little rubber waterproof membrane popped, compressing under his fingertips. The pop gave him the tactile sensation of triggering his remote-control

SLAMs, but the lack of explosion was a rumbling, en-gulfing silence that punched the Executioner in the gut. The clipboard's owner was coming closer, and Bolan's radio-controlled munitions had no radio signal to deto-nate them. He took a deep breath, addressing the mili-tiaman in his halting Arabic, counting on the Janjaweed officer attributing his lack of fluency on being a con-verted tribesman. "Sorry, this was yours?"

He held out the clipboard and its owner took it, con-centrating on the pages to see if anything was out of place. His concerns about losing vital orders and maps were more pressing than studying Bolan's face in the darkness. "Dimwit, what made you think you had any…"

The militiaman's nose wrinkled as he caught of whiff of Bolan's recent bath. Bolan didn't need a translator for the next few words. "What the fuck is that smell?"

The Executioner strode in tight with the African, as if to look over his shoulder, then jammed the otherwise useless radio detonator hard under the guy's ear. The solid-state transmitter's frame punched hard into the carotid artery, sending a stunning jolt through the Thun-der Lion's brain. Bolan held the man as dazed eyes turned up, focusing on him, finally recognizing the Executioner as an intruder. Unfortunately, the blow with the blunt detonator had caused such trauma to the main artery feeding the brain that a brutal hemorrhage surged through the side of his head. The ruptured blood vessel disgorged blood under high pressure into the brain pan rather than feeding oxygen to the lobes. The militiaman was unable to cry out to alert his brother soldiers, let alone move his feet. Bolan dragged the injured man along and sat him on some sandbags out of sight of the busily preparing artillery crews.

Bolan drew his folding knife. "Sorry that you suffered."

The point of the combat folder punched through the back of the man's neck, slicing into the trunk of neural fibers that formed the lowest centers of the African's brain. The traumatized artillery coordinator released a dying sigh of relief, and his eyes went blank and lifeless. Bolan laid the corpse back, propping him up so that he appeared to be resting. He took the papers in the clipboard and stuffed them into a pocket of his load-bearing vest. The clipboard was left in its former owner's lap. He took a moment to check the detonator for its malfunction.

He opened the battery case and noticed that one of the metal leads hadn't been engaged by the end of the battery. The spring had been shoved hard to one side. He bent the spring back and reinserted the battery carefully, taking the opportunity to look at his LASH, as well. He discovered that the wire lead from the ear and throat mike had been separated somewhere along the line. Bolan wiped crud off the lead and shoved it hard into place.

James and Encizo were keeping each other informed about their preparations. The column of militiamen was on the move, and Bolan checked his watch. The doomsday numbers were almost up for the refugee camp.

Bolan pressed the firing stud on the SLAM remote.

Hell broke loose as the five munitions that Bolan had planted shattered the barracks and detonated palettes of 120 mm ammunition with apocalyptic force. The ground shook with the simultaneous blasts, ten kilograms of high explosive augmented by gas mains or earth-rocking heavy shells. The shock wave from a nearby pile of prepped ammunition tossed Bolan onto his back, spilling the dead coordinator into his lap. The 120 mm shells, each weighing close to fifty pounds, were tossed like toothpicks. The rounds that flew off the initial blasts hadn't been set off by the miniature munitions, but their mass was sufficient to tear five-foot holes through prefab buildings or to crush human beings into paste. A roaring column of flames smeared up through the night sky. Around the compound, screams of agony and terror slowly became audible over the fading roars of detonations.

Bolan heard Calvin James tell Rafael Encizo that the enemy was in motion. He consulted the map, then scanned the compound.

A bank of 120 mm heavy mortars, nestled behind a wall of sandbags, caught his eye. Militiamen had abandoned their posts to deal with the effects of Bolan's sabotage, racing to help wounded friends or to deal with fires caused by hot shells setting buildings aflame. Such concern for brother soldiers would have touched the Executioner's heart, had not their mortars been sighted in on fifteen hundred unarmed, disease-ravaged Sudanese whose only sin was not kneeling in submission to Islamicist fanatics. Bolan reached the tubes and began adjusting their aim. A change of only a few degrees meant that the 120 mm mortars would land hundreds of yards short of their initial targets. Whether that was enough to rain hell down upon a mechanized assault force was unknown for now, but the Executioner didn't have time to fire spotting rounds.

The six tubes, reset, would have to be enough to give Bolan a spread of fire. The mortars were fired by dropping a shell into a tube where a detonator popped, launching them. With six of them, the Executioner had a form of rapid-fire artillery that he wouldn't have had anywhere else. The large field pieces had required teams of five to ten men to load, aim and fire. The mortar shells, though they shared the same diameter as the heavy guns, didn't have quite the same punch as the big howitzers. Bolan dropped the first shell of a scooped armful, then sidestepped to feed the second, repeating the process until he reached the sixth tube and his arms were empty.

"Striker, you there?" Encizo asked seconds later.

"Affirmative," Bolan answered. "What's the damage?"

"The first shot you dropped landed thirty yards behind the last vehicle. You need to adjust…" the Cuban began. "*Caramba!* What have you got?"

"Six tubes, no waiting," Bolan said. He moved swiftly to the second and third tubes, dropping a shell into each. "Are the last few rounds getting too close to Cal's defenses?"

"No. Whatever your adjustments, they're right on target. The technicals have taken a hell of a beating. Cal's boys are cutting loose with a 12.7 mm and turning a troop transport into a sieve," Encizo announced. "What's your situation?"

A chatter of an assault rifle raised a spray of sparks along one of the 120 mm mortar tubes. Bolan ducked. "Bitturumba's boys know that they have a wolf in their fold. I might need a ride out of here. You up to it, Elee?"

"I'm on my way," Aslin answered. "Hang tight."

Bolan took the VEPR down from his shoulder as more enemy guns opened up, sandbags shuddering under the rain of bullets. He'd bought the refugees some breathing room, but now the fanatical fundamentalists were onto him, and they wanted him dead.

CHAPTER ELEVEN

After the mayhem of the abandoned airstrip and the battle for the defense of the refugee camp, Elee Aslin thought she'd seen everything that could be unleashed in the face of all-out war. Then she saw the ruins of the Thunder Lions' firebase clawing up out of the ground, shattered remains of buildings standing like naked, fire-charred ribs, the skies above a gruesome smear of ash and dust spreading like a pool of blood.

"God in heaven," Aslin whispered as the carnage unfolded in greater detail the closer she got to the ruined militia compound. "What happened?"

"Colonel Stone," Rafael Encizo answered.

Blistering streams of automatic fire streaked across the battlefield, like a laser light show. Now and then, an explosion would punctuate the distant exchange, a fresh blossom of ejecta hurling men aside like cape dogs off a raging wildebeest's back.

"I'm going to land on top of his position," Aslin announced.

"No. We'll attract too much enemy fire, and Stone

would be exposed for too long when he climbed aboard," Encizo countermanded. "We'll stay about forty yards outside the perimeter closest to the mortar nest he's in."

"He'll be exposed trying to get through the fence to us," Aslin warned.

"Not him," Encizo said. "Park us at about forty feet off the ground. I'm going to lay down some cover fire to let him know we've got his exit strategy covered."

Aslin's brow furrowed.

"Don't worry," Encizo told her. "Stone never goes into a place he doesn't know how to get out of. If he'd done that, his war would have been over decades ago."

The WHO pilot brought the Huey to a hover outside the fence, hoping that the Cuban was right.

THE EXECUTIONER SWUNG up his VEPR and removed all doubt from the Thunder Lions that he was not one of their own, raking a squad of men ruthlessly with chest-stitching sweeps of 7.62 mm slugs.

Militiamen twisted under Bolan's swift precision bursts, collapsing into bloody heaps of lifeless meat after their seconds-long death dance. From the sandbag-protected mortar nest, the Executioner had a momentary advantage of cover and good firing arcs against his enemy. The advantage wouldn't last longer than the first flight of enemy grenades, however. For now, Bolan let his marksmanship create a buffer zone that would hold the Thunder Lions at bay, outside the range that they could throw their hand grenades.

Thunder Lion rifles ripped impotently at the packed contents of the sandbags, the relatively low-mass, low-penetration 5.56 mm rounds unable to generate enough momentum to multiple sacks of packed soil. The mortar nest had been heavily fortified to minimize shrapnel spray from an accident with the ammunition, so few small arms could get at Bolan through the heavy cordon. Only an indirect weapon could get past the low, thick wall to hurt the Executioner. At the range he held them, only a grenade launcher or another mortar nest could dislodge him.

The thought of another mortar nest gave Bolan an idea, and he glanced at the stacks of 120 mm ammunition by the tubes. The shells would have more than enough power to even the odds against the massing militiamen surrounding him. He grabbed a mortar tube and hauled it to the sandbag wall, resting it just a little above horizontal. A second quick trip to retrieve a crate of shells provided everything he needed. Both trips took only thirty seconds, lengthened by a pause to punch out another short salvo of rifle rounds at the riflemen to keep their heads down. Bolan hurled a shell into the mouth of the simple artillery pipe. The extreme low angle of the mortar tube prevented the shell from traveling more than fifty yards, but that had been the Executioner's goal.

The 120 mm warhead struck a section of a barracks where riflemen had been taking cover. The shell's detonation violently excavated a massive cavern through the structure, scattering the enemy gunmen who'd thought they were safe. Bolan cleaned house with his VEPR, taking down fleeing soldiers who were receiving a taste of the overwhelming death and destruction they had wreaked upon countless Sudanese citizens. Some weren't lucky enough to escape the splintered chunks of prefab walls that tore through them as effectively as fragmented shrapnel wire.

A puff of smoke lit up in the distance and Bolan hit the dirt, recognizing the muzzle-flash of an RPG-7 rocket grenade. The 110 mm shell slammed into the thick mount of sandbags. Bolan was lucky that the enemy gunners decided to utilize an antiarmor round that had been designed to cut through thick tank armor with searing heat. The sandbags smothered the explosion so that no lethal fragments struck the big American, but the concussion still rocked him.

Bolan swung his mortar tube toward the other end of the rocket-propelled grenade's smoke trail and hammered off another 120 mm round before the grenadier could reload his weapon. The heavy artillery warhead landed short of the gunner's position, but its detonation hurled up a wall of flying dirt between him and the enemy. The Executioner hosed the cloud with a series of short bursts from his rifle.

As good a tactic as the improvised close-range artillery fire was, it was merely a stopgap measure. Once the Thunder Lions recovered from their confusion, they would move in and overwhelm him.

"Striker, we have your marker," Encizo stated. "We have a visual on you."

"I hear the Huey and your LMG," Bolan returned. "Stay where you are. I'll be making my break soon enough."

"Aslin's getting a little edgy up here, worrying about you," Encizo noted. "What's the delay?"

Bolan scurried under the cover of Encizo's door-gunning to place the last of his SLAM munitions, reset to "motion detection antipersonnel" mode. While the SLAM wasn't a curved shell of ceramic packed with ball bearings and notched fragmentation wire like a

Claymore mine, the one-kilogram munition's disk-shaped explosive payload could produce a crippling shock wave. It would buy Bolan an extra few moments to make his retreat. "Be careful. I don't think I took out the RPG man that fired on my position, and there might be others in the area."

"What's the plan?" Encizo asked.

"Lay down a line of fire from your RG-6," Bolan said. "I'll light up my path. Just have Elee land fifty yards out once your launcher runs dry."

As he spoke, the Executioner swiveled the mortar tube and fired another 120 mm package of destruction through the reinforced chain-link fence. The high-explosive round vaporized planks, barbed wire and steel wire in a blow laden with apocalyptic power. The crushing blast also raised screams of suffering from that direction. The Thunder Lions had tried to flank the lone crusader, and for their effort, their bodies were riddled with splinters and jagged chunks of metal. Bolan cut loose with the VEPR, raking the side of mortar nest away from the hole he'd blasted. The "hail Mary" spray of autofire caught another squad trying to sneak at him from the opposite direction. With a quick pump of his MP-203 grenade launcher, he stuffed an incendiary shell into the 40 mm tube. He triggered the weapon, coring the group of paused riflemen with a liquid flash of intense heat, thermite searing through flesh to the bone beneath. The temperature was so great that the ammunition in the militiamen's guns and spare magazines cooked off, bullets flying wildly as gunpowder detonated.

Encizo's grenades started slamming into the Thunder Lions' stronghold now, Bolan's signal to begin firing writ clearly for the Cuban. The nightmarish racket of detonations and death screams ratcheted up even louder.

"Welcome to your judgment," the Executioner whispered, starting his retreat. To one side, a SLAM was triggered in its mine format. The detonating packet of explosives spit out a cone of bone-pulverizing force that tossed a trio of hapless corpses a dozen feet into the air. Bolan emptied another VEPR magazine into the remainders of the assault squad, which had tried to sneak up on him. He gave the shocked survivors no chance to gather their senses and continue their surprise attack.

Flames licked from the earth surrounding the mortar nest, a deadly testament to the hell that the violent militia had brought upon itself through its genocidal campaign of murder and rape. For too long, the Executioner had been too busy to give the mass-murdering forces of the Sudanese militias his full attention. There had been a brief splash of hope when the Ethiopian military sent an expeditionary force into action, driving the slaughtering fanatics from Khartoum. The militias hadn't folded, however, and their killing ways continued, only slightly abated. Now, it was Bolan's time. He was here to collect a blood debt from the agents of ethnic cleansing. The pile of corpses he'd created this night was merely a small down payment on what they owed.

Bolan raced through the hole he'd torn in the fence, Encizo's light machine gun chattering from the side of the Huey. The Cuban's powerful arm reached out and hooked Bolan's, hauling him up into the Huey. Aslin pulled back on the collective, rocketing the helicopter into the choking smoke created by the Executioner's swathe of carnage.

"Oh, man," Aslin muttered, shocked. Stunned words poured from her mouth into the intercom microphone. "Where were you when these bastards started killing folks?"

Bolan could tell that she was blown away by the apocalypse churning in his wake. Encizo reloaded his RG-6 and speared more 40 mm shells into the Sudanese infantry manning the firebase. It was a spray to keep heads down, though a few were popped handily from shoulders when grenades exploded beneath unsuspecting bodies.

"A lot of people who've lost loved ones to the Thunder Lions can rest easy tonight," Aslin added.

Bolan watched the fiery wound he'd torn in the African grasslands. "I'm not going to stop until they can all rest without fear of Bitturumba's butchers. The Thunder Lions will never hurt anyone again."

"The guys in that camp sure as hell won't," Aslin whispered, steering back toward the refugee camp.

THORMUN BITTURUMBA LOOKED at his firebase, a former nest of ground-shaking, army-crushing artillery, and saw the damage that had been wrought upon it in the space of a single evening. Five hundred of his best artillery men had used the fortress as an impregnable linchpin holding the line against the Ethiopian military's interference in Sudanese affairs. Now he looked at bent and twisted gun barrels, mangled by detonating ammunition. Around them, charred corpses littered the ground like the shells of nuts. He swallowed as he saw a severed arm gnawed on by a honey badger. The general pulled his big Desert Eagle and fired a shot at it, but the tough little mustelid jumped aside from the limb, avoiding being cored by a .50-caliber handgun bullet. It hissed at Bitturumba as he fought to ride the weapon's massive recoil, then raced through the broken ground before the big commander could aim another shot at it.

"An omen," Kartennian noted.

The Turk's words were sandpaper on the raw wounds in Bitturumba's ego. "Don't give me that mystic bull-shit, you moron!"

Bitturumba looked back to the relief companies he'd brought in to bolster the devastated artillery battalion and rebuild the shattered compound. A squad of men suddenly disappeared as a hidden SLAM, placed the night before by the lone warrior, cut loose, triggered by their passing. One man staggered drunkenly toward the general, his face peeled back to display his skull beneath. The horrific remains of the mutilated man tried to talk, but he had no lower jaw, tongue hanging like a grisly necktie from a cavitated face. He tumbled into the dirt.

"By the Prophet!" Kartennian spit. "Even hours later, he is claiming lives!"

Bitturumba's brow furrowed. "They should have expected booby traps and other sabotage."

"And the others?" Kartennian asked. "This was an impenetrable fortress. Your rivals assailed it countless times with their mightiest formations and weapons, and you turned them back every time. But one man somehow passed through your guards and gates as if he were a ghost, and reaped hundreds of lives!"

Bitturumba's chest muscles tightened, the tendons on his neck standing taut like steel cables. The Turk's critical yammering was stomping his last remaining nerve. He sought to diffuse the insulting jihadist's superstitious mewlings with simple logic. "This was impregnable against every conventional assault, but a smart, determined man could have figured a way. I have teams checking to see if he dug a tunnel in or used a pole vault. He could have even snuck in aboard one of our light field artillery from the first trap."

"Your gate security checks everything," Kartennian countered. His dark eyes were wild with fearful speculation.

"Looking under the chassis of an SUV is one thing, not everything," Bitturumba said. "A lapse of attention could have given the warrior his break. He also could have had the stomach and endurance to slip through the sewage runoff."

A lieutenant walked up, carrying a charred snorkel. "We found this under one of the sabotaged barracks. It was near a latrine drainage tunnel."

Bitturumba nodded, dismissing the militiaman. He then turned and fixed Kartennian with a wrath-filled glare. "He found a hole, and he took it. He is not a ghost, merely smart, resourceful and determined. Spare me your superstitious blatherings. Sorcery exists only in fantasy, not real life."

"Mock me if you dare," the Turk responded. "But one man, a white man, managed to walk around caked in your men's feces unnoticed?"

Bitturumba pinched a meaty wad of forehead between his fingers, finding himself uttering a prayer for strength in the face of ignorance. "Logic is a wonderful tool in reconstructing your gibberings about magic, moron. But then, what would a fanatical twit such as yourself know of logic? You're no brighter than the idiots in Kenya who think they can transform into leopards by wearing animal skins."

"You dare compare Islam to those heathen animalists? The Koran is a font of scientific knowledge!" Kartennian protested.

Bitturumba laughed spitefully. He decided to give in to his anger, finally fed up with the line of bullshit that the Turkish jihadist was shoveling toward him. "Your idiot holy book preaches that the Earth is flat, and the sky is a canopy stretched between mountains. You morons believe that the world is a handful of centuries old."

Kartennian trembled with rage. The angrier the Turk appeared, his olive skin reddening so much Bitturumba thought he'd suffer a coronary, the calmer and happier the Thunder Lions general felt. Nothing helped a miserable mood like spreading it around. "A...a true Muslim would never speak—"

Kartennian's proclamation of faith was cut off by Bitturumba's thick fingers clamped around his throat.

"I might be your ally, and I might pretend to believe in your fairy tales, but remember this, you ignorant sap. You should examine your experiences over the past few days. Does a myth have to be more important than your goals?" the general questioned. "Because if you spew one more of your ignorant lies about how your god grants you victory so easily that you don't have to use that lump of shit between your ears to think, I swear to you that I will not only kill you, I will rape your daughters and nieces, then pass them on to my men. If God can protect you and yours from that, then you'll know in death that you really were right. But do you really want your journey to paradise to run through my torture chamber? Because right now, in this place, I am the lord, your god."

Kartennian's face was purple, his eyes bulging from the force with which Bitturumba squeezed him. When the general let him go, the Turk collapsed to his hands and knees, vomiting and trying to gasp in lungfuls of air. Kartennian glanced up, shaking in abject horror at the towering mountain of muscle that seethed with disdain for his existence.

"My apologies. I forgot where I was."

Tears burned down the Turk's cheeks, and Bitturumba could smell the acrid stench of urine and feces. He'd have to watch the fundamentalist fool, now that he'd laid his allegiance to the Islamic supremacists in simple language. Right now, though, he had more important things to worry about.

The other militias were still high on their excitement at attacking the Expeditionary Force's main headquarters, despite the bloody losses the Ethiopians had inflicted upon them. Bitturumba had to make certain that they didn't see the loss of his artillery fortress as a sign of weakness.

There was also the threat of the lone warrior who'd wrought devastation on his forces. Thankfully, Baldr was almost here, sent by his brother to support, not replace, Bitturumba's effort against the interfering crusader. He'd tap the top-flight assassin's skill in removing the fundamentalist idiot Kartennian in a manner that wouldn't offend the Turk's allies in the Middle East or tip off his "fellow" Janjaweed forces in the Sudan.

Right now, Bitturumba had one thing going for him. The Thunder Lions had led another assault on the Ethiopian Expeditionary Force, and it had been a mighty effort. The foreign intruders had suffered some losses, but not to the extent that the Islamic supremacists would have preferred. Bitturumba could easily spin the failure to be on the part of the other Janjaweed warlords. The Sudanese didn't know, or care, that the assault on the WHO contingent and the refugee camp had been the general's main focus. He had brought in four companies of fresh troops to repopulate and rebuild the fortress, which would give him stature, showing them that he'd suffered nothing more than a minor setback. He could also pass off the destruction as the concentrated firepower of the Ethiopians' artillery units, counterattacking. Scars were a mark of honor and manhood among African warriors, and the "wounds" caused by the previous night's debacle would make him even more glorious in the eyes of his peers. The Thunder Lions were still a vital fighting force, and unassailable in reputation. Bitturumba's position had barely been affected.

That wouldn't last if Kartennian recovered his spine, or if the mysterious warrior struck once again.

Bitturumba's phone rang in his pocket, and he plucked it out. "Yes?"

"He's here," Major Sanu Korunda stated. "Do you wish to speak with him?"

"Give him my secure number," Bitturumba ordered. "He has his own means of private conversation."

"Yes, sir," Korunda replied.

MACK BOLAN DRIED HIS HAIR from his second shower in six hours. He'd just awakened from an energy-restoring catnap, and still felt the crawling unease of concentrated sewage seeping in his pores, despite the scrubbing he'd given himself after he'd first returned to the refugee camp. James brought him a mug of rancid but hot coffee. Used to the swill that Aaron Kurtzman brewed, Bolan sipped from the offered cup without complaint. Compared to the taste of sewage that had seeped in around the bit of his snorkel, it was almost palatable.

"Most people at least make a face when they taste my coffee," Tanya Marshall quipped.

Bolan offered her a grin. "I thought the WHO fought against things that rotted stomachs."

Marshall laughed. "I'm sorry I haven't met you yet. I'm Dr. Marshall. Colonel Stone?"

"Brandon," Bolan answered. "Any good news on the medical front?"

"We're still running comparison tests on the samples that Cal had flown in," Marshall said. "The chemical coding of the viral DNA seems similar, but with so many degraded gene markers thanks to the virus's decomposition, it's hard to make a decent match."

"We'll see if the antibodies formed by our survivors reacts to the batch we have here," James added. "If there is a positive reaction, we'll get to work on producing a vaccine."

"One which needs to be mass produced," Bolan countered. "Gearing up for production requires time and effort. There could be a large window of opportunity for any group that's already gained control of the virus. Infection could outstrip any vaccine production we can arrange."

"Do you always like to snatch defeat from the jaws of victory?" Marshall asked.

Bolan frowned. "It's my job to prepare for the worst-case scenario. We have a small chance, and it's going to take a lot of work to make sure it remains a viable response and not a string of false hope."

Marshall nodded. "We're still working on all of our options against the disease, not just the stuff your people sent."

"Didn't mean to be a killjoy, Doctor," Bolan apologized.

"Elee, my friend, tells me you've been taking another approach to finding the cure," Marshall added. "How's that going?"

"Not much progress so far, but I'm keeping my eyes open," Bolan responded. "I'll do my best to bring you back a live sample in its suspension."

"But you'll be doing your best to take out the production and distribution of the disease," Marshall noted. "Still, if Bitturumba has a cure for his pet microbe, you'll probably bring it to me still clutched in his cold, dead fingers."

Bolan raised an eyebrow. "Wouldn't that compromise the sample?"

Marshall shook in a brief chuckle. "Depends on the container he's holding at the time."

"It's heartening to see that your Hippocratic Oath doesn't extend to mass murderers," Bolan replied.

"It's bad enough the fat fuck has been slaughtering and raping his way through this country the old-fashioned way," Marshall answered. "But naming a brand of Ebola after his murderous followers?"

"Don't worry," Bolan replied. "Tonight, we have a good chance of locating the production facilities. I intend to make his form of disease extinct. Both micro and macro."

"The Ethiopians have been after him for months. What do you have that they don't?" Marshall asked.

"More liberal rules of engagement."

"You don't strike me as liberal, Colonel Stone," Marshall observed. "But then, I don't think politics is your focus."

"Protecting the innocent is," Bolan explained. "Everyone's entitled to their ideas, as far as they don't harm anyone else. When they cross the line, I step up to stop it, left wing, right wing, beak or tail."

Marshall looked to James. "I swear, I could see the flag unfurl behind him as he spoke."

James grinned. "He has that effect when he takes the time to talk. Tanya, I'm going to have to excuse myself from any more research."

The green-eyed doctor nodded. "You've helped our research so much, but I could tell that you were champing at the bit to get back to the front lines."

"Save a cup of coffee for me when I get back," the Phoenix Force medic told her.

Marshall gave James a quick, not-so-chaste kiss. "For luck." She winked.

CHAPTER TWELVE

Cartagena, Spain

The warehouse had long since devolved into ruin, abandoned decades ago. It wasn't empty, though, as the two bidders had each brought ten dark-dressed men laden with submachine guns and pistols to protect them. The air was tense, but most of the uncertainty came from Igor Sharpova, whose overheated face was etched with disgust that another man was attending the auction. Despite having nearly a squad of trained fighting men flanking him, he kept his eyes focused on the Libyan with edgy intensity. Colonel Mhousid Kaffriz was a sharp contrast to the uncomfortable and miserable Russian who was weighted down with his heavy beard and body armor. Kaffriz seemed almost at home, dressed smartly in a beige linen suit that flattered his lean, athletic build. His beard was neatly trimmed and sculpted to match his jawline, a cut designed for comfort while still allowing himself the manliness of a chin covered in hair. Though Cruz had initially entertained the idea of wooing only the Russian with promises of continental domination, Kaffriz's counteroffer had sparked his interest.

"I thought we had a deal," Sharpova protested once Cruz no longer felt like drawing amusement from the Russian behind the anonymity of a video camera. "We were a sure thing."

"Mhousid has a home-field advantage, it seems," Cruz said. "He's got access to quite a bit of oil and diamonds in his little sliver of continent. He can afford to match your bid."

Sharpova's rat eyes narrowed at the familiarity in Cruz's utterance of the Libyan's first name. "Money? Is that all you're concerned with?"

Cruz shrugged. "I know they say that money can't buy happiness. But apparently the people who said that never bought a really good blow job. That makes me really happy. His money buys that just as well as yours, Igor."

The Russian glowered. "You son of a bitch."

Cruz smiled. "Igor, please. It's Thormun whose mother was the ball-slicing bitch. My mother was just a money-grubbing, gold-digging debutant."

Sharpova's lips curled back from his tobacco-stained teeth. "I want the virus! I want it!"

Cruz scratched his left eyebrow, wincing at the shrillness of the Russian's demands. "Jesus walks! You sound like a two-year-old. Mine! Mine!"

The Spaniard sighed for effect, then glanced at Kaffriz. "What do you say, Mhousid? Think you can play nice with others and share?"

Kaffriz chuckled at the proposal's absurdity, but shook his head. "Why should I have to pay full price for only half the product? And why, for the love of all that's holy, would I have to worry about someone else fucking up my end of the deal by possibly allowing his version of my golden gun fall into the wrong hands? This hairy bastard screws up, and suddenly Interpol and the WHO get a hold of the virus and can reverse engineer a cure."

Cruz shrugged. "You see my dilemma." Cruz sighed. "Two buyers, and they both want exclusive rights."

"You offered me Africa!" Sharpova screeched. His hand dug for the gun in his waistband. The Russian contingent was suddenly illuminated by the angry red glares of dozens of laser sights. Sharpova and his bodyguards jumped back, as if burned by the negligible heat of the pencil-thin targeting beams.

"Behave, Igor," Cruz warned. "You can always walk away from this."

"Bastard!" Sharpova roared. "You fucking little bastard!"

"Igor, you really need to remember your research if you're going to pull an insult out of your ass," Cruz said. "My mother and father were married. Thormun was just some one-night stand."

"Stop mocking me, you prick!" Sharpova yelled.

"Be a man," Cruz groaned.

"It's amazing this troglodyte has lasted this long." Kaffriz sighed.

"I refuse to pay more for something I've already bought! You have my money," Sharpova snapped, glaring at his Libyan competition.

"No. What you gave me was your opening bid. But don't worry, it's a credit in your favor for when the auction begins," Cruz explained.

Sharpova grabbed the lapel of his jacket, seizing it to his lips. "Open fire!"

There was only stunned silence in the wake of the Russian's barked order.

"Damn you! Open fire!" Sharpova repeated.

Cruz pulled a small walkie-talkie from his pocket and hit Send. "Hector, I don't think Igor will be happy until you oblige him."

"Hector?" Sharpova asked softly, the anger fading from his reddened face.

A thunderbolt slammed into Sharpova's right arm, the .338 Lapua Magnum round severing the limb in a messy splash of torn muscle, shattered bone and spraying blood. The Russian spun, collapsing to the warehouse floor. Sharpova gurgled, his eyes wild and wide from the explosive shock of the high-powered rifle round.

The bodyguards let their weapons clatter to the concrete, hands rising in surrender. Laser-aiming points still glowed on their torsos, reinforcing the knowledge that their ace in the hole had been trumped. Their incentive to remain armed and threatening disappeared as their employer flopped helplessly in the dust, blood gushing from a severed artery.

"A team of snipers," Cruz announced with a smile. He took a deep breath and repeated himself. "A team of fucking snipers."

Sharpova looked up pleadingly from the floor, his bald head drenched in sweat. Cruz's smile disappeared, and his olive features seemed to darken as his glib tone faded. "You were going to have some fucking little rent-a-thug aim a gun at me? Me? *Me!*" Cruz bellowed. "I can understand someone aiming at their competition, but you pointed your guns at *me!*"

Cruz drew a Llama .45 pistol and leveled it at the wounded Russian's face. Spittle sprayed from Sharpova's gibbering lips as his remaining hand tried to clamp off the tide draining from the bloody stump that used to be his right arm. "You had a gun pointed at me! Say something in your defense!"

"I just wanted the virus," Sharpova croaked.

"I'd give it to you now, but I'm too angry to see straight," Cruz growled. "Besides, this is more fun."

He fired the .45, the bullet plowing into the juncture of flesh and bone between Sharpova's thighs. Arterial blood gushing out of the nearly half-inch hole in his loins. The Russian wailed incoherently in pain. Cruz triggered the big black Llama again, plopping a second 230-grain round into Sharpova's intestines. The Russian curled into a fetal ball, his bowels releasing as his digestive system was ruined in the big bullet's passage.

"Please," Sharpova whimpered. "Mercy."

Cruz lowered the hammer on the .45, snorting in derision. "Mercy? Mercy! Fuck you, 'comrade.'"

The businessman slipped the Llama back into its hip holster, then turned to address Kaffriz. "Come on, Mhousid. There's got to be a place much more hospitable to doing business than here in the presence of an expiring heap of shit."

Sharpova saw his bodyguards run to a far exit. Cruz, the Libyan and his men made a more leisurely exit. He grimaced, torn by agony. The phone in his pocket was wet and slippery as he reached for it, but he managed to pull it out. It had taken three tries to open the compact cellular unit, slick blood keeping him from getting a good purchase on the flip cover. His strength was fading swiftly, but he managed to press the speed dial.

He'd programmed the phone to send an emergency text message in such a situation.

With his dying breath, Sharpova cursed Alonzo Cruz, sending the signal to inform the West of the pharmaceutical baron's relationship with the Thunder Lions and his complicity in the lethal virus's creation.

Satisfied that he'd begun Cruz's downfall, avenging his betrayal, Sharpova surrendered to death's cold embrace.

KAFFRIZ APPROVED of the new meeting locale, a quiet little boardwalk café, cooled by coastal breezes. He reclined comfortably in his chair, sipping at his chilled iced tea. "Our situation has become much more tenuous. The Russians, though impulsive and headstrong, tend to be thorough when it comes to arranging revenge for perceived betrayals."

Cruz nodded, a wistful smile flickering at his lips. "I'm positive that Igor had a contingency plan in case things turned to shit. That's why my people are preparing to move our operation to wherever in the world you need it."

The late-afternoon sun dipped closer to the crystal waters of the Atlantic Ocean. Kaffriz took another sip of his tea, tracing his finger through droplets of condensation on the surface of his glass. "Libya, naturally. How much room would you require?"

Cruz laid down a small notebook. Kaffriz flipped it open, seeing pages of technical specifications written in the Spaniard's neat, concise hand. "I've always been prepared for the eventuality of rapid departure, as well as the possibility that I'd need to set up production facilities in less than ideal technological surroundings. Currently, the entire operation is highly mobile. It's based in Germany for the moment."

"How much transport do you need?" Kaffriz asked, slipping the notebook into the breast pocket of his beige linen jacket. He picked up a slice of lemon and gave it a twist into the tea to liven up the beverage. "Or do you have planes at the ready?"

"I'll only need a good airstrip capable of handling three cargo jets," Cruz responded. "Also, it might be in our favor to bring in my brother."

"Thor Bitturumba would be an honored friend in General Ammuz's New Libyan Order," Kaffriz offered. "The Thunder Lions will be welcomed in our maneuver to oust the weakling who leads our once-proud nation."

Cruz nodded. Given how things had built to a head in the Sudan, with the interference of Ethiopians and Americans, a change of venue would allow his brother to regroup. "Thor will be pleased, as well."

Kaffriz nodded and took another sip.

Satisfaction rested on the Libyan's face. Things were looking good.

Darfur, Sudan

THE SUN WAS SETTING as Calvin James and Rafael Encizo rendezvoused with the Executioner. The trio took a few moments to compare notes from their individual reconnaissances to form a clearer picture of the kind of security and opposition they would be facing at Bitturumba's center for biological warfare.

"The facility is spread out across a full acre, composed of prefabricated container buildings that are mostly barracks and offices," Bolan announced. "The fence is fifteen feet tall, and it's built right on the tarmac, making digging beneath it nearly impossible.

There are militiamen in the four corner towers. Two men each tower, one manning a sniper rifle, the other manning a Type 67 Chinese General Purpose Machine Gun. Between the guard towers, they control an 800- to 1000-yard stretch of empty ground, thanks to the 7.62 mm R round for the 67."

"From the preponderance of French small arms and Peugeots converted to technicals," Encizo stated, "there's very little doubt that this is a full-blown, legitimate Thunder Lions' operation. The hangar is defended by a platoon of riflemen, and the airstrip is being patrolled by two technicals, while we have another circling the compound."

James wrinkled his nose. "I've got some bad news. There's a battalion of militiamen deployed about four hundred yards to the west of the compound. They have troop transport trucks and technicals under camouflaged cover, and the men are utilizing the uneven terrain and trees to remain low profile. They're not resting, either. They seem ready for a signal to attack."

"I noticed. From their equipment, they're more likely assembled from Bitturumba's newly acquired allies," Bolan stated. "He's using his push against the Ethiopian forces and his acquisition of the virus as a rallying point. It'll make things difficult for us. One gunshot, and we'll be trapped between the Thunder Lions and their allies."

"So we're going to have to be quiet breaking in," James said.

"Not we," Bolan corrected. He drew a rough scale map of the compound and the militia battalion position in the dirt. He poked the soil in two places to mark where he wanted Encizo and James to go. "I need you two to stagger here and here between the battalion and the camp. If I end up making noise, and Bitturumba's force gives the signal, you two will have to open up to provide a temporary holding action for me."

"How long?" Encizo asked.

"Anything longer than a minute will end up with all three of us being ground into hamburger," Bolan said. "If I can't make a retreat within forty-five seconds, then your support fire won't help me on the way out. The spots I've set up for you have not only clear fields of fire, but solid extraction routes with plenty of cover for your retreats."

"And you're between the hammer and the anvil the whole time," Encizo grumbled.

"My favorite place to be," Bolan said with a smile. "Set up." He handed the Cuban his rifle and spare ammunition. The Executioner would need to be stripped down for speed and stealth. His suppressed Beretta and .44 Desert Eagle were enough to carry the day if necessary. Unfortunately, if he had to resort to the noisy heavy pistol, he'd be endangering the two Phoenix Force operatives when they began their delaying action.

James and Encizo took only a few minutes to announce over the hands-free radio that they were in position. Bolan took off on their signal, a living shadow slithering through the night. The sun had set an hour earlier and the sky was a thick deepening purple, which lowered over the lone warrior like a protective cloak. This was going to be another standard infiltration run, which meant that just about anything could happen. Nothing ever went as expected on one of these soft probes. So many infiltrations had opened up into a wild tangent, leading him into a deeper, more dangerous conspiracy, that the Executioner had burned away every ounce of complacency in his heart of hearts. Bolan expected that he'd find a lead into Bitturumba's technological support. It wasn't racism that informed Bolan's opinion about outside interference being responsible for the production of the lethal microbe that the Thunder Lions' general used against his helpless Sudanese victims. The scientific skill to process such a murderous plague required advanced laboratories, which were in short supply in the Sudan.

The facility did appear to have a small high-tech container building with vents on top and an air-lock umbilical leading to a decontamination chamber at its only entrance. It was unmistakably a transportable bioweapon facility. Bolan had seen setups like this countless times, encountering such porta-labs before. When they appeared in the dark corners of the Third World, they were harbingers of only suffering and death.

The potential for contagion release was a strong threat should a firefight break out. The compound was relatively isolated from nearby villages, and should a containment failure occur, the only likely victims were the seven hundred fifty troops inside the compound or nested to the west. Those "victims" had been mass murderers, dedicated to slaughtering, torturing or raping non-Muslims in a genocidal campaign that had been waged for the past several years. Bolan and his allies had their respirator masks to filter out the deadly airborne spores, so only the terrorists would suffer if the wind was right. If the breeze changed direction, however, and a warm thermal lofted the practically weightless viral microbes into the night sky, then thousands of noncombatants would be doomed. There was also the possibility that the battalion troops and the compound garrison were equipped with their own carbon-fiber filter masks. As much as Bolan would have preferred to strike a crippling blow against the radical religious enforcers, he wasn't going to risk unleashing a hellish plague into the countryside.

The architects of atrocity and abomination would have to face their judgment by more conventional means.

"Striker? Can I call you that?" Elee Aslin's voice crackled over his hands-free set.

"Sure, Elee," Bolan replied. "What's up?"

"I know you're worried about that battalion getting in your way," Aslin noted. "What about the Ethiopians?"

"I'm not certain their artillery units will be accurate enough to hit them and only them. Cal and Rafe are dangerously close to them, and a stray shell could cause a contagion breach and spread spores instead of destroying them," Bolan answered.

"Who said anything about big guns?" Aslin countered. "Okuba and I have been burning up the radio talking about it, and there's a mechanized platoon rolling toward our position. He says they have BTR APCs, whatever those are."

"Heavily armored vehicles," Bolan translated for her.

"And they have jeeps with machine guns. It's a small strike force Okuba put together," Aslin continued. "Six jeeps and three APCs, with full loads of troops."

Bolan mused on the situation for a few minutes. "They would be heavily outnumbered once the militia reacted in full force, but there's a good chance that they can cause some casualties and provide a good distraction for me. You're in communication with the platoon now?"

"Let me hook this up." Aslin's voice cut out for a moment. There was the sound of a few clicks and crackles, and the next sound Bolan heard was Okuba speaking.

"Colonel Stone?" The man sounded as if he were in a vehicle.

"You're feeling well enough to be on patrol?" Calvin James interjected.

"I'm sitting," Okuba replied. "Colonel Murani feels that the Expeditionary Force owes you a large favor, Stone. We've got three BTRs and half a dozen technicals at your disposal. Point us at the militia, and we'll give you the best mobile punch that the Ethiopian military can assemble."

"A battalion would have the firepower to chew you apart," Bolan warned.

"If we were intending to make this a fair fight, you'd be right," Okuba answered. The reply brought a smile to the Executioner's lips. "This fucker Bitturumba has been tossing cheap shots at us all year long. It's time to show him what an Ethiopian assault force can do. Besides, we've got six RPG teams who have just too much ammunition to carry home with them."

Bolan felt his heart stir. The Ethiopian people had been on the receiving end of worldwide apathy and United Nations incompetence during their infamous drought of the late eighties and early nineties. The nation had turned itself around, and when the Darfur genocide grew intolerable, the brave, hardy people had moved in and sent the fundamentalist Islamic mechanics of slaughter packing. The African warriors used the same force of arms that, half a century before, had driven Benito Mussolini to use poison gas to even up the odds in his invasion of Ethiopia. The Executioner was proud to have such a courageous fighting force on his side. "You're hired, Okuba. I'll have Cal give you directions where to start the fight. The tactics are simple. Hit them hard, then fall back. The only ones dying today are Janjaweed."

"We will not disappoint you, Colonel," Okuba answered. "I'll even pray to Anansi, the Grandfather Spider, that he sends you all of his finest trickery to slip you in Bitturumba's sheets undetected."

"The great trickster god has taught me much over my years, Okuba," Bolan said, graciously accepting the well-wishing prayers. "But thank you for putting in the good word for me."

Bolan knew that with the Ethiopian's initial salvo, the Islamist militia would be in a scramble to recover its honor, sending a bloodthirsty hunting force after them. The Ethiopians would be able to outmaneuver the confused and ponderous battalion. He'd let James direct traffic, pointing the EEF mechanized platoon to provide the maximum effect for minimum risk.

All that left was for one lone Executioner to hit the bioweapons lab, infiltrate it, retrieve a deadly sample, avoid a containment breach and finally destroy Bitturumba's production of Ebola Thunder.

It wouldn't be a piece of cake, but Bolan knew that if he pulled it off, the murderous militia would swallow a gut full of stomach-busting justice.

CHAPTER THIRTEEN

Calvin James refused to let the gnats of concern worry him into life-threatening distraction. He had been given the reins on this phase of the mission, providing cover for Bolan's stealthy infiltration and guiding Okuba's Ethiopian road force to utilize their firepower to sucker punch the Islamist militias. Rafael Encizo was three hundred yards away in his sniper hide, his VEPR assault rifle converted to "light machine gun" mode to make the most of his position.

"Just give us the word, Striker," James whispered as he laid out a string of 40 mm grenades for his rifle's MP-203 compact grenade launcher. The shells were high-explosive, antipersonnel rounds, and the smart-ass in him couldn't resist taking the acronym for them— HEAP—and turn the splayed battle rounds mentally into a "heap of shit" intended for the militiamen. Eight 40 mm bombs, each capable of flattening soldiers in a twenty-yard circle, waited for the launch of their ninth "brother" as it rested in the breech of his underbarrel-mounted launcher.

It had been several minutes since Bolan's last transmission, and while James knew that a successful infiltration took time, he still had to fight against his impatience. It was a hard struggle, made more difficult by the need for stealth and stillness on his own part, lest he give away his position to the five hundred soldiers waiting in the distance. He remained silent, though, holding off tics of anxiety that gnawed at his nerves, trying to break loose. Boredom wasn't a factor here, as adrenaline coursed through his bloodstream like a stampede of wildebeest. His attention was held solidly by observation of his surroundings, keeping track of dozens of enemy soldiers who would notice him if he made just one simple mistake.

James waited for Bolan's command to unleash hell, hoping that he was good enough to pry the brave warrior from the jaws of death.

ANSON REINHARDT ITCHED for a cigarette as he passed through the checkpoint in the fence to begin his perimeter patrol. However, once you were in Heinz Baldr's employ, you had to learn to put aside your petty addictions in terms of smoking and drinking. Though they were no longer under military command, there were still rules of discipline. Cigarette smoke made a sentry easier to spot, and the act of lighting up ruined the ability to perceive opponents in the dark.

Reinhardt had a grudging respect for the Austrian. The man had good organizational skills, and he had put Reinhardt on the track to some good-paying private jobs. This one in Africa was only the latest in that long line. He was receiving plenty of hazard pay, protecting a laboratory container in the middle of the Sudanese conflict. He also got to play with some great high-tech toys, like the brand-new Fabrique Nationale SCAR-H rifle. The heavy-caliber version of the compact weapon was the newest product that the famed Belgian arms makers had put out. Accurate, yet portable, packing enough power to stop an angry leopard, let alone a far more fragile human being, it was a great tool. Hands-free radio communicators and top-line ceramic plate-augmented body armor, which kept him cool even in the African heat, were all great things to try out. Sure, he was in close proximity to a box full of death plague, but since it had a forty-five-percent survivability rate, and even the simplest filter masks protected against the air-borne spore's ravages, he felt that he was in good shape.

Plus, the night before, he'd been able to score a great kill on a leopard. Reinhardt wore the alcohol-desiccated testicles, member, claws and fangs of the once-proud beast on a necklace underneath his body armor. A smile crossed his lips at the thought of being so hard, he wore the balls of a fucking big cat around his neck. It was one thing to keep souvenirs of the humans he'd killed, but people, even if they had guns, were weak and soft prey. A leopard was a natural killing machine, thousands of years of genetic engineering making it one of the true kings of Africa, as opposed to the lazy lion. Leopards hunted alone, not like lionesses who traveled in packs to bring down a single opponent.

This animal wasn't alone, however. He'd heard the mournful growls of the leopard's mate—Reinhardt wasn't sure if he should call a female leopard a bitch, but he liked the idea anyway—as he took his hunting knife to the male's carcass. Outside the fence, it was him, alone with the enemy. He kept his suppressor locked on the end of his SCAR-H, anticipating the possibility of having the fangs of the leopard queen added to his necklace soon.

That would be one hell of a trophy.

"Come and get it, bitch," Reinhardt whispered.

AT FIRST, BOLAN COULDN'T BELIEVE his eyes as he spotted Reinhardt. He had to be one of the few white men in this region of Africa, outfitted for combat and smeared with camouflage greasepaint to help him blend into the surrounding grasslands. Now, closer to the compound, he was able to recognize a mix of European and Asian troops among the Africans. The Executioner observed the white mercenary and realized that the commando was not in uniform, nor packing the standard Thunder Lions' service rifle. He had a brand-new model FN assault rifle, hardly common hardware even among a force that utilized the FAMAS front-line service rifle. The SCAR-H was new, developed after the turn of the millennium, as opposed to the 1978-vintage FAMAS. The design that this commando carried was so new that it was still in the adoption stages for service across Europe and the U.S. That meant that whoever was bankrolling the bioweapon security force had high-level connections and serious money to equip his team with the latest and greatest.

The sentry also had good situational awareness; his eyes scanning the long grass and tree line, Reinhardt had a hunter's gaze, looking for the slightest blade of grass out of place. If Bolan's stealth had not been honed across countless battlefields across the globe, he would have been noticed by the high-tech commando. Bolan tapped his throat mike to let James and Encizo know he was sending a quick, one-word message. "Pro."

He left it to James to pass on the information to the rest of the group that there were highly trained killers stalking the perimeter of the camp. The sentry had his own hands-free communications setup. That kept Bolan from making a move and eliminating him. Normally the Executioner would have taken the guy by surprise and taken his place, but it was one thing to slip among tired and bored Russian gangsters by posing as one of their own. Even using the shadows and greasepaint to infiltrate a distracted African militia would be relatively easy. The rifleman patrolling the camp perimeter was in constant communication, and even the brief death grunt of reaction to a silenced Beretta bullet or knife blade would alert the rest of the security force.

It took quick reflexes and keen observational skills to remain in the guard's blind spot, but Bolan managed to skirt Reinhardt's attention and get closer to the compound. He toyed with the idea of letting James and company open up on the emplaced militiamen right then and there, providing a distraction, but the trained mercenaries would clamp down their security even more tightly, prepared and anticipating such a feint. There was a trail that the guard traveled upon, leading to a gap in the reinforced, barbed wire–topped fence surrounding the compound. The facility itself was well-lit, offering little secrecy for the Executioner if he attempted to walk through. He'd only end up filling the sights of commandos posted inside the fence.

There was a grunt off in the distance, punctuated by an animal snarl. It came from back where the sentry had gone. Bolan whirled and saw the guard thrashing as a black figure tore into him.

"Oh, God! Get it off me! Get it off me!"

The black panther atop Reinhardt slashed at the high-tech mercenary, razor-sharp claws slicing past Kevlar body armor and between ceramic trauma plates. Those hooked knives tore into the soft, vulnerable flesh underneath, parting muscle down to the rib cage in powerful swipes. The midnight-furred female leopard had bounded from the darkness onto the human intruding into its territory. Two of Reinhardt's partners rushed to the entrance that Bolan had dismissed moments before the big cat had attacked.

"God! She's back to get her mate's balls!" one of the mercenaries shouted. He brought his rifle to his shoulder, ready to shoot at the killing machine as it shredded Reinhardt's flesh and broke his bones.

"Don't shoot!" the other guard warned, pushing the rifle muzzle down into the dirt. "Anson's still under that fucking thing! Plus, you'll blow the trap! The militia will move in early!"

The first guard growled in frustration at his shot being thrown off.

Angry yellow eyes met Bolan's for a moment, then glanced toward the two men standing at the gate. The leopard launched itself like a rocket, fangs and claws bared for ferocious combat, and Bolan whirled, pulling his silenced Beretta with a speed and grace put to shame by the sleek black shape cutting through the air. The leopard and Bolan's 9 mm round struck at the same time, the cat taking down the guard who'd dared aim at her with his weapon, and the suppressed bullet smashing through the nose of the other sentry. Both humans fell, one with his brain drilled out by the Executioner's shot, the other with his head nearly torn from his shoulders by the strength and claws of the big cat. Neither man managed to release so much as a gurgle of warning to their allies.

Bolan rushed to the man he'd shot and pulled the radio off his vest. The leopard stepped slowly, nonchalantly, off the chest of the mercenary it had killed, lapping some gore from the yawning stump of the man's neck. As Bolan plugged in a spare lead to the radio, the yellow-eyed jungle queen regarded him silently.

"What the fuck? Report! Reinhardt! Gomez! Perun!" A bellowed roar came over the radio. "Call in!"

Bolan kept the sound off as the cat raked her claws into the soil to clean them off. Her rage abated, burning eyes looked around the well-lit compound. Her interest was fading in the affairs of the humans. Bolan had taken only the radio unit, leaving the men with their weapons, knowing that three disarmed corpses would raise alarms as jungle cats didn't have a need for assault rifles. The leopard gave the face of Bolan's gunshot victim a violent swat, her claws obscuring the gunshot wound. Maybe it was an act of postmortem revenge, but by marking the target, she had disguised the Executioner's presence. She stared at the warrior for a moment, then bounded off into the jungle.

"It's a fucking leopard!" someone called through the radio. "Shit, two leopards!"

In the momentary confusion following the big cat's assault, Bolan's midnight-black silhouette and swift, agile movements had bought him a few more seconds of anonymity on his infiltration. The Executioner appreciated the irony that cutting-edge technology and precision combat tactics had been undone in mere moments by a creature that had remained essentially the same for the past hundred thousand years. Humankind still had a long way to go to outdo the beasts of the jungle. Only Bolan's nonhostility toward the great predator had bought him a pass on fighting off fang and claw. He wished the cat prosperity and emotional healing for the loss of her mate.

As he did so, he raced toward the bioweapons lab and ducked into the air lock.

"Damn it! One of the cats got into the safety seal!" came a bellow over the radio. It took a moment for Bolan to realize that he was listening to a mix of languages he was familiar with, his razor-sharp mind translating from Spanish and German with equal facility.

"Wait for him to come out? Because we aren't inoculated against the fucking bugs they're growing in there," another man replied in Italian. The security force seemed culled from all across the European Union. It didn't matter who they were, though. All of them were well-armed and would gun down Bolan in a heartbeat. He had only a moment of protection as the guards were unwilling to risk contagion by firing at the cat they believed had infiltrated the lab.

Bolan had his filter mask in place over his nose and mouth. He'd been emboldened by the knowledge that he was only vulnerable to infection through his respiratory system. That vector was kept safe, thanks to the impassable armor of carbon fibers that would hold the microscopic airborne spores at bay. Even a bloody laceration wouldn't allow infection.

"Is anyone inside, damn it?" another guard asked. "Get on the same language here, you idiots!"

"The lab's shut down for the night," the Italian responded in his broken Spanish.

"Fucking morons!" a man with a heavy Turkish accent bellowed. "The virus is only dangerous if you inhale it. Put on your filters!"

"What about wounds?" one guard asked.

Bolan allowed the guard force to dither as he went about his task. He had only a few more seconds left before the gunmen realized that the predator among them wasn't merely an animal. He had to find a viable lab sample before they made that discovery and burned him to the ground under a hail of heavy-caliber bullets. He did, however, switch to his com-link with James and the others.

"Pour some fire on it," Bolan ordered.

"Do it!" James bellowed.

Bolan had his Beretta ready to repel any intruders. In the meantime, he saw an empty centrifuge that had been set up for allowing the breeding of the virus under controlled conditions. Small samples would be separated and put into new culture vials. Those cultures would be matured, then inserted into an aerosol suspension that fed and kept the virus alive until dispersal via air-burst munition or the simpler, equally effective airborne dusting methods that had brought him and the others to this facility.

Through the metal walls of the lab container, he heard a rumbling of distant thunder, and recognized it as the opening salvo of Okuba's RPG gunners. Six thermobaric shells detonating at once was an unmistakable cacophony. Over the guard's radio, he heard the dismay of the security force.

"Shit! It's a distraction!" the Turk's voice boomed. "Get in that lab now! That's no fucking cat!"

Too late, Bolan mused. He had already found the secure refrigerator with its heavy locking mechanism.

Bolan traded the Beretta for his Desert Eagle and fired a .44 Magnum slug through the mechanism. The stealth portion of this mission was decidedly over, so the need for silence had been obviated. The refrigerator popped open with a sigh, and the Executioner found test tube breeding samples inside.

A guard appeared at the air-lock door and Bolan whirled, throwing him a 240-grain hollowpoint through his open mouth. A spray of brain matter and gore exploded into the face of the gunman behind him, the blinding spray eliciting a cry from the dazed mercenary. The shocked sentry suddenly found himself struggling under the deadweight of his partner. Bolan fired again, the Desert Eagle tearing open the merc's throat in a shredding swipe of death.

With a tangle of two corpses blocking the air lock, Bolan had a relative moment of leisure to enact his sample extraction. He stuffed a stopper into the mouth of one test tube, then wound a strip of cloth around the glass vial. He plucked out an empty Beretta magazine and removed its baseplate. The top of the magazine had been sealed over with a thick closure of duct tape, and the cloth provided cushioning for the test tube as it was slid into its armored steel new home. The setup had been concocted ahead of time to provide protection for the deadly glass of microbe-laden death. He further protected the sample by inserting it into a waterproof, reinforced pocket of his battle harness.

He fished out a thermite grenade from his supply of munitions. The bomb was already wrapped with a worm of plastic-explosive detonation cord around the body of the thermite canister. A radio detonator was lodged in a thickness of the volatile putty, and Bolan had the trigger switch in another armored pocket. The virus wouldn't be able to survive the 4000-degree heat generated by the thermite charge, but just to make sure, Bolan put a second and third grenade into the refrigerator with the rest of the samples. The three of them would cook off with enough power to match one half of the temperature of the surface of the sun. The bioweapon lab itself would be scoured of life with a single press of a button.

Bolan went to the two recently created corpses and stripped them of their ammunition and one of the SCAR-H rifles. The presence of European mercenaries, unfortunately, meant that the triggering of his improvised decontamination device would not mean the extermination of Ebola Thunder. Bitturumba was still a menace, as well, even without his stockpile of biological weapons. All Bolan had was a viral culture with which the World Health Organization could work to map out a vaccine and treatments.

The Executioner hadn't even stepped out of the lab yet.

The doomsday numbers tumbled as he felt the lab container shaken by a detonating rocket grenade.

LIEUTENANT JOLU OKUBA'S thumbs ached from holding down the spade-shaped paddle trigger of the massive 12.7 mm DShK heavy machine gun. Beneath him, the jeep lurched, making his arms, from knuckles to shoulders, ache as he swung the powerful thirty-pound weapon on its pintle mount. His only saving grace was that the mounting protected his body from the awesome recoil. The militiamen that he'd raked with the last 600-round-per-minute burst all stayed down, even though he'd only hit one in four of his targets. Okuba was lucky to hit that much given the racing technical's jostling.

However, the men he did hit were torn violently asunder by the passage of two ounces of steel-jacketed lead as it obliterated flesh and bone. Even a normally survivable wound like a shoulder or thigh hit was turned lethal as each bullet carried more than six tons of kinetic energy along with it. A weaker round like the 7.62 mm NATO had less than one-sixth that kind of punch, only displacing tissue and perhaps breaking bone. The monster force of the 12.7 mm bullet was more than enough to rip off limbs and burst arteries feeding arms and legs. Bodies hit square on the torso suffered explosive crushing on all internal organs. Men saw their buddies ripped to shreds by the heavy machine-gun fire put out by Okuba and five other gunners, and they took cover behind the thickest barriers they could find.

Okuba's RPG teams had also wrought horrendous destruction among the enemy militia's rear flanks. The fat 105 mm warheads flew with lightning speed and stunning accuracy, detonating in a flash of thermobaric force. The explosions produced ten-meter kill radii in the ranks of the emplaced soldiers. In one salvo, six twenty-meter circles of death were opened up in the unsuspecting assault force. The TBG-7V warheads dispersed clouds of aerosolized fuel across the 10 mm radius dome, soaking the very atmosphere with high-octane flammability. A secondary charged detonated less than a heartbeat later, igniting the dome cloud and producing a high-pressure explosive wave that obliterated everything inside the epicenter of the explosion. Objects outside the total kill diameter received a steamroller of concussive force that could crumple the armor on anything short of a tank. With dedicated loaders, the RPG gunners were able to lance off twelve of their thermobaric kill blasts into Bitturumba's ambush force before they all reached unassailable cover.

Unfortunately, after the first dozen detonations, the militiamen had scattered, making it harder to take out amassed forces of the enemy battalion. No matter. The Ethiopians had turned their rocket-propelled grenades toward enemy technicals and troop trucks, devastating half of their transport capability in the space of a few seconds.

"Forty-five seconds! Disengage!" Okuba bellowed. His assistant hung another ammunition box on the DShK. The lieutenant dragged the disintegrating link belt of ammo into the breach, then closed the action. Thumbs stabbed down on the spade lever, triggering a new hose of high-caliber death in the abatement of his team's 60-round RPG hammering. The rocket crews retreated into their BTR-60 armored personnel carriers. The armored vehicles were far from silent, their 20 mm cannon and 14.5 mm superheavy machine guns spitting out short bursts to cover their roving technical backups. The KPV Soviet superheavy machine guns spit out rounds even larger and more powerful than Okuba's 12.7 mm hell blazer. The 14.5 mm bullets were a mix of armor-piercing and high-explosive incendiary rounds that not only shredded enemy vehicles, but left them blazing. The burning shells had been excellent target markers for Okuba's RPG rocketeers. The 20 mm cannons fired the equivalent of hand grenades at 250 rounds per minute, keeping the disorganized battalion off guard and scattered.

Even with this hellish onslaught of firepower, the

enemy forces had suffered only one hundred fifty casualties. The sluggish battalion stirred to life, turning to meet the challenge thrown down by the Ethiopians.

Okuba kept his promise to Bolan, and the mechanized platoon retreated from the Sudanese predators as they scrambled to fight back. Half their vehicles still maintained enough mobility to take up the chase, which meant that Okuba's men were going to be pursued by at least two hundred angry Islamofascist radicals in trucks and technicals. It would be a hairy chase, but the BTR-60s and VAZ-46 jeeps were more than up to the task of racing across the rough Sudanese terrain that they'd picked as their extraction route. The uneven ground would snarl up the more road-bound Peugeot pickups and jeeps utilized by the militiamen.

Okuba combined his fire with that of a BTR-60's KPV machine gun to slash a Renault troop transport truck to ribbons as it attempted to lead the charge after the Ethiopians. The militia convoy snarled up in its effort to take pursuit, slowed by its disorganization and massive size, but the enemy technicals were able to skirt around the blazing, shattered transport truck and its slaughtered payload of fanatical troops.

"Godspeed, Colonel Stone," Okuba prayed. Everything was up to the big American now.

CHAPTER FOURTEEN

"Oh, God! Get it off me! Get it off me!" Anson Reinhardt's voice screeched over the communications network, jarring Kartennian from his tense vigil, awaiting the arrival of the American soldier.

"God! She's back to get her mate's balls!" That one had to be Perun, Kartennian assumed. The Turk had needed to restrain his fury with Reinhardt, because the night before, the German mercenary under Baldr had wasted ammunition and broken operational security to shoot a leopard that had wandered too close to the compound. The boastful fool had mutilated the animal's corpse, and now wore its genitals and natural weapons on a leather thong around his neck.

Obviously, nature was getting its revenge upon the cruel mercenary, Kartennian felt.

"Don't shoot!" another guard, Gomez, warned. "Anson's still under that fucking thing! Plus, you'll blow the trap! The militia will move in early!"

At least some of Baldr's so-called elite had working brain cells.

Suddenly a series of grunts and animal snarls exploded across the radio.

"What the fuck? Report! Reinhardt! Gomez! Perun!" Kartennian bellowed. "Call in!"

Nothing. There were several tense moments of silence. He glanced to Heinz Baldr, who stood at the window, rifle held in low ready in one hand, field glasses in the other. "It's a leopard! Shit, two leopards!"

"Two?" Kartennian asked, keeping his transceiver on mute. "But the cat had a mate. Leopards don't travel in threes!"

"All I know is what I saw," Baldr growled. "Just take a look."

There was more blathering on the electronic party line. For a crew of highly trained professionals, the appearance of a wild animal or two threw them into a panic. After far too many moments of dithering chatter, Kartennian's patience broke. "Fucking morons! The virus is only dangerous if you inhale it. Put on your filters!"

He turned and glared at the Austrian that Cruz had sent to bolster Bitturumba's forces. "What in the flying fuck is wrong with those bloody idiots? A loose cat wanders inside the wire, and they piss themselves like little children!"

Baldr kept his watch on the situation, SCAR rifle clamped in his fist so tight, his knuckles were white and bloodless. "A goat-fucking moron like you has no place disrespecting my professional soldiers."

"Perhaps your father engaged in bestiality, Christian…" Kartennian countered. He caught Baldr's cold gaze, which dared the Turk to go further with his planned insult.

"What about wounds?" a French mercenary called back.

"Listen to them!" Kartennian bellowed. "Thor thought your rods were going to be worth shit against the American? They can't even handle a pussycat!"

Baldr shrugged. He seemed to be waiting for something. Kartennian's hand dropped to the Browning Hi-Power nestled in his hip holster, instinctively picking up on the machinations churning behind the Austrian mercenary's cold blue eyes. A snap of the thumb strap and the comfortable handle of the handgun levered into his grasp.

"Drop the rifle, errand boy," Kartennian ordered, leveling the pistol at Baldr's stomach.

Baldr regarded the Turkish jihadist, but let the FN rifle slide gently to the floor. "You'll need me to take out the intruder. Like it or not, I am the best thing you have on your side."

"I wasn't born yesterday, Heinz," Kartennian grumbled. "Alonzo Cruz and Thor Bitturumba may have gotten to where they are by pulling the shit over everyone else's eyes, but mine are gifted by God himself to see through lies and duplicity. Let the sheep fall for their constant stream of bullshit, I have the teachings of the Prophet to guide me!"

Baldr watched the 9 mm muzzle leveled at a spot just above his navel. The mercenary was filled with more quiet resolution than Kartennian had originally credited him for.

Maybe the Austrians weren't the mealy-mouthed weaklings that the Imams had said all Europeans were,

Kartennian thought. Then he remembered how Bitturumba had shown his true colors, vomiting up a vile spewage of hatred and lies against the unblemished truth of the Koran.

"Who was it who sent you to slay me? Thor? Cruz?" Kartennian snapped, waving the barrel of his gun with erratic abandon. "Tell me, and I will make this as painless as humanly possible."

The only answer was the rolling of Baldr's eyes as he held up his hands in surrender. Kartennian's rage built until distant explosions triggered a flinch. The roar of RPGs and heavy machine guns blazed out their death song, and with the Turk's finger on the Browning's trigger, the 9 mm pistol barked in sympathy. Baldr folded over, clutching his stomach in pain as soon as the Browning barked its savage message.

Kartennian grabbed his radio, his higher consciousness finally processing the cacophony going down outside. "Shit! It's a distraction! Get in that lab now! That's no fucking cat!"

The Turk rushed to Baldr's side, rolling the wounded man onto his back. "Oh, no. I need answers, lackey!"

Baldr's face was a twisted mask of agony, so Kartennian knew he had the freedom to glance away from the downed mercenary.

Through the tree line, the Turk saw the sparks and flashes generated by machine-gun fire and rocket explosions. Bitturumba had assembled an impressive force, the cream of his rival Janjaweed commanders' fighting men. Four separate companies of battle-hardened troops, all united for the sole purpose of taking down a solitary man. For a moment, Kartennian entertained the fantasy that the American was coming through that cordon of warriors alone, chewing through five hundred troops just like the unstoppable juggernaut that he'd seen in several American movies. It was the only concept his mind could wrap around for the moment, an incredible engine of destruction, with a cannon locked in each fist, plodding through rifle fire and grenades that bounced off his skin like grains of rice.

Only then did a brief flash of reality kick in for Kartennian. No man possessed the invulnerability to wreak such horrendous damage in an honorable, face-to-face conflict. The truth was more likely based on superior maneuvering and strategic positioning, a combination of good, solid cover, lateral movement and skilled marksmanship making up for sloppy battlefield tactics. The Turk frowned. The thought of such a warrior fighting to destroy the infidels, rather than against the Islamicist revolution, was a heady dream.

Kartennian felt something hard jam him in the crotch just behind his scrotum.

"I'm wearing body armor, you son of a bitch!" Baldr snarled in furious explanation. The Beretta locked in the mercenary's fist exploded, a hot muzzle-flash searing Kartennian's testicles. The 9 mm round struck in the halfway point between the Turk's anus and his scrotum, but the round-nosed bullet bounced off the heavy bone of his pelvis, careening away at an angle that plunged through his bowels and burst from his stomach just below his sternal notch. On its way out, the 9 mm pill ripped through intestines, filling his stomach with agonizing fire. The jihadist collapsed to the floor of the office, clutching his ruined guts.

Baldr rose on shaky feet, glancing out the window for a moment. Where Kartennian made the mistake of not restraining him, the Austrian pinned the Turk down, grinding his heel cruelly into the gunshot-ruined belly, letting his weight crush down on already heavily damaged internal organs. "That shit hurt, you slimeball. Where the fuck did you get off shooting me?"

"Bitturumba…sent you…kill me," Kartennian gurgled.

"Well, yeah," Baldr confirmed for the Turk. "But fuck! That hurts!"

"Go…hell," Kartennian croaked.

Baldr opened fire with the Beretta, emptying half a dozen more bullets into Kartennian's upper chest. "You first."

Balder was tempted to blow the Turk's face off, but he needed the Muslim world to believe that it was the American, not Bitturumba, who had been responsible for Kartennian's execution. With the Turk cast as another martyr to the mythic warrior's crusade, Bitturumba would be able to rally thousands of avenging brothers to the cause of exterminating the deadly mystery man.

The Sudanese suddenly started opening fire on the compound. The lab container disappeared in a detonation that jolted Kartennian's office, almost knocking Baldr off balance. A wall of Sudanese fire hammered into the camp, but it managed to pull the mercenary out of his reverie. Around the airstrip, Baldr saw one of the patrol technicals in flames, yet still rolling slowly across the tarmac. A transport helicopter burned, split in two by a mortar shell.

"Time to evac, people!" Baldr ordered. "This shit's gotten serious!"

Running as fast as he could, the Austrian mercenary

reached the line of remaining aircraft. Baldr threw himself in the side door of a heavy transport helicopter, satisfied with a job mostly well done. With Kartennian dead and Ebola Thunder presumed exterminated, Baldr's task of confusion and disinformation was done for the night.

It was time to leave the charnel house behind.

CALVIN JAMES AND Rafael Encizo held their fire as the remaining vehicles of the emplaced Sudanese militiamen took off after Okuba and his men. James waited, knowing that Okuba would further thin out the enemy herd that he and his Phoenix Force partner would have to hold off. The pair had given themselves several more minutes on-site, able to support the Executioner for that much more while he was still trapped within the confines of the compound.

"Cal to Striker, we're still on overwatch," James said into his radio. "I've converted your rifle to can formation and will provide sharpshooter cover."

"What about Okuba?" Bolan asked.

"He's leading what's left of the militia on a chase that would go great with that Benny Hill music," Encizo explained. "The fundamentalists are literally tripping all over themselves trying to get a crack at the Ethiopians."

"How many left behind?" Bolan quizzed.

"A hundred and fifty to two hundred," James noted. "I've got targets in compound. They're covering your air-lock escape. Two more got in on my blind spot. Shall I engage?"

Bolan took a deep breath. "Go for it."

James milked the trigger on his VEPR. The 24-inch

heavy machine-gun barrel had been installed and its stiffness and extra length gave the Phoenix Force rifle-man the reach he needed to drop a low-sound profile bullet into the back of a mercenary's head. The steel-cored, spoon-nosed bullet spread out like a flower on contact with hard bone, creating a sloppy kiss of metal to brain matter when the hardened heart of the slug punched through the fractured skull and whirled through the cranial cavity like a blender. Brains inside the shattered skull were scrambled and whipped into a slushy froth.

The camp security reacted to James's opening shot, whirling as one. James felt that it was too bad for the compound commandos that their reflexes weren't enough to sidestep his second and third bullets, the sub-sequent armor-piercing rounds carving through head bone on two more of them, cutting down the odds against Bolan even further. The corner guard towers lit up with their machine guns, but James's silenced VEPR gave them nothing to aim at other than a subtle super-sonic crack.

Ironically, it was the spray of unaimed return fire that arced into the ranks of Bitturumba's ambush force. On the heels of Okuba's blitzing hammer storm, the militia whirled and returned fire, ignoring the hidden Phoenix Force snipers. The Sudanese focused a re-lentless storm of bullets, grenades and rockets on the camp. James looked on in horror as explosions and bul-let strikes walked in an unstoppable line toward the bioweapons lab where the Executioner had been pinned down.

When the first RPG shell rocked the container's wall,

James felt certain that he'd been the one responsible for the death of the Executioner.

"Mack!" James roared as a blossom of molten fire split the porta-lab in two.

THE EXECUTIONER KNEW that if he wasn't careful, he'd carry lethal contagion back to the World Health Organization facility embedded in the fibers of his blacksuit and on his skin. Bolan had a plan for that contingency, however. Wielding the FN SCAR-H, he kicked open the air-lock door and fired into the decontamination chamber's ceiling. He'd seen nozzles built into the overhead segments of the umbilical and while observing the compound, he also had noticed that the enclosed corridor had tanks of decontaminant fluid installed on top. Bolan's salvo of assault-rifle fire punched holes in the ceiling and the tanks above them. The bullets released jets of cleansing bleach and antiviral disinfectant, which instantly soaked Bolan to his skin. Droplets stung into his eyes, causing his tear ducts to burn. Tears released in overtime to wash the caustic astringents from his eyes, but it was not as bad as being dosed with tear gas, as he'd done over the years. The Executioner endured through the painful burning in his eyes, already having his vision clear thanks to the cleansing tide from his tear ducts.

James's shots had bought Bolan a quick gap in the attention of the massed security forces. Bolan raced out the other end of the air lock and leaped through the night like the leopard that had sown the confusion to help him infiltrate only moments earlier. The corner guard towers blazed away with sniper rifles and heavy machine guns, giving the soldier a pang of dread that his Phoenix Force partners had come under fire.

Bolan reloaded his depleted SCAR and leveled it at a nearby guard tower. He was glad that the high-tech mercenaries had used the SCAR-H variant, with its higher power, long-range 7.62 mm NATO rounds. The authoritative rifle swept the closest sentry tower, bullets smashing through wooden slats shielding the distracted gunners. The devastating punch of the rounds, deformed on their journey through thick planks, produced horrendous wounds in the gunmen, silencing the pair of powerful weapons seeking out Bolan's allies.

That's when he realized that the compound was shaking as the remaining militiamen who had been left behind in Okuba's wake cut loose with everything they had. In their rage and the need to gain revenge for a perceived betrayal, the Janjaweed fundamentalists disregarded the threat of infection and contamination, launching portable mortars and rocket grenades in addition to heavy machine-gun bursts through the heart of the camp. A churning cloud writhed like a waking dragon, then surged forward through the facility. Bolan lurched to his feet, knowing that he was only a few seconds away from the snarling serpent of destruction slithering toward him. When the transport container that made up the structure of the bioweapon shook violently, the Executioner's thumb stabbed the firing stud on his remote detonator.

The shock wave floored Bolan as a white-hot lance of liquid flame burst through the roof of the lab. It was split in two by the detonation of three thermite grenades and the militia's incoming artillery fire. Seared by a fire nearly half the temperature of the surface of the sun, metal melted into fluid, atmosphere vaporized, broken down into its molecular components, and most importantly, microbes incinerated and died in the cleansing flames. By the time the heat reached Bolan, his soaked blacksuit and exposed flesh were dried out instantly. Had he not been drenched by decontamination sprays, his skin would have suffered far more than mere cracks and singes by the rolling blast furnace of superhot air.

Screams of confusion and dismay erupted from the compound's defenders. The Executioner knew that the cargo he carried would provide a road map to the WHO, safe in its sealed pocket on his assault harness. However, it would be useless if the mercenary crews gunned him down. Self-preservation was only icing on the cake, but a global threat was far more important than his lone life.

A merc swung around the smoldering cloud of ash raised by the immolated biolab. Having had no time to reload the SCAR, Bolan drew his Desert Eagle with lightning speed. The European rifleman was half-blinded, coughing from smoke and dust, giving Bolan the drop on him. The .44 Magnum slug took the man through his open mouth, blowing his neck bones into splinters and ripping the spinal cord right out of his brain. The Executioner dumped the empty magazine from his rifle and slammed home a fresh one.

Bolan realized that in the rush to escape the air lock, his earpiece had popped out of his ear. He reinserted it.

"Striker to Phoenix, pull out!"

"Mack? You're okay!" James cheered.

"I feel like I fell asleep on a barbecue grill, but I'll live," Bolan answered. "I've got the sample. Pull out and get to Elee."

"We're a bit busy right now," James said. "We were getting a little payback."

"I told you—" Bolan began, but he bit back his frustration. His friends had been worried about him, and it wasn't something that he could blame them for. More than once, the Executioner had shut down emotionally, transforming into a killing machine over the loss of a beloved ally. He examined the situation as it stood. Two of the guard towers closest to the militia had been blasted to splinters, while the tower across from the one that Bolan had eliminated was still focusing its firepower on the turncoat Sudanese.

Bolan rushed to the ladder to climb up and man the tower's machine gun. Movement in his peripheral vision registered just as Bolan reached the base of the sentry structure. He whirled and dropped to the dirt in reaction to an enemy's approach. From the ground, Bolan saw a quartet of Bitturumba's black-uniformed Thunder Lions race to intercept him. He triggered a short burst from his SCAR, a trio of bullets punching through one of the Africans, stopping the first one cold. The 7.62 mm rounds tunneled through the guts of the lead rifleman, stopping him as if he'd collided with a brick wall. A second gunman stumbled over the dead man's splayed legs. The clumsy trooper landed face-first in the dirt, sparing him the effects of Bolan's rapid follow-up shots, which raked the other two gunmen across their upper chests.

The tripped gunner had lost his rifle, but there was a gleaming blade locked in his fist. With a fierce leap, the Thunder Lion was on top of the grounded Bolan, who had twisted in time to not be caught and pinned by his opponent. The African's strength was nearly as great as his leonine namesake, smashing the rifle from his adversary's grasp. The Executioner grabbed the Sudanese's wrist, stopping the descending spear-point blade as it hovered inches over Bolan's heart.

"When you get to hell," the militiaman growled, "tell them that it was—"

Bolan cut off the knife-man's boastful message to the afterlife with a snap of his knuckles, sinking them deep into the Sudanese's larynx. Voice box crushed and windpipe collapsed, the militiaman's lips burbled with bloody pink froth. Bolan wrenched the knife around hard, punching the blade back into its owner's gut. With a surge of strength, he dumped the dying man in the dirt. There wasn't anyone else approaching quickly, so the Executioner retrieved the fallen SCAR and scrambled up the ladder.

"Cal? Rafe?" Bolan grunted.

"We're still kicking," Encizo responded. "But the bad guys are pouring on the heat."

"I'll take it off you," Bolan promised as he scurried into the gunner's nest. The Type 67 General Purpose Machine Gun was mounted on a swiveling tripod, and the remnants of its 100-round belt dangled, undamaged by the Executioner's nest-clearing salvo. Knowing he could hose rounds on target out to nearly one thousand yards, he turned on the Sudanese militiamen. The heavy 7.62 mm Russian rounds made the mounted machine gun buck vigorously, wanting to lift the 25-pound weapon off its mounting, but the searing line of slugs raked viciously into a squad of soldiers trying to assault James's position. The weapon ran dry, but Bolan was familiar with the Kalashnikov design, feeding it a fresh belt in the space of seconds.

James utilized the breathing room the Executioner

had bought him to slam a 40 mm grenade into the ranks of soldiers threatening to overrun Encizo. Once the Type 67 was back online, the streams of autofire from both Bolan and the stocky Cuban combined to rip into enemy forces. In a stroke of luck attributed to the confusion known as the fog of war, the remaining guard-tower crew found themselves following the line of tracers from Bolan's GPMG to direct their own fire. The sentries who had been set up to kill James and Encizo found themselves in the role of unknowing protectors. The mistake was such a stroke of favor that Bolan felt no need to take out the gunners.

With the trio of machine guns providing ferocious volumes of blistering firepower, backed up by the heavy sniper rifle and James's grenade launcher, the Sudanese hardmen were softened into panicked retreat.

The trap had been broken, and with the smothered influx of fire lancing into the camp, the remaining mercenaries rushed to waiting heavy transport helicopters that had survived the initial conflagration. Three shattered shells of obliterated aircraft stood on the airstrip, bleeding smoke into the night sky. Others, presumably Bitturumba's embedded Thunder Lions, poured into their surviving jeeps and trucks. There weren't many rats left to abandon their burning, sinking ship, but the guards in the far tower quickly joined them.

"We'll hook up with you," James said. His voice momentarily took on a shaken timber. "I thought that I'd goaded those fucks into killing you."

"I'm not dying that easily," Bolan responded. "Elee, you've got enough smoke to cover your approach."

"I'm on my way," Aslin responded. "Do you always leave this much devastation in your wake?"

Bolan scrambled down the ladder. "If I have to, yes."

"Okuba just contacted me." Aslin sighed with relief. "He's given the Sudanese the slip after wrecking a few more of their vehicles. He'll meet us back at the refugee camp."

The Huey swung in to land, but Bolan's attention was on the departing European mercenaries. He had shaken loose the shadowy conspirators who had been bolstering Bitturumba's ascension to power in Africa.

"Colonel?" Aslin asked over the radio.

Bolan turned away from the fleeing flight of helicopters.

He had found the shadow operators once. He would find them once more.

They had to pay for the plague and suffering they'd unleashed.

CHAPTER FIFTEEN

Stony Man Farm, Virginia

Aaron Kurtzman looked over the recent information coming into the Farm's War Room off the CIA intel ticker. It seemed that the Russian field office had been inundated with files that contained information about a *mafiya* arms deal with an African militia. That by itself wasn't news to the Stony Man cyberwizard. Mack Bolan had been on that case for nearly a week now, tipped off by his contacts within Russia about the black-market germ warfare shell shipment. Bolan and Kurtzman were aware of the broker for the international arms deal, an Igor Sharpova. While the Executioner cleaned up the scene in Africa, Kurtzman was hard at work with his computer team searching for the Russian gangster utilizing cyberspace. Sharpova had a date with judgment in his future, one long overdue in both Kurtzman and the Executioner's opinion.

That date was put indefinitely on hold, now. Thanks to a GPS tracker built into Sharpova's cell phone, Cartagenian constables had discovered the Russian's bullet-riddled, mutilated corpse on the floor of an abandoned factory. The Russian criminal had bled to death from brutal injuries, which had been calculated to induce a slow, agonizing demise. Only a herculean effort had enabled the dying mobster to reach his cell phone and get the ball rolling on the data pouring through the CIA's Russian offices.

The discovery of Sharpova's corpse in Spain, and the release of notes tying pharmaceutical entrepreneur Alonzo Cruz to a hard-line, former Soviet military officer, combined to inform the Stony Man cybernetic crew that it was Cruz who may have been the engineer of Ebola Thunder. Another bit of information that Sharpova had spilled to the CIA was the name of Thormun Bitturumba's father.

It was Antonio Cruz, Alonzo's father.

Kurtzman felt his blood grow cold at the prospect of a drug company magnate being the half brother of an African warlord responsible for rampant slaughter and destruction. The CIA, on the other hand, was releasing the opinion of their analysts. The brains back at Langley had immediately produced a report that Sharpova's information had to be fabricated from whole cloth, given the highly public nature of Cruz and Bitturumba's feud. Cruz was a very vocal opponent of the European Union's apathy toward the Darfur genocidal crisis. Bitturumba had made his "street cred" with the Sudanese Janjaweed by decrying the loudmouthed European who had no right to call for interference in African or Muslim affairs. The war of words, plus Bitturumba's aggressive and successful Thunder Lion militia, had combined to make the towering general a lightning rod for attention among Africans tired of the outside world using their nations as playgrounds.

According to the analysts, the sudden burst of data had to have been an action on a rival company's part to discredit Cruz and Crusade Pharmaceuticals. Cruz had gained international acclaim among citizens of the EU who felt powerless over the tales of atrocity coming out of the Sudan. Cruz's humanitarian persona had garnered Crusade Pharmaceuticals contracts and free advertising, which pushed him to the top of the European stock markets in terms of value. Cruz made no bones about his work in Third World nations, moving medicine and money into Africa, the Middle East and Asia. The name Crusade Pharmaceuticals had given him enormous controversy, as devout Muslims saw the appellation as an insult based on centuries of intrusive warfare in the Middle East. Apparently, that didn't stop Cruz from doing the right thing, winning over moderates and gaining Western allies for his "in your face" attitude toward violent jihadists. Donations flooded through Cruz's coffers almost too fast for Interpol to keep track of all the money.

"If this is true," Price said, looking at the data over Kurtzman's shoulder, "all that charity would make an excellent money-laundering cover."

"And get this. Only a few days ago, Cruz said that he had his factories set up to begin production of a vaccine for Ebola Thunder," Kurtzman read. "All he wants is a sample of the virus, and his scientists will use it as a road map to create a treatment. He claims to have been in contact with the World Health Organization and feels such a strategy is feasible since there are strong indications that the virus has been artificially manufactured."

Price's eyes narrowed as she looked over the business report. "We should take a look at Cruz's money trails. Crusade Pharmaceuticals has a lot of euros flowing into Africa at the moment, and if we can trace a solid link between charity funds and a radical Islamic militia, we might have the basis for going after him with presidential sanction."

"Even if it's just circumstantial evidence, Striker would go after Cruz with or without approval," Kurtzman said. His mind raced for a moment, darting back to the night that the Executioner and his Phoenix Force allies engaged not only the Thunder Lions, but the Egyptian cell of the Muslim Brotherhood in Alexandria.

"Akira," the computer wizard called, referring to the Farm's premier computer hacker, "I need you to tap Egyptian intelligence. Look for large influxes of funding to terrorist cells in Alexandria over the past week. Something that would be enough cash for the Brotherhood to send eighty members out on a private hunting party."

"We have fresh information coming in from the Sudan, Aaron," Carmen Delahunt spoke up. The vivacious redhead was a former FBI agent, recruited by Brognola when she was searching for a greater challenge. "The EEF has moved in on the site that Striker hit just a few hours ago. They found European nationals among the dead, so the Ethiopians are transmitting digital camera images over to Interpol, looking to see if they can link the dead with anyone in their files as either terrorists or mercenaries."

Kurtzman rolled his wheelchair over to Delahunt's workstation. "Anyone in the batch that we know?"

"Mostly small fry. Mercenaries from England to Russia. All of them have been sanitized, as well, no corporate ties to any legitimate professional military organizations or private security firms," Delahunt said. "Hold on. Someone doesn't fit in."

Delahunt scrolled through the image stream until she came upon the photograph of a swarthy Middle Eastern man. "Does he look familiar?"

Kurtzman frowned. "Run him through the recognition filters. He looks more Turkish than Arabic."

Delahunt ran the facial recognition software. It took only five minutes to come up with Kedzi Kartennian. "Ninety-five-percent match, due to burn damage on the face and the slackening of facial muscles in death. Blood drainage caused some problems, too, but reconstruction is close enough for us."

Kurtzman nodded. "I know the name. He used to be part of the conduit between Azerbaijan and Iran. The mullahs used him to support revolution in the former Soviet states. Things eventually got too hot for Kartennian when Russia asked the Turkish government for help finding him. Since then, he's dropped off the map."

"And he's popped up in Africa," Price interjected. "Apparently the mullahs wanted to keep their asset, but Eurasia's too dangerous for him. That explains the Muslim Brotherhood showing up in force, too. Iran and the Brotherhood both want a far more radically Islamic fundamentalist government installed in Egypt."

"Well, their link is cold and rotting in Africa." Kurtzman sighed.

"With Iran footing the bill for their Egyptian brothers, they felt the urge to bring in a whole army," Delahunt mused. "Not that it helped. We also picked up a rumor that one of the names that terrorist organizations have attributed to Striker was active in Egypt. His reputation was enough to be the impetus for a massive mobilization of forces."

Price shook her head. "We go to all this trouble to make Striker an anonymous figure, removing his background and history, and the Russians, the Jihad, the Asian crime gangs and the South Americans make up their own legends about him."

Delahunt chuckled. "Criminals and terrorists are a superstitious and cowardly lot. Though the Executioner has long since been reported dead, his spirit still lives on."

"They have enough proof in terms of corpses and ruined plots to believe that something is out there killing them off," Kurtzman added.

"Interpol has been looking into Cruz, mainly due to some suspicious deaths among his business rivals within Crusade Pharmaceuticals," Delahunt said. "They couldn't come up with anything that would be the basis of prosecution, but that could just be because Cruz can afford quality help."

Huntington Wethers spoke up. "High quality." The tall, dignified former professor of cybernetics at Berkeley was a valued member of the cyberteam, and his research techniques were second to none. "His current chief of executive protection is a former member of Austria's COBRA antiterrorism initiative. Heinz Baldr."

Price's eyes flashed with recognition. "I remember his resignation. I read a flagged item that said he'd engaged in moonlighting for some Saudi and Pakistani firms. That was a conflict of interest with his governmental duties, since his work for those companies entailed training methods similar to the Austrian counterterrorism forces. The Saudis and Pakistanis had tenuous ties to al Qaeda, but nothing definite. In the end, the Austrian government couldn't, or wouldn't, prosecute Baldr, and he was discharged. He now takes jobs within the private sector."

"That was about the time Alonzo Cruz started rising through the ranks at Crusade," Kurtzman added. "It could be a coincidence…"

"It's not," Price proclaimed. "This web's just gotten a lot more tangled. Jack's already left for Africa?"

Kurtzman nodded.

"Then let's let Striker know that he's got a road trip to Germany coming up," Price said. "Get this data to him ASAP."

Darfur, Sudan

THE WHO LAB TECHNICIANS didn't waste time asking where Tanya Marshall and Elee Aslin had gotten the viable Ebola Thunder culture. After making certain that the pair were free of contagion and possible symptoms, they tore into their work. The process involved breeding the virus so that they had a series of experimental samples for running treatment protocols. Though the lab workers were silent and focused, Marshall knew her fellow scientists. There was a living fire deep in their eyes, minds charged with electric excitement at the tools for salvation that they'd been handed.

Marshall grinned as she, Stone, Aslin and Farrow watched the lab team through a glass partition. "They're as giddy as schoolgirls."

Bolan allowed himself a chuckle at her momentary levity. "So the microscopic war looks like it's drawing to a close."

Marshall's smile faded. "You're still worried."

Bolan rubbed his jaw. "I'm thinking that the men who gave Bitturumba that concoction didn't limit themselves to one variant strain. The WHO could be breaking their backs developing a cure for a disease that will never be used again. In fact, the next bioweapon might not have anything in common with Ebola Thunder."

"So why this whole big deal of creating a health crisis specifically geared toward putting the world on alert?" James asked.

"Headquarters gave us a call earlier and I have a hint," Bolan said. "Alonzo Cruz and Crusade Pharmaceuticals."

Marshall's eyes narrowed in concern. "You're kidding, right? Cruz gave us half the equipment in this laboratory, and most of our technicians are former employees of his."

"I'm not," Bolan said. "Rafe has been in communication with our higher-ups, and my usual pilot is being sent here to ferry me to Bonn, Germany."

"Crusade has done a lot alongside us," Marshall explained. "I need to come along."

Bolan frowned at the thought. "Chances are that Cruz will want to cover his back. He knows I'm coming for an emergency meeting with him in regards to discussing his response to the current Sudanese plague crisis."

"This would be more the World Health Organization's purview, though," Marshall replied. "I'll get on the phone with Cruz and defuse things."

"Defuse things?" Bolan asked.

"If he is a killer, he might be a little off balance if he's expecting you to come in like James Bond, but then he ends up with two actual medical personnel. Besides, I can help you look more legitimate," Marshall replied.

"Dr. Marshall, it's going to be a very dangerous situation," Bolan said. "I'd prefer not to put you in harm's way."

"Really, Colonel?" Marshall asked. "Do you think that I came to Africa because it's fun and safe to deal with plagues here? If what you're saying is correct, Alonzo Cruz has created a global menace by releasing his artificial spores into the wild. Given the speed at which microevolution takes place, there's a possibility that a vaccine-resistant, respiratorily infectious variant could mutate in the near future. Right now, thanks to you, the Sudan is relatively safe, but what about the rest of the world? That's kind of my job. World health. Protecting the health of the citizens of the world."

"Which is why I'm going to interview Cruz," Bolan answered. "Considering the people he's working with, however, you could come to serious harm."

"And Africa's been so safe, what with Janjaweed death squads roaming the countryside, wild animals and an airborne variant of Ebola?" Marshall inquired. "Germany can't be any more dangerous than sitting between an Ethiopian Expeditionary Force and armies of Islamofascists bent on genocide."

Bolan frowned. "Make the call. But you listen to what I say. Everything I tell you is to keep you alive and healthy."

"So what am I supposed to do?" Aslin asked.

"Right now, you're temporarily in the employ of the USAMRIID, and you'll be ferrying around Ruiz and Farrow," Bolan said, nodding at James and referring to the cover identities of the Phoenix Force commandos. "Just because Bitturumba's currently on the ropes does *not* mean that he's out for the count. I'm certain Bitturumba and his brother Cruz—"

"They're brothers?" Marshall asked. "That's ridiculous!"

"Half brothers, actually," James confirmed.

Marshall looked as if someone had drained the blood from her face. "Why is one brother helping us while the other's killing everyone in sight?"

"Because, while he's been giving all this charity out, he's been raking in private donations to help with the cause," Bolan stated. "Cruz is benefiting from his philanthropic ends."

"And sadly, so is his brother and others who are much less than philanthropic," James added. "Our researchers have traced some charity money to a recent account deposit for the Muslim Brotherhood."

Aslin's nostrils flared. "No, they're most definitely not deserving of charity. My father dealt with those jackals once, and he never felt spiritually clean after making their acquaintance."

The quartet walked out of the lab center and ran into Rafael Encizo, who was jogging up to them. "Jack just flew into Nyala. It'll take a couple of hours for the plane to be refueled and prepped for the next leg of the trip."

Aslin glanced over at Bolan. "You sure that you're not going to need me up in Germany?"

"Elee, I need you to be here for Rafe and Cal. They're not just my subordinates, they're my team, and I need to have them in good hands. You've flown us through some harrowing times, and like it or not, chasing down Bitturumba, even if he is on the ropes, is going to be dangerous."

Aslin nodded.

The Executioner gave the woman a slight smile. It

was time for the Bolan blitz to make its journey to the home of the lightning war—Germany.

BITTURUMBA HANDED BALDR a cold beer from his cooler. "A little celebration?" the Austrian asked.

"Thrilled to not only have Kartennian out of my hair, but to be done with Ebola Thunder," Bitturumba replied. He ran his thick fingers up over his clean-shaved pate, then chuckled. "So to speak."

"We could have set our watches by how reliably the American showed up," Baldr said. "But he didn't come alone."

"I heard. I'm sorry for the loss of your men," Bitturumba stated.

Baldr took a draft of his beer. "They were just fodder, even if they didn't know it. Kartennian began to suspect something was up when the guards encountered a leopard. I wouldn't lose any sleep over them."

"A leopard?" Bitturumba asked.

"It provided a distraction for the interloper, but don't get any ideas about the mysticism of it," Baldr explained. "The thugs I'd hired had shot her mate the night before."

"I take it that the American escaped," Bitturumba mused.

"Alonzo just called me. Apparently the World Health Organization and the U.S. Army Medical Research Institute for Infectious Diseases are sending representatives to meet with him. Originally, it was just the AMRIID, but Dr. Marshall said she's accompanying a Colonel Stone to Germany. It's officially to bring him their data to produce a vaccine."

Bitturumba bellowed out a laugh. "A vaccine for an

otherwise useless disease. But the stock market will see that deal with the WHO, and piss themselves trying to pick up Lonzo's shares. My little brother will be drunk with money."

"And what about you? You've lost a lot of men, and the virus will be worthless once the vaccine becomes available," Baldr questioned.

"The disease increased my recognition, but you should know that I have my own cannon fodder. The Janjaweed thugs that took that brutal pounding from the American soldier and his Ethiopian allies were made up of the cream of the crop of my closest rivals," Bitturumba said with a chuckle. "My enemies have lost their finest troops, while mine are setting up for two trips."

Baldr grinned. "So you're going through with the plan to move into Chad?"

"First, we have to pull a little face time in Libya," Bitturumba said.

"Spreading out and conquering the world, one African nation at a time," Baldr mused. "After Sharpova bit the dust, I figured that the writing was on the wall that General Ammuz was far more receptive to your ideas."

"The Janjaweed have a few of my companies among their number, and they're filling in the ranks as I maneuver my troops into Gharb Darfur and Shamal Darfur. The Ethiopians might have gotten as far as Khartoum in the northern half of the country, but we have Shamal and Gharb to ourselves," Bitturumba said. "The other warlords want to take the fight to the EEF and its positions in Janub Darfur, but so far, they're just hammering themselves senseless all along the 12th Parallel."

"So you go to Libya for a peacekeeping mission, and you lose your position here in the Sudan?" Baldr asked.

"Khartoum is already twisting in the wind, being so weak that they can't kick the Ethiopians out," Bitturumba grumbled. "But, I have some advantages. Ammuz has significant pull among many of my rival commanders. Those he doesn't, we will deal with by delivering them to the world court."

"The genocide ends under your rule," Baldr noted.

Bitturumba nodded. "My act of mercy, aiding my brother Muslims in Libya and Chad will find me with a changed heart."

"And it won't hurt that the Janjaweed will move into Chad to get some payback for the 2005 conflict," Baldr added. "You set up a puppet regime there…"

"The love for me," Bitturumba said, arms spreading widely, "will make me the president of this rotten little nation."

"I thought you said you were done with Ebola Thunder," Baldr said. "So what's the crisis in Libya and Chad?"

"Variants. Variants necessitating that two fierce rivals, Cruz and Bitturumba, set aside their differences for the good of all humankind," the general explained.

Baldr laughed. "Oh, that's wickedly beautiful."

"When will you be leaving for Libya to oversee Alonzo's operations?" Bitturumba asked.

"Not for a while yet. We have to get the plague going full steam, then General Ammuz will have his transport planes bring in the lab containers from Germany," Baldr stated. "Right now, we're counting on your end of the operation to begin spreading trouble on the coast. Tripoli, Surt, Banghazi…"

Bitturumba nodded. "I'll be flying to Al Uwaynat to

meet with the general a little later today. That will be taken care of."

"What about this Colonel Stone who's going to see Alonzo?" Baldr asked.

Bitturumba thought for a moment. "It's most likely the cover identity for the man who's been worrying me since the lost shipment in Alexandria. We've baited him against us, and now he's baiting us, waiting to see what our response is. The smart thing would be to just let him sit on his thumbs in Germany, but the shitty thing is, he'll be right in Lonzo's backyard. He'll know that the labs aren't there to provide a cure."

"Undoubtedly," Baldr said. "If he's there, checking on the Bonn operation, that means he's onto Crusade Pharmaceuticals. Doing nothing would be suicide because he'd be following the trail back and maybe pick up on the Libyan angle."

Bitturumba grimaced. "What have you got around Bonn?"

Baldr thought for a moment. "There's my security team, and they really are the best. They also have links to local gangs of neo-Nazis and skinheads. They tap them for deniable operations, but they can mobilize up to fifty men. You have any help?"

"I can go through Kartennian's contacts in Europe. Neo-Nazis and jihadists don't mix too well, however," Bitturumba replied. "It'd have to be done in waves. Do we know what airport he's coming in from?"

Baldr nodded. "Crusade Pharmaceuticals' field near Bonn. I have a member of my security team who is a German-born Arab. He was my tie-in who got me on the trail to Kartennian."

"So we have that prick to blame?" Bitturumba asked.

"Kharo's a good egg." Baldr defended his man. "He can scare up some muscle from local fundamentalists."

"While you have the security team and the skinheads waiting to pick up the slack if Kharo's contacts fail," Bitturumba said.

"Stone will have his work cut out for him," Baldr said. "Here he had the advantage of grenade launchers and heavy machine guns as well as support from the Ethiopian military. An attack on him in Germany will make him more vulnerable because I simply can't see him carrying around a bag of assault rifles in a civilized nation."

Bitturumba quirked an eyebrow. "If your lads have access to automatic weapons, so can he. I know that American self-defense experts advocate the use of tennis-racket carriers to conceal a folding stock semi-automatic rifle."

"Concealed rifles?" Baldr asked, dismay drenching his words. "I knew they were called gun nuts…"

"Mostly for unobtrusive transport to their car, not for just walking down the street," Bitturumba corrected. "Remember, this Stone is a military professional. Any tricks your mercenaries know for hauling assault rifles to their jobs in the heavy gun-control environment of Europe are most likely going to be old news and standard practice for him."

Baldr nodded. "No wonder you're the general. Have a safe trip, Thor. I'll get my men to work on this."

Next stop, Libya, Bitturumba mused as he finished his beer.

CHAPTER SIXTEEN

Bonn, Germany

Robert Kharo's lips were drawn tight around the butt of his cigarette, a serpent of smoke crawling into the air from the burning ember, as if to play lookout for the German-born Syrian. Kharo's eyes were scanning the tarmac, expecting the arrival of the Gulfstream 150 jet coming in from the Sudan. He was at one of the corporate air terminals that Crusade Pharmaceuticals had spread throughout Europe, part of Alonzo Cruz's network of travel arrangements that kept him from riding on regular passenger flights. It was so much easier for representatives of the World Health Organization and the Army Medical Institute for Infectious Diseases to fly into Bonn on his airstrip rather than come through the international airports. Sure, there were a couple of customs officials and in the tower, there was a German aviation official, but there was no incentive, as with an airline-run terminal, for the government to provide security forces. Private mercenaries, much like Kharo himself, manned this field.

Corporate money paid for hangar and terminal security, and Kharo was impressed by the manpower on hand. He suspected that the men in uniform, standing sentry over the terminal, were all likely veterans of German military special operations teams or police counterterrorism squads.

Dressed in a black suit with a chauffeur's cap, Kharo was secure that no one would think twice about his presence. He was part of Heinz Baldr's elite corps of bodyguards, but he also served as a driver. The man's goal this day was to deliver Dr. Marshall and Colonel Stone to the lion's den.

Kharo's confederates were in a pair of pickup trucks on his chosen route, positioned to intercept the limousine. A dozen men, armed and ready, were poised to hit a guest of a "hated anti-Islamist," Alonzo Cruz. The trucks would swoop down on the limo like wolves bringing down a doe. It would be all over in the space of a minute, and Kharo would undoubtedly be injured, but he'd live, and heroically strive to call the police for help.

Colonel Brandon Stone, USAMRIID, and Dr. Tanya Marshall, World Health Organization, would be torn to pieces by armor-piercing rifle ammunition, their bodies too shredded to be identifiable in the wake of the brutal assassination.

The plane taxied across the airstrip, crawling to a halt at the hangar.

Kharo flicked his cigarette out the window. It was showtime.

"A PLEASURE TO MEET you both," Kharo greeted Bolan and Marshall as they entered the corporate terminal for Crusade Pharmaceuticals. "I'm your driver, Robert Kharo. You can call me Rob."

"You know who we are," Bolan answered brusquely. "Mr. Cruz said he didn't have much time before he left Bonn, so forgive my lack of small talk."

Kharo raised his hand, nodding in agreement. "Say no more."

He took their bags and placed them in the trunk of the stretch limo. He held the door for the woman, Marshall, while Stone helped himself into the back of the vehicle. Kharo jogged to the driver's seat and slid behind the wheel.

"I know a shortcut," Kharo stated.

"So do I," Bolan replied. The driver looked back and into the muzzle of the Executioner's Beretta. "Get into the back with us, Rob. And keep your hands where I can see them."

The man paused for a moment. Bolan lashed out, grabbing a fistful of collar and yanking back violently. Kharo's head bashed into the ceiling of the limo. It was a stunning blow and the next thing that the driver knew, Bolan had taken the .357 Magnum revolver out of his cross-draw holster. With a powerful shrug, the warrior hauled the dazed Kharo into the passenger compartment over the driver's partition.

Within moments, Cruz's agent was hog-tied with plastic cable restraints on his wrists and ankles.

Marshall looked on in surprise. "How did you know?"

Bolan tugged open Kharo's white uniform shirt, revealing body armor. "It's illegal for civilians to have certain grades of concealed body armor, no matter what their job. Even bodyguards are limited to lower levels of ballistic protection than certain firearms utilized by the German Federal Police. Rob here is wearing armor rated to stop an AK-47's rounds. I could tell from the bulk around his chest, and the discomfort of his movements when he was carrying our bags."

Marshall frowned. "He would have driven us into an ambush?"

Bolan nodded. He stripped Kharo of his armor, then handed the vest to Marshall. "It might not be much, especially if Cruz is sending people with weapons that can cut through these windows. Those rounds might be too much even for this particular vest."

Bolan and Marshall both crawled over the partition and into the front seat. Bolan hit the control, and the bulletproof shield slid up between passenger cabin and driver's compartment. He'd sealed Kharo into the back, stripped of the folding knives the man had in his pockets and the revolver in his ankle holster. Bolan clicked on the GPS unit on the dashboard and examined the route that was programmed into the device.

"What are you looking for?" Marshall asked.

Bolan poked the screen where the road took the bend. "Ambush. This is where Kharo set us up to be murdered."

Marshall tilted her head inquiringly.

"It's an isolated area with relatively little traffic, but it has two roads that feed onto it. Both of those roads are partially concealed by terrain features, allowing them to sit hidden," Bolan explained as he studied the map, looking for an alternate route.

"Something tells me that you're not going to avoid that spot," Marshall said.

"Would you leave a foreign object in an injury to cause an infection later on?" Bolan asked.

"Meaning that the people Cruz sent are dangerous, and have to be dealt with immediately," Marshall agreed. "Otherwise they might hit some other limo, or get into a shootout with the police."

Bolan pulled the limo out of its parking space. "Stay in the seat well when I tell you to. The glass won't be much protection, but the dashboard and car body will."

Marshall sighed, nervous. "Since I know you've done this plenty of times before, I'll just let you do what you do best."

Bolan gave her a reassuring smile as he pointed the limo toward their next deadly encounter.

Darfur, Sudan

RIDING SHOTGUN in the VAZ-46, Calvin James knew that the struggle against Bitturumba and his Thunder Lions still had a long way to go. Overhead, in the World Health Organization Huey helicopter, Elee Aslin and Rafael Encizo played the Ethiopian convoy's eyes in the sky. Lieutenant Jolu Okuba grinned as he sat just behind James, ready to jump up to ride the big DShK machine gun mounted on the steel pintle pole.

"Having fun?" James asked.

"All this exercise is good for my tired, achy bones, Cal," Okuba replied. "And we're hot on that big bastard's tail. By midnight, Thor Bitturumba will be dead."

James took a deep breath. "Don't get cocky, Jo. The Thunder Lions are wounded and being chased. Dangerous is just the top of the list of adjectives that I'd apply to them."

Okuba frowned. "We have six mechanized platoons

in motion. Six times the firepower that we had when we shot the hell out of a whole battalion."

"We're also six times more obvious as a target," James responded.

He keyed his radio. "Rafe, what's the word from up on high?"

"The convoy you're pursuing is still a good distance ahead, but they are slowing down as they approach a passage between two plateaus," Encizo said.

"Damn," James snarled. "Jo, give the colonel a quick call. We're heading into a trap."

Okuba looked dubious, but got on the horn to Colonel Asimo Murani. "Sir, Dr. Farrow and Captain Ruiz say we're being baited into an ambush."

Murani's deep voice responded over the radio. "Let me speak to Farrow."

"Colonel, they're leading us right into a narrow canyon up ahead," James said. "It's a highly defensible position. They could hold off a force ten times as large as us easily."

"We get bottlenecked, and we're easy to pick off," Murani agreed. "What's worse is that our armored personnel vehicles won't be able to maneuver in that canyon. We could jam up the whole column with one or two good shots, and then be picked off at leisure."

"But if they keep going, we'll lose them," James grumbled. "I don't want to risk your men, but we could lose Bitturumba's men in the confusion."

"So what's the plan?" Murani asked.

"Rafe can provide air support, and we could send our more maneuverable forces into the fire," James said. "We can avoid enemy fire just by going full speed on the canyon floor, but they could take us out with just small arms. That can work in our favor, though, because when the enemy pops out to shoot us, they'll be exposed to you."

"I know the WHO would throw a fit, but I have a couple good machine gunners who can ride in the doors," Murani mentioned. "Anyone leans out, my boys could take their heads off. If—"

"Screw that 'if,'" Aslin interjected. "Captain Ruiz has used this as a mobile gunnery platform enough times over the past few days to qualify me for the U.S. Air Force. Hell, I'd strap rocket launchers on board if you had any."

Murani chuckled. "The RPG is a rocket launcher, but it'd be tricky to shoot it out of the side of a helicopter."

"Actually, not really," Encizo stated. "For a broadside, we'd risk backwash burns from the RPGs, but if we fired parallel to the cabin, firing toward the nose or the tail, we'd be able to fire at will."

"That could definitely work," Murani said as he thought about it.

The convoy rolled to a halt, and Aslin landed the Huey.

Murani shook hands with James and Encizo. "So how many? Three jeeps?"

James shook his head. "Make it one through the eye of the needle. The rest of the convoy can then set up at standoff distance. The 12.7 mm and 14.5 mm machine guns have a range far beyond what the Janjaweed small arms and RPGs can reach, and provide intensive cover for the closer jeeps and any rocket teams you put in at, say, a 100-meter point. Elee, Rafe and your men in the helicopter will give overwatch, but if the Thunder Lions' column has antiaircraft weapons, we need the BTR-60s' 20 mm cannons to take them down. The big guns you have are our best compromise of long-range punch and firepower. Elee and my jeep will come up hard and fast to flush the enemy positions. The Thunder Lions will see our backup jeeps coming after us and think it's a full-on charge."

"You'll be at risk," Murani warned. "For my men."

James looked at Okuba. He smiled at his Ethiopian friend. "You've done so much good for this region that anything less on my part would be an insult to you."

"Just don't die," Murani admonished. "I don't want the U.S. Army mad at me."

James nodded. "That won't be a problem."

The Phoenix Force commando wished he were as confident as he sounded.

Al Uwaynat, Libya

THE MEETING OF GENERALS seemed like a communion of titans. General Aldreh Ammuz was as tall as Thormun Bitturumba at six feet five inches. With his barrel chest and shaved skull, Ammuz could have been Bitturumba's brother had it not been for his olive-skinned Mediterranean features and the scruff of black foliage lining his lantern-shaped jaw. Bitturumba possessed a softer, rounder face, and his light brown skin betrayed the mix of Spanish into his African blood. Their big hands met in a clamp where the two men tested each other's grasp. Mutually satisfied with their counterpart's prodigious strength, they relaxed and shared a broad grin.

"Welcome to Libya, brother," Ammuz said officially. "I presume your flight was satisfactory."

"It was indeed," Bitturumba replied. "I fear that the

trek of my forces across Shamal Darfur will be a far harsher journey."

Ammuz nodded. "I could arrange for easier transport. A thousand kilometers, six hundred of them through arid desert, would be far too costly for even the most efficient mechanized force."

"It would be most appreciated," Bitturumba responded. "We won't need to bring more than three or four battalions across to Libya."

"And your plan for Chad?" Ammuz asked.

"I have a division in Al Junayah. They have been holding the military of Chad at bay with my fellow Janjaweed leaders. Plus, we will not need a direct application of force with my brother's weaponry," Bitturumba explained. "Neither Libya nor Chad is in the position they need to be to benefit from any cures being funneled through Crusade Pharmaceuticals and the UN WHO."

Ammuz grinned. "And as a good man, you will send your Thunder Lion warriors to assist in disaster relief."

Bitturumba bowed. "My Muslim brothers, stricken by disease, need my help and protection. I weep for the loss of Khadaffi to the plague, but will succor his successor, General Ammuz, in restoring peace and order to our neighbors to the northwest."

Ammuz's smile was broad and appreciative.

"You've been practicing," he noted slyly.

Bitturumba chuckled. "Of course, terrified refugees flooding from the north and the east into Chad will spread contagion throughout their nation. There, terrorism and riotous lawlessness will force the military from their border."

"Whose terrorists, yours or mine?" Ammuz asked ironically.

"Both, but it doesn't matter. We can steer the blame solely on dissatisfaction with the government in N'Djamena," Bitturumba said. "Reeling and unable to control the confusion in the wake of the plague, Libya's new leadership will accede to pressure from the European Union to provide humanitarian aid."

"Pressure built by Alonzo," Ammuz added.

Bitturumba winked, acknowledging his counterpart's perception. "And in my new role as an African peacekeeper, I, too, will embrace Crusade Pharmaceuticals' efforts to help contain a multinational crisis. Lonzo and I will publicly kiss and make up. The Europeans embrace me as a reformed leader, because I then crack down on my fellow Janjaweed, ending the Darfur genocide. The Ethiopians invite me to the peace-talk table. You and I install a puppet government in N'Djamena, and the three of us now control a coalition of four nations. Lonzo will easily win the top seat in Spain, you have Libya, I go to Khartoum as the new African messiah of peace, and our pawn is Chad. Crusade Pharmaceuticals gets billions in UN grants to support their plague abatement efforts."

"You think big," Ammuz replied. "Messiah, eh?"

"An ironic title, my friend," Bitturumba answered.

Ammuz threw back his head and roared in triumphant laughter. "And how do we spread the plague up on the Mediterranean coast?"

"The same way we will spread it in Chad, the Central African Republic, the Congo, Uganda…"

Ammuz raised a thick black caterpillar of an eyebrow. "You *do* think big!"

"You won't get Ebola Thunder. You're getting a new disease that transmits via all new disease vectors," the

Sudanese general explained. "Ebola Thunder really is dead now. But Lonzo didn't load his gun with only one bullet. The CAR through Kenya will catch a two-pronged variant, a version that survives in the water supply and another version that can be carried by humans in their respiratory system. Given the old version's fifty-five-percent lethality rate, we took that trait and built in personal immunity for carriers, coupled with airborne infectious vectors. Libya, then in the future, Egypt, will catch the carriers as well as spores spread by aerosol dissemination. But that is entirely up to you. Frankly, my interests lie more toward the south. You have the whole of the Mediterranean to play with."

"And what if the U.S. or Israel gets suspicious?" Ammuz asked.

"Israel's sojourns into Lebanon of late has defanged the nation of its critical powers. With Iraq, the U.S. is not just spread thinner than their leader's lies, but they have been bathed in the juices of hypocrisy before they can even say shit about us actually going in and performing humanitarian aid," Bitturumba explained. "Their 'rescue efforts' were preceded by missiles and artillery. Our rescue efforts will be honest disaster relief."

Ammuz grinned. "So for now, we play it cool."

"We play it cool forever," Bitturumba said. "This is a house of cards that we are building here. We even sneeze on another African, we'll be found out as war profiteers and plague mongers. A missile loaded with killer bacilli launched at Israel will collapse our entire ruse in the time it takes for international news to pop off its first headline."

Ammuz frowned, disappointment darkening his mood. "So we suffer the Jews and their blasphemy."

"Stealth and treachery will always defeat brute force, my friend," Bitturumba reminded the Libyan. "Libya can become Israel's friend, but that does not mean other enemies need stand idle on the sidelines."

Ammuz's eyes lit up. "How long would all of this take?"

"I see the collapse of Libya taking about a week, but Chad and the other African nations will require more milking," Bitturumba replied. "Your connections will make things much easier, which is why you bought in as an equal partner."

"So when the central African states are thrown into chaos, it will be Libya's technology leading the way, flying in relief on our fleet of Soviet castoff aircraft," Ammuz replied. "And then, in repayment, we receive slices of natural resources."

"Fair payment, not tribute to conquerors, but rewards for heroic rescuers," Bitturumba said. "General or President Ammuz, the heroic face of New Africa, champion and defender. You will be the golden god, the good guy, and not just Africa will love you. You'll be a star across the globe, bringing Libya out of its regime of terrorist sponsorship."

"Why not you?" Ammuz asked.

"I've been too hard for too long. They'll love me in Khartoum, though, and throughout Africa, but I am satisfied to be your sidekick, the one who you redeemed, the madman turned back to a saint," Bitturumba said.

"When shall I start bringing in your people?" Ammuz asked, excited.

The plotters, now brothers in blood, schemed long into the night.

CHAPTER SEVENTEEN

Bonn, Germany

The Executioner had discovered Kharo's backup weapon, a folding stock SIG-SAUER 556 carbine, tucked under the driver's seat. After a quick examination, he pronounced the weapon fit for action. It was a semiautomatic-only weapon, but the punch of a 5.56 mm rifle bullet was still far more effective than three rounds of 9 mm from his Beretta machine pistol. He also found a bullet-resistant attaché case under Marshall's shotgun seat.

"Keep it over your head," Bolan suggested as he loaded the SIG 556 and flicked off the safety.

Marshall nodded. "That looks like them now."

Bolan looked out the windshield, not bothering to inform the WHO doctor that he'd seen them already. The black pickup had four men sitting in the back, but the Executioner knew that the quartet in the bed and the men in the cab were only half of the total ambush force. He hit the brakes the moment he was within two hundred yards of the waiting vehicle. The men were watching the highway from their vantage point behind the small hillock, searching for Kharo's stretch limousine. The truck, behind a small, grassy knoll, was hidden from the main road that would eventually merge with this current paved strip. Bolan had rolled up behind them. He had already studied the terrain. This current stretch of asphalt had been barely used, no cars passing in either direction.

It was perfect, allowing the Executioner to have his combat stretch, a free area where he could bring all of his skill and firepower to bear on an enemy force. Bolan pulled the limo onto the shoulder, then opened the car door. He left the engine running, shouldering the sleek, ultramodern SIG 556 and placing the front sight of the rifle on the head of one of the waiting militiamen two hundred yards away. Somewhere, on an access road across the highway, another squad of assassins waited in another pickup. Bolan knew the kind of ambush planned as it was a standard guerrilla operation utilized by terrorist groups across Europe and Central America. The plan was simple and effective, allowing the ambushers almost unlimited superiority due to speed and violence of action.

Unfortunately for the jihadists in the truck, Bolan had perfected his own finely honed ambush tactics. He just needed one thing to ensure that he wasn't opening fire on a road maintenance work crew sharing some beers on a lunch break. He dropped his aim and pulled the SIG-SAUER's trigger. The carbine's bark was unmistakable, but Bolan's initial round slammed into the tailgate of the pickup where the supersonic bullet destroyed itself on sheet metal. The swarthy men riding in the truck bed removed all doubt of their involvement in Cruz's assassination plot by dragging up Kalashnikov rifles from the floor. As soon as Bolan saw the familiar profiles of the AK-47s wielded by the gunmen, he set to his task of eliminating the would-be murderers.

The Executioner locked on to one gunman and speared two quick 5.56 mm projectiles through the angry face of the extremist, his brains vaporizing into a pink cloud squirted out of a hole shattered through the back of his skull. The AK-wielding corpse vaulted back as a residual chemical charge remaining in his spine triggered a convulsion as he died. The Arab killer's body pinned an ally against the cab of the pickup.

Working the trigger swiftly and smoothly, Bolan targeted a second terrorist, stitching him from sternum to nose with three quickly fired rounds. Heart, larynx and brain each absorbed 65-grains of copper-jacketed hollow-tipped lead moving at just under 1000 meters per second. Against steel, the bullets were relatively ineffective, especially at two hundred yards. However, against meat and skeletal structure, they produced enormous tissue destruction and cavitation. The second gunman toppled sideways, shoved out of the way by an aggressive rifleman who fired his AK one-handed and from the hip.

Bolan sighed as the storm of 7.62 mm slugs chewed into the asphalt almost one hundred yards short and to the right of his position. Not even a ricochet touched the armored limousine door that he used as a combination of bench rest and shield. Bolan fired a few shots at the sloppy rifleman, but they missed him as the pickup suddenly lurched forward into the road. He glanced over to Marshall, the attaché case held behind her head as if to ward off rain. Her green eyes flashed back to the Executioner.

"Get down, trouble's coming," Bolan warned as he slid behind the wheel. He threw the idling limo hard into Reverse as the doctor tucked herself under the dashboard. The pickup whipped around into a U-turn, racing to charge down the limo's grille. Bolan let the enemy gunners close the distance, waiting for their driver to commit himself to the collision course. When the pickup's engine shuddered into higher gear, settling into its charge and accelerating, the Executioner cut loose.

Where the terrorist gunman tried to score one-handed hits with an unslung, unbraced full-auto Kalashnikov, Bolan had his SIG-SAUER 556 braced and indexed on the limousine door, even as he accelerated into Reverse. While it was no match for 800 rounds per minute the full-auto SIG was capable of, the Executioner hammered the pickup with fifteen shots before rounds tore through the windshield and into the driver's chest. The dying man's final reflex wrenched the wheel hard to one side, too fast for the truck's forward momentum.

Marshall glanced above the dashboard in time to see the left front tire snag under the pickup's acceleration force. Momentum, tripped up, needed somewhere to go. Unfortunately for the men in the back of the truck, that meant that the bed turned into a catapult. Bodies, living and dead, launched from the pickup's bed, flying in a high arc that, to her eyes, easily reached fifty feet. The pickup slammed into the asphalt with such force that the cab folded under the chassis. If the gunman riding shotgun was still alive behind the bullet-riddled windshield, Marshall pitied him, because he was crushed violently on impact.

Then the first body that had been launched from the

pickup bed struck the road and burst like a ripe tomato, gushing gore onto the blacktop. Marshall's stomach turned at the sudden explosion of organs ejected through shredding skin. She saw a second body landing in the grass at roadside, but before she could get a better look at that particular impact, Bolan grabbed her by the neck and pushed her down into the seat well.

Safety glass detonated and Marshall's ears ached with the unintelligible howls of the man who had punched through the limousine's windshield. Blood sprayed down the collar of her blouse and Bolan grunted, the limo shaking as if he were punching something. Splatters of shredded skin dribbled over the edges of the attaché case, but finally the ear-piercing wails died out after three seconds. It seemed as if it had lasted an eternity.

"You okay?" Bolan asked, putting on the brakes. He dumped the near-empty mag out of the SIG carbine and reloaded it in one swift motion.

Marshall looked out from under the bulletproof valise. She saw bloody teeth littering the cup holders just behind the emergency brake. The hood and dashboard were smeared with thick, sticky crimson, at least the hood she could see around the fractured glass of the windshield. Luckily, there was a good opening, three feet wide, in the glass. "God have mercy."

"Someone had better," Bolan said. He swung the SIG around and used the folding stock to smash out the shattered remnants of the windshield from its frame. Marshall saw a bloody shambles of a human being struggling to get to its feet in the middle of the road ahead. Bolan slammed the limo into Drive and the front fender smashed the barely alive gunman. "Down, Tanya."

Marshall looked at him in horror, then saw a second pickup tear onto the road four hundred yards downrange.

"Going down," she said with ashen conviction. The roar of the SIG blasting away in semiautomatic thundered on her eardrums, but it didn't hurt or disturb as greatly as the agonized wails of the unfortunate opponent who'd ended up embedded in the windshield.

The limo lurched violently, metal grinding metal, and the horrid thumps of more bodies sounded as they bounced off the roof of their ride. Over the screech of crumpling fenders, the clatter of weapons and the drumbeats of men glancing off the car, she heard the wet sticky crunches of shattering bones and the gurgles of terminating lives. Marshall held herself tightly, eyes clenched shut, forcing herself not to imagine the horrors wrought by the warrior behind the wheel.

"Stay in the car, Tanya," Bolan said softly. She felt the limo lurch as his weight left the vehicle.

Marshall didn't move. She jerked in response to distant mercy shots, and she knew that her companion was emptying rounds into mortally wounded enemies. She stayed put under the dashboard. She didn't realize she was crying until her cuffs grew wet with tears.

Bolan got back behind the wheel, then guided her to sit up, putting an arm around her trembling shoulders.

"I asked for this," Marshall whispered, tightly wound.

Bolan's brotherly hug stilled her tremors. "No. You asked to help save lives. Not to be present at an atrocity."

"Horrible," she muttered.

"I know," Bolan agreed. "Hopefully it's over."

Marshall's emotional armor broke and she buried her face in his chest, sobbing.

Darfur, Sudan

LIEUTENANT OKUBA WAS behind the wheel of the jeep and Calvin James stood, manning the ponderous DShK 12.7 mm machine gun mounted in the bed where the backseat would normally have been. Both men wore helmets and heavy flack jackets, the most resilient body armor available to the Ethiopians. In the African heat, they rarely wore the armor due to the risk of heat prostration and dehydration. The presence of enemy Type 67 and heavier machine guns necessitated the bulky protection for the pair.

Not that the flack jackets would provide much protection from a direct hit by an enemy 12.7 mm bullet. The big fifty that James manned was designed to punch through the thick shells of armored personnel carriers. His and Okuba's steel helmets and body armor were like gossamer in comparison to the rolled, multilayered alloy plate that the DShK and its brethren were designed to defeat.

"Hit it!" James commanded. Okuba hit the gas, the support jeeps lurching into action just behind him. Aslin's Huey took off from its idle, rocketing ahead of the pack easily. The VAZ-46 jeeps couldn't match the sheer acceleration power of the twin turbo shafts of the hulking UH-1 helicopter. Gunners hung on in the sliding side doors of the bird, strapped in and making certain the helicopter was bristling with firepower. Already the PKMs spit out chattering torrents of full-auto fire into the canyon to get the Janjaweed miltiamen's attention.

Fat 100 mm warheads rode on cottony columns of smoke trailing from their launchers, spearing up from the mouth of the gap. Elee Aslin saw the incoming salvo of antiaircraft RPG fire and climbed hard, lifting the Huey up and over the initial round of explosive rockets. James stabbed the spade triggers of his DShK, signaling the start of suppressive fire as he launched a blistering storm of 12.7 mm slugs at the growing cloud that pinpointed the base of three RPG rocket trails. The other jeeps and armored personnel carriers threw in their opinions on the impropriety of the Thunder Lions for shooting at the WHO pilot. James watched as the canyon mouth came alive with roiling blossoms of orange where incendiary 14.5 mm and high-explosive 20 mm cannon shells detonated on the boulders that the Sudanese hard force had taken cover behind. James looked to the helicopter, seeing where smoke contrails lanced down from on high into the canyon. The Huey-mounted RPG crews had opened fire on Janjaweed gunners in the gap.

So far, the initial wave of firepower had rocked the Janjaweed defenders into silence, but James suspected that it was bait for a trap. The plan had to go as was laid out, otherwise it would be more than he and Okuba coming under hostile enemy fire. With more targets barreling across the canyon floor, the potential for more casualties loomed. The agile VAZ would stand a chance with the support fire from the heavy weapons of Murani's mechanized platoon and Aslin's improvised airborne gunnery platform. The mouth of the gap loomed closer and James knew he was at the point of no return.

Behind him, fiery streams of bullets lashed at the canyon ledges, arcs of tracers flowing like horizontal rain to pepper the Thunder Lion sniper positions on the cliff walls. By now, the Thunder Lion garrison was opening up, aiming to crush the column of vehicles that they had hoped would roll into the killing box. Muzzle-flashes blazed in the shadows and James flinched as the steel plates bracketing his 12.7 mm weapon rang under the incoming fire. The Phoenix Force commando opened up, sweeping as many positions as he could, but the air was thick with dust and smoke, the results of all that firepower pulverizing rock and flesh alike. Targeting became more difficult, especially as Okuba swerved wildly and violently, zigzagging the speeding Vaz to make the enemy have to work harder to hit them. Big bullets rocketed from the DShK's muzzle, slamming more into rock walls than enemy bodies, but James's fire, illuminated by tracer rounds, made it easier for the more stable and stationary gunners left behind to rake the enemy nests with ruthless marksmanship.

A 20 mm shell detonated low, hitting just to the right of the speeding VAZ. Okuba yelped in pain and surprise as shrapnel buffeted his side.

"Jo!" James snapped. "You okay?"

"Not bleeding!" Okuba answered, keeping up the breakneck pace through the brutal gauntlet of the Thunder Lions and their fellow Janjaweed militiamen. "Keep shooting!"

James swung the DShK, a ripsaw of death lashing out left and right as fast as he could swivel, keeping the bursts short to make the most of the nine-yard belt feeding from the box hanging on the big gun's side. However, the 12.7 mm whirled faster now, the weight of the disintegrating link disappearing faster and faster now. Bodies rained off the ledges of the canyon like toys tumbling from shelves. The VAZ jolted and bounced as its big knobby wheels struck corpses that landed in its path.

PKM machine guns erupted, raining death from the sides of the WHO Huey, a broom of hot lead knocking ambushers from their emplaced positions on the cliff walls. Meanwhile, Murani's RPG crews spiked 40 mm shrapnel rockets into the canyon. The Janjaweed had been hoping to reenact the Spartan defense at the infamous Hot Gates, drawing an opposing force into close quarters where numbers and firepower were secondary to position and cover. James tore the fangs out of that plan, because even if friendly shrapnel flew in indiscriminate sheets that rattled against their flack jackets, area-effect weapons like explosive cannon rounds and incendiary shells worked to jar the enemy from their positions. By drawing the Thunder Lions into shooting first, the Phoenix Force warrior had taken away their advantage of surprise, and the Ethiopians pumped massive volumes of shrapnel, concussive force and whizzing machine-gun bullets into the canyon.

With the addition of the Huey as an alternate vector of incoming fire, and James's gun as a target marker, he'd lessened the Janjaweed's concealment. Explosive rounds, thrown at what would have been secure positions, detonated above and behind their cover. Fragments rained down even the thickest of boulders, ricocheting off rock walls and down into the backs of gunners. The canyon was quickly becoming drenched in blood and littered with the bodies of the slain. The VAZ was rolling slower now, though, and James's DShK locked empty. As he bent to retrieve the RG-6 grenade launcher from beneath a heavy bomb blanket at his feet, James noticed smoke jetting through bullet holes in the jeep's hood.

The multishot 40 mm grenade launcher burped out white phosphorous rounds into Janjaweed positions on their ledges. The militiamen were now behind the jeep, and James swung the DShK around to continue to utilize the armor plates on the heavy machine gun. Okuba and he had passed through the initial five hundred meters of canyon where the Thunder Lions had set up their killing box. James's RG-6 hammered out its searing 6-round salvo of WP shells. They detonated, creating burning white clouds that flashed in the distance. Flaring, raging spheres of flesh-melting hot metal shrapnel bit into the bodies of machine-gun crews and infantry positions along the gap's cliffs.

A rain of full-auto thunder chopped into the VAZ, but James had leaped behind the body of the jeep, only just barely avoiding being shot to ribbons. The vehicle shook under the onslaught as Okuba lay curled behind the wheel well of their swiss-cheesed ride. James crawled to the Ethiopian lieutenant's side.

"Jo? Jo!" James called. He saw that Okuba's face was bloody, lacerated by shrapnel. A burbling wet gash welled up, thick crimson dripping from under one ear. Immediately, the Phoenix Force medic applied direct pressure to the wound.

"Took a bad hit, I guess," Okuba replied. "You should be shooting back."

"Shut up, Jo," James ordered. "You do *not* have permission to die."

The VAZ vibrated under the Janjaweed hammering. James ignored the fierce onslaught, packing gauze into the vicious cut on Okuba's neck. It was surface damage, thankfully, flesh and skin peeled aside, but the plucky EEF lieutenant's arteries and jugular were unharmed. A gash had been torn along Okuba's temple, just under his helmet, a reason for the Ethiopian's dazedness. Satisfied that his friend wouldn't bleed to death, James unslung his drum-fed VEPR from the back of the jeep.

Encizo and Murani's gunners had seen the VAZ come to a smoky halt, and they threw down a withering storm of firepower, buying James enough cover to retrieve his weapon and spare ammo. The VEPR opened up, its muzzle-flash burning like a miniature sun in the shadows. Now that he was stable, behind stationary cover, James was able to more easily target enemy positions. Unfortunately, the Janjaweed gunners now had James's range and position, and opened fire on him. Dust flew up in choking clouds as hostile bullets peppered the canyon floor and the rattling chassis of the jeep. James felt a round ring violently off his helmet, the impact bouncing his brain around inside his skull. The VEPR slipped out of his stunned fingers, and the Phoenix Force pro was dazed by the sudden hit. Okuba shoved James to the ground and took up the drum-fed rifle, opening fire on the militiamen, continuing to keep their attention divided three ways.

The stunned Phoenix Force fighter struggled to sit up, but Okuba barked at him. "Stay down! You'll get your damn fool head shot off!"

James pulled his Beretta out of its holster and climbed behind the rear fender. He took aim and opened up, adding his puny 9 mm rounds to the rock-and-roll mayhem of the VEPR. The torrent of full-auto fire from Okuba drew the Janjaweed's attention. Explosions engulfed the far mouth of the canyon, flaming fingers of machine-gun fire clawing the cliff walls. A massive bulk of smoke and dust was raised by the concentrated hammering of a dozen 20 mm cannons, a dozen more RPG launchers, and scores of rifles and machine guns. Lead and death poured into the gap in a molten flood of devastation that flowed toward James and Okuba. Explosions, autofire and death screams had turned the canyon into a shuddering hell zone as the Ethiopian mechanized force scoured the Sudanese militiamen from their positions, inch by painstaking inch. It was a sign of the intensity of Murani's advance that the Thunder Lions ignored James and Okuba to fire at the Ethiopian column as it tightened its deadly grip slowly on them.

Death was inexorably wrapping around the throat of the Janjaweed defenders.

James stuffed his sixth and final 15-round magazine into the butt of his Beretta and looked back at Okuba. Dread filled him as he saw the Ethiopian slumped on the ground, the full-auto rifle gone silent. He crossed to Okuba and saw where an enemy bullet had crushed a hole between his eyes.

"Goddamn it, not again," James cursed, his voice cracking with sadness.

On unsteady legs, he grabbed up the VEPR and slammed home a new drum. He swung the chatterbox toward the militiamen and opened fire. His shoulder ached from the vicious recoil, but the Phoenix Force warrior didn't let pain hold back his avenging fury. James fanned the rear flanks of the enemy gauntlet, stitching lines of bullets into spines and heads.

It was a cold-blooded tactic, but the Janjaweed had

earned far worse deaths by their uncountable acts of cruelty and brutality against unarmed Sudanese. James also was honest enough with himself to admit that he was caught up in the grips of a blood rage over the loss of a friend.

The VEPR ran dry and James dropped it, continuing on with his Beretta.

"Calvin!" Encizo's voice broke over the radio, cutting through his haze of fury. "Calvin! It's over! We've cleared the canyon!"

James lowered the empty Beretta in his trembling hands. "They killed Jolu."

"Sit tight, man," Encizo ordered. "Keep it together."

The empty pistol dropped into the dirt, clattering on the floor of the canyon. Only distantly did he realize that he'd taken a bullet through his right shoulder, and that his arms and legs had been slashed bloody by shrapnel. As the adrenaline would fade from his bloodstream, he'd feel the full extent of his injuries, but the rush of combat, fear and anger had numbed him to everything on the physical level.

That didn't keep the death of Okuba from feeling like a bullet through the heart, however.

CHAPTER EIGHTEEN

Bonn, Germany

"Are you feeling any better?" Bolan asked Tanya Marshall.

She was still shaken, trembling almost as if she were suffering from hypothermia, but she managed a terse nod. "That was just a little intense."

Bolan rested a comforting hand on her shoulder. "No. That wasn't a little intense. I usually don't end up driving around with a human being jammed into my windshield."

Marshall looked at him, still holding herself against an out-of-place chill. "Well, it would get you pulled over by the cops more often. And you are supposed to be low profile."

"Especially if I just lean out and ask, 'Something wrong, Officer?'"

She made a disgusted face. "Normally, I hate all that gallows humor shit. How can you joke about mutilation and death?"

"I don't, but I'm used to it," Bolan said. "But even my coworkers have to vent."

"I never thought I'd ever trivialize death," Marshall replied.

"You're not. You're lessening the stress of the situation with humor," Bolan noted.

Marshall shuddered, but this time as she kept her laughter from sounding off loudly.

"There. Now you've got a psychic defense mechanism in place to forget whatever you did manage to see around me," Bolan said.

Marshall nodded. "That does work. It's sick, and twisted, but it works."

"Good," Bolan said. "Now, I don't want you to take this the wrong way."

"You want me to stay behind in the car when you go after Cruz, right?" Marshall asked.

Bolan smiled. "No problems?"

"None at all. This isn't over by a long shot, is it?" Marshall asked.

"Kharo had the full trip plotted into his GPS," Bolan said, tapping the blood-spattered device's screen. "Plus, while you were resting, I asked him a few questions."

"Torture?" Marshall asked, tense.

"That's not my style, but he got a good, long look at some of my recent handiwork," Bolan replied. "When he saw the one who made that dent, started singing."

"So Cruz and Bitturumba have a backup plan?"

"More trouble up ahead, but this time, I'll keep you out of harm's way. Did Elee teach you anything about rifles?" Bolan inquired.

Marshall nodded. "She taught me on an AK-47. They are a hell of a lot easier to hit things with than a pistol."

Bolan started the car. Now that Marshall's emotional turmoil had died down, Bolan could continue driving to

Crusade Pharmaceuticals' Mobile Laboratory Research Center. Despite the wrecked windshield and the drying blood puddled on the dented hood of the limousine, the vehicle was still in fine running condition. An armor plate had been situated behind the limo's grille, providing shielding for the engine and battery. Bolan kept a pair of folded rifles—Kharo's SIG 556 and a borrowed, collapsing stock AK-47—handy near his leg under the steering wheel. He had also retrieved the Desert Eagle from its spot in his luggage.

He pulled the limo onto a small dirt road and parked it. He showed the SIG 556 to Marshall, demonstrating the safety mechanism, bolt charge knob and reload function, which were highly similar to the AK-47, from which the SIG was derived. "It should be easy for you to reload the rifle, but if you need more than thirty shots, back out and drive back to the airport and to Jack."

"What about you?" Marshall asked.

Bolan patted his war harness, pockets stuffed with spare magazines for his arsenal. "I intend to return all of this borrowed ammunition to Cruz."

Marshall shuddered as the Executioner left her in the limo.

Al Uwaynat, Libya

GENERAL ALDREH AMMUZ could scarcely contain his excitement as the ventilated container that Thor Bitturumba had brought with him was unveiled. The container had air filtration systems, pumping in atmosphere while being kept under negative air pressure to prevent the spread of infectious microbes. There were four men inside, visible through a hermetically sealed window, with an electronic speaker set up next to the frame. All of them looked like hale and healthy Mediterranean men who would fit in on the streets of Tripoli without undue scrutiny.

"Meet your four horsemen of the apocalypse," Bitturumba introduced.

"Actually, we're more pedestrians and commuters," one of the men joked. "But we'll bring all the fun that a horseman can bring, just for less cab fare."

"Four doses of pestilence," Ammuz noted. "I assume that they are fine for physical contact."

Bitturumba grinned. "They are small men for a reason. What better way to disguise respiratory and bodily fluid isolation precautions than behind a burka and veil?"

Ammuz's eyes narrowed, the corners of his mouth turning up in a wild smile. "Using the Muslim culture's misogynist flaws against the narrow-minded."

Bitturumba raised an eyebrow. "Oh?"

"Please. Don't pretend to buy into the superstition mongering concocted by Saudi Arabia and Iran to make use of overzealous 'true believers,'" Ammuz said. "I'll have you executed if you say it outside this room, but I have no more interest in some baby rapist's prattlings about the moon god than you do."

"I knew there was a reason we got on so well," Bitturumba noted. "Moon god?"

"Ah, you don't have the historical context from which the fanatics have spawned their lies," Ammuz said. "Mohammed was looking to found his own cult of personality, but he needed the backing of a powerful tribe. The Sabeans were those power brokers, but they didn't want to have to redo all their decorations. They followed a pre-Islamic pagan moon god called Allah.

Mohammed wound a string of contradictory lies to keep the peons befuddled. My uncle was at the 1950s dig in Hazor, back when it was still Palestine, where they discovered the pagan temple of the little moon god that would blind a billion sheep."

Ammuz noticed that even the four men in the container truck were grinning. "I take it they're not Muslims?"

"How else could I find four men who would dress as women?" Bitturumba said. "The fanatics make excellent pawns, but these men are intelligent, capable operatives. They're immunized against the plague and totally anonymous. They can spread contagion all along the coast to cripple entire cities, not just Tripoli."

"Once we're done, we return to a neutral zone, take the treatments necessary to eliminate our contagious conditions, and disappear into Egypt," one of the plague hosts explained.

"Self-administered treatments," another plague host added. "We won't endanger your forces, General."

Ammuz smiled. "Good. In that case, we'll arrange for your transport to Tripoli in a few days." He paused, then addressed Bitturumba. "This will put both Cruz and you back in your corresponding homelands before the new plague crisis breaks out, ensuring that you maintain plausible deniability."

"Good," Bitturumba said. "The boys won't be uncomfortable in there. The container is designed to comfortably house them. The quarantine setup is airtight, so to speak, and they have plenty of distractions to make use of their downtime. Just remember to use the food port there."

"That will be my responsibility," a familiar voice said. Ammuz grinned as Heinz Baldr joined the two generals.

Bitturumba shook Baldr's hand. "We were just talking. You haven't gone to oversee the situation in Bonn?"

"Lonzo felt I'd be more effective here," Baldr stated. "Besides, there's not one but two ambushes set up for Colonel Stone in Germany, and even if he does somehow manage to evade all that, what's he going to do to explain to the Federal Police the pile of corpses left in his wake? Fighting off one war without incurring the attention of the BND or GSG-9 would be something, but the forces I have on hand back at the Mobile Laboratory Research Center can throw up a fight that would be heard for miles."

"Colonel Stone?" Ammuz asked.

"The man we believe might be the American soldier," Bitturumba replied.

Ammuz nodded. "I lost several good friends in Alexandria to him. And I am familiar with the rumors spread about him by my government."

"I'll make certain this little package is safe and secure," Baldr said. "And add my own men to your defenses."

"You think there might be more trouble?" Ammuz asked.

Bitturumba nodded. "Historically, the American soldier is allied with a team of commandos."

Ammuz nodded. "Libyan special operations units have encountered opponents of a similar description. At least before they disappeared forever."

"Covering all the bases," Baldr said.

"Just secure my presents," Ammuz said, patting the container of contagion. "I doubt I'd need bolstering that much."

Baldr and Bitturumba shared a glance. Bitturumba addressed the issue. "This Stone is one nasty fucker. He's trumped everything we've thrown at him so far.

Our only saving grace has been that we're mobile. Stone might be up in Europe now, chasing down leads, so we've got a good cushion against his finding out about the Tripoli operation."

"You're still concerned," Ammuz pointed out.

Bitturumba nodded. "He's tough and smart."

"We'll just have to be lucky," Ammuz said.

Bitturumba smiled. "Fortunately, gods make their own luck, Aldreh."

Mobile Laboratory Research Center, Germany

THE EXECUTIONER RETURNED to his natural environment as hunter, not bait. He melted into the trees that surrounded the isolated scientific facility situated about five miles southwest of Bonn, Germany. In his skintight blacksuit, he moved with catlike stealth. From his position, he saw an airstrip capable of handling military transport planes the size of a C-130 Hercules with ease. Dotting the compound, laid out in neat, orderly grids, were duplicate transport containers, similar to the laboratory that he had obliterated just the night before. They were inactive, their vents silent, and air-lock umbilical corridors were retracted against the sides of the individual units.

They were unmistakable, nonetheless. Bolan's brow furrowed at the sight. How Alonzo Cruz would have tried to deny that his transportable lab designs were identical to the one that Bolan had destroyed was something the soldier didn't even begin to fathom. All Bolan knew was that he saw dozens of minilabs, each capable of breeding contagion on a wholesale basis. If Cruz wanted, he had enough mobile labs to sell to the far corners of the Earth, perfect for every high-bidding terrorist organization or unscrupulous government that had enough money to afford it.

If Bolan had doubts that the containers weren't meant for creating cures, but producing catastrophe, the proof came in the form of a patrol of hard-eyed, head-shaved and tattooed toughs armed with machine pistols. The young men were almost as heavily armed as the Executioner himself, but their rough, undisciplined look and patrol parameters were evidence that they didn't belong to any official part of Crusade Pharmaceuticals' security operation. He closed with the patrol, shadowing them easily.

All doubts faded when one lifted his radio to his lips. "Where the fuck is the limo? I'm getting bored waiting for Stone and the bitch."

"You'll get your shot at Stone and Marshall soon enough," came the reply. "Be patient."

"Fuck." The leader of the four-man patrol snarled, stuffing his radio roughly back into its belt pouch.

Bolan pulled his fighting knife silently from its sheath, sizing up the quartet of skinheads. Already his mind was calculating angles on how to take down these amateur-hour mercenaries swiftly and quietly. He decided to hit the thug with his finger resting on the trigger of his weapon first. Bolan was on them in seconds, the nine-inch Bowie blade carving down through the young gunman's forearm. The neo-Nazi's disembodied hand and the machine pistol dropped into the grass. The lost limb's former owner gawked at the fallen body part, the sudden slice so quick that he didn't even register a flicker of pain.

The Executioner left the stunned skinhead to contemplate his severed hand, looping his other arm into a noose that wound around a second gunman's throat. Utilizing the momentum generated by his two hundred pounds lashing forward at literally breakneck speed, he twisted the hapless sentry's head sharply. Bolan's steel-toed boot swung in a vicious arc that connected under the jaw of a third man. Bone shattered under the impact, driving splinters to stab through the windpipe of the armed street tough. The skinhead grabbed his crushed throat and broken jaw, blood pouring into his lungs as well as cascading over his lower lip as he was dead on his feet. The guard's machine pistol lay in the grass, forgotten.

The fourth and last armed sentry heard the rustle and crackle of multiple breaking bones behind him and whirled in reaction. He struggled to bring up his assault weapon to shoot the big black shape that had whipped through his partners. Bolan had his Bowie reversed in his fist even as he closed in on the last neo-Nazi. He speared the razor-sharp blade right through the center of his face. The thick, powerful knife crushed through the thin maxilofacial bones around the nose as if they were crackers, carving deep into his central nervous system. Dead on his feet, the final armed thug dropped his gun. Bolan twisted the Bowie out of the center of the corpse's face, and the body slumped into a useless mass of dead meat on the trail.

Bolan wiped the knife on the body's clothing, then turned back to the first man he'd dismembered. The wounded sentry stood looking at his exterminated brothers, his jaw slack at the idea that they had been so swiftly taken out.

"Don't kill me," the young man whimpered. Bolan snapped a cable tie from his harness around the stump of the youth's forearm. He pulled it tight enough to tourniquet the wound, but the neo-Nazi was already in shock. Still, stanching off the flow of blood would prevent a needless death. Bolan was ruthless, but he would never consider murdering an unarmed enemy.

"Go home," Bolan warned. "You lucked out."

The skinhead nodded, listening to the embodiment of death address him in German. He stopped and picked up the grisly union of his dismembered hand and the machine pistol. He held the gun up to Bolan. "I just want my hand back."

Bolan pried the lifeless fingers from their death grip.

"Keep the gun," the young German whispered. He turned, clutching his lost hand, and ran for his life, racing back toward Bonn.

The Executioner headed into the woods to look for more of the street thugs.

ALONZO CRUZ PACED, waiting for the arrival of Colonel Stone and Dr. Marshall, going through cigarettes as if they were jelly beans. He paused from smoking like a chimney only long enough to pull out his cell phone to check for new text messages, not trusting Heinz Baldr's lieutenant, François Carmacy, to give him a straight answer. Baldr was with Bitturumba and General Ammuz in Libya, personally taking responsibility for the manufactured biological wave of death intended for Tripoli.

"I should have never come up with this stupid plan," Cruz grumbled.

"Just relax," Carmacy said, trying to soothe Cruz's nerves. The Spaniard glared at Carmacy, and the mercenary was glad that looks couldn't kill. He turned away from the angry Cruz and looked over Kaffriz warily. The Libyan's bodyguard contingent was milling around outside the main office. Ten men with concealed pistols and small submachine guns were a slight increase in the force around the Mobile Laboratory Research Center, but Carmacy didn't know about their military training. He wasn't certain if he could trust their professionalism, but that only inspired a nagging thought about the street toughs that Baldr instructed him to bring in. The neo-Nazi street-gang members knew how to brawl, batter and even murder, but they were not disciplined line troops. Carmacy's security contingent, however, was discharged cream of the crop of military and police organizations across Europe.

"Pardon me, sir," Carmacy said. He stepped to the doorway and brought his radio to his lips. "Report in."

"This is patrol four. We haven't seen fuck all," a young German voice replied.

Carmacy waited for a moment, anticipating more replies. Instead, he received only silence. "Where are the rest of you?"

Quiet.

"Report, damn it!"

Finally, the coldest voice that the lean French mercenary had ever heard broke the silence on the radio. "We're sorry. The punks you have been trying to reach are no longer operational."

Terror wrapped its long, chilling, crushing tentacles around Carmacy's heart and his eyes widened with alarm. He whirled to warn Cruz and Kaffriz when a distant rifle crack sounded. Something smashed into his shoulder blade, throwing him to the floor of the mobile office container. The merc's mind raced frantically. He'd lost the use of his right arm instantly, and apparently his warning was no longer necessary as the businessman and the Libyan officer dived for cover behind office furniture. Kaffriz's fist was stuffed with a Heckler & Koch USP pistol. Carmacy tried to work his lips, to push the words out to ask for help to be pulled to cover.

That's when the boots stomped down on his legs and back.

Kaffriz's bodyguards, Carmacy realized just as a heel crushed his neck bones, plunging the hired gun into oblivion.

BOLAN'S FIRST SHOT WAS LOW and a little to the left. He'd intended to catch the mercenary at the office in the back of the head. Normally, the Executioner avoided cruel tactics like shooting to wound, but the range was so great for the AK-47, and the sights had been cranked out of alignment with the old barrel that he wasn't capable of getting a confirmed kill with a single shot. Still, the panic sown among Alonzo Cruz's security men reared like a wild horse. A squad of Arabs trampled the man he'd hit, so Bolan was aware that the trap was nothing less than a means of eliminating his interference so a greater conspiracy could rise. Bolan's borrowed AK barked four more times, cutting down two more heavily armed mercenaries who had been confused by the initial sniper round. Two other men had been saved by their body armor.

The Executioner didn't have time to lament the inadequacy of his chosen sniper weapon. He rose and took off down the hillside as the security force homed in on the sound of his rifle. Bullets stabbed up at the now-empty sharpshooter roost, gunmen spraying wildly as Bolan's black-clad form knifed through the dark green foliage. Leaves and branches rustled under the leaden wind whipping up from the research center. The

Executioner flicked the selector on the AK to full-auto and cut loose from the waist. It was a sweep of suppressive fire, not directly intended for taking down enemy targets, but Bolan's initial rounds drilled into the face of an armored sentry who had rushed to intercept him at the section of fence at the base of the hill. Other gunmen saw their ally's head detonate, helmet gushing off on a spout of hot gore.

With an underhanded toss, Bolan dropped off a SLAM charge at the base of the electrified security fence. Fifty thousand volts was sufficient to detonate the high-tech bomb, electric current sparking off a kilogram of RDX explosives. The bomb went off with earth-shaking force. Links of the wired fence rocketed along at bulletlike speeds, cutting arms and legs on three mercenaries who were otherwise protected by their body armor. The trio collapsed from their crippling injuries. Bolan swung through the hole he'd created in the electrified perimeter. He'd taken the moment that the SLAM went off to reload the Kalashnikov, giving him more than enough firepower on hand to rake the downed gunmen at close range. Their cries of pain terminated, steel-cored bullets through their Kevlar ending all worries about shredded, useless limbs.

"What the fuck are we paying you for?" Alonzo Cruz bellowed. He fired a handgun from an office window before hands reached up and seized him back behind cover.

CHAPTER NINETEEN

From the heart of Africa to the heart of Europe, the Executioner had followed a trail of conspiracy, deadly microorganisms and mercenaries. Now, here at Crusade Pharmaceuticals' German branch, the Mobile Laboratory Research Center, Bolan had discovered a further branching of the intercontinental plot with the sighting of armed Mediterranean men rushing into the office. The warrior had carved through several of Cruz's high-tech mercenaries and had devastated a platoon of brutal skinheads surrounding the facility. But now, Bolan was in the lion's den. The electrified security fence was breached, torn wide open by high explosives, and he was inside the perimeter with dozens of paid, professional gunmen.

While Bolan was distracted by Alonzo Cruz's angered challenge, an armored gunman burst from cover. The warrior's reflexes were in prime condition, and even though the mercenary was on top of the Executioner, Bolan turned the AK around and smashed the steel stock hard under the helmeted gunman's chin. The metal butt plate crushed windpipe and splintered mandibular bone in one killing stroke. Bolan grabbed the dying man and hauled him up as a shield. Enemy shooters cut loose on Bolan's position. Their fire wasn't sufficient to cut through a Kevlar-clad corpse. Still holding the dead man as a shield, he grabbed his rifle. A pull of the trigger unleashed a full-auto salvo that hosed Cruz's gunners, driving them behind cover.

The Executioner plucked grenades off his shield's vest, and let the carcass fold into the dirt. A guard took a shot at Bolan with his MP-5, but the soldier was already slipping behind protective cover. The aggressive mercenary charged toward Bolan's last-known location, and ran straight into a double-tap from the Executioner's .44 Magnum Desert Eagle. Body armor stopped one 240-grain mangler, but the second shot struck the mercenary's right cheek. Like a steam shovel, the wide-mouthed hollowpoint excavated a canyon through the sentry's head.

Heavy machine guns bellowed as their operators finally got the ponderous, tripod-mounted weapons turned around. The big blasters had been focused on the gates at the facility entrance, a part of a plan to turn his and Marshall's limousine into a collander with streams of heavy-caliber, full-auto belts of armor-piercing ammunition. Bolan raced toward new cover as the container he'd taken shelter behind absorbed hundreds of metal-shredding rounds.

The Executioner had gotten out of the arcs of fire of the big guns and he paused for a moment. He set another of his SLAMs to "antipersonnel mine" mode and lodged it under a container, its infrared motion detector beam facing out into a corridor between the portable labs.

The inert status of the laboratories' vents and lack of active infection precautions gave Bolan a free rein to raise as much hell as he pleased without fear of releasing contaminants. He then baited his trap, targeting a single mercenary downrange and hosing off half a magazine's worth of ammo toward him. The steel-cored 7.62 mm AK rounds made quick work of the guard, even through his body armor, thanks to sheer volume and the superior penetration power of the cartridge. It drew the attention of a half-dozen guards who cut loose with their weapons. Bolan retreated under their advancing fire, drawing the mercenaries right into his killing box.

The six guards moved in unison, finally reaching the waiting SLAM. Their bodies broke its infrared trip-wire beam. A belch of searing flame vomited out of the antipersonnel munition, lifting two of the armored men as if they were rag dolls. The concussive jet of deadly force hammered them into the container across from the high-tech mine hard enough to leave deep dents in the shape of their bodies in the heavy rolled steel of its casing. The two men were instantly dead. A third wailed as his left arm had been shorn off at the shoulder by the guillotine blade of energy hurled out by the SLAM. The others were staggered, spared instant death by their body armor, their stance and their positions. They were still blinded and deafened by the thunderclap ripped off with the power of 2.2 pounds of compressed and shaped RDX.

The Executioner charged the stunned mercenaries, having reloaded his Kalashnikov once more, and he hammered out a death song. Caught flat-footed in the haze from the mine detonation, the trio of surviving, uninjured hardmen and their one-armed partner shook under the ferocious onslaught of Bolan's salvo of steel-cored retribution. The AK ran dry and Bolan let it drop on its sling, pulling a pair of confiscated MP-5s from their low-slung spots at the small of his back. The twin German machine pistols had been taken off the neo-Nazis from the perimeter patrols. They had been stuffed with armor-piercing BAT ammunition, and the Executioner used them on a backup quartet of Baldr's mercs who had been rushing to support the explosion-rocked first squad.

Nine millimeter bullets knifed through Kevlar and into vulnerable organs that their bullet-resistant armor had been meant to protect. Firing an automatic weapon in each hand wasn't a valid tactic for most men, but Mack Bolan had enormous physical strength to control the 9 mm weapons in full-auto recoil. The distance to the mercenaries was measured in a handful of steps, and they were all clumped up in a narrow space. All of those factors combined to allow the Executioner to burn down his opposition by four more corpses, left lying in twisted sprawls at his feet.

A machine gun swung around and its operator unleashed a firestorm of hell while his support crew cut and ran, fleeing the wraith in black who'd viciously gutted their coworkers. The gunner held down the trigger, swiveling the muzzle to try to dislodge Bolan with a hose of 7.62 mm NATO slugs. While Bolan admired the man's courage, his situational awareness left much to be desired because Bolan had just evacuated the position that was the focus of streams of firepower. The Executioner primed a grenade and fired it like a fastball down the blind spot formed by the mounted gun's armor plating. The end of the valiant mercenary's defense was punctuated by the bellow of six-and-a-half ounces of explosive turning into energy, twin shells of fragmentation being released by the fuse's burn-down.

Bolan reloaded the HKs and looked to the office that Cruz had last been seen in. Libyan bodyguards burst from the door, their guns blazing, but they ran right into the Executioner's braced machine pistol. Bolan emptied one of the 9 mm subguns, then let it drop on its strap, lifting the second and draining it into the pouring procession of Libyans that appeared in the doorway, slaughtered by short, quick bursts. The Mediterranean gunmen were sitting ducks, making a foolish final charge to try to overwhelm the man in black. Their corpses struck the ground only slightly slower than the brass raining from the breech of Bolan's autoweapons.

The soldier cast aside the empty HKs and pulled his Desert Eagle, advancing on Cruz and Kaffriz.

"Listen, Stone! I know this looks bad, but we have a lot of money!" Cruz shouted. It was typical. Cruz wasn't a man who had an actual political ax to grind. His motivation was quick and easy cash filling his wallet, so any semblance of dedication flew out the window when it came time to negotiate for his life.

The Executioner drew closer to the office. He triggered the big .44 Magnum pistol twice, knocking holes in the side of Cruz and Kaffriz's shelter.

"Stone! Damn it! Let's do business!" Cruz yelled.

"Fine. You want a deal? Bring the two thousand or so victims of your disease back from the dead," Bolan called. "Once they're walking around and healthy, taking care of their families again, then we'll talk business."

Bolan kicked a body off the steps leading up into the office. He looked at Carmacy, the man he'd shot. The frightened Libyan bodyguards had crushed him to death in the wake of the initial sniper attack on the compound. Lifeless gray eyes stared accusingly into the office. In their reflection, Bolan saw the Spaniard and the Libyan cowering out of sight. Both were unarmed, but there was a handgun lying on the floor, just in range for Kaffriz to reach for it.

"No deal?" Bolan asked.

"Then what do you want?" Cruz pleaded.

"Surrender or death. No bribes. And no fighting your way past me," Bolan announced.

"And what after surrender?" Cruz asked.

Kaffriz reached out for his USP on the floor. Bolan fired the Desert Eagle through the filing cabinet, having gauged the Libyan's position by his reflection in the dead man's eyes. Kaffriz jerked, his shoulder mangled by a big fat .44 Magnum messenger.

"After you surrender, then you make your deal," Bolan said. "Tell me what I want to know, and your judgment comes to you painlessly. Keep quiet, and I don't allow you to die for a long time."

Sobbing in terror, Cruz came out with raised hands.

Darfur, Sudan

JAMES'S SATELLITE PHONE warbled, and Encizo plucked it from his friend's pocket.

"Calvin?" It was Bolan.

"No, Rafe. Calvin suffered a major concussion, and he's got a machine-gun bullet in his shoulder," Encizo answered. "I'm here with him while he's getting patched up. What's new, Striker?"

"Trouble with a capital T up in Libya," Bolan explained. "I've taken prisoners, and have some new intel."

"Libya," Encizo replied. He consulted his mental maps. "The Shamal Darfur has a broad border with Libya. Chad, too. That's where the Janjaweed has been engaging forces on the border, as well as along the Gharb Darfur border."

"There are plans for Chad, as well," Bolan confirmed. "But Bitturumba and Cruz first have a plot to hand Libya over to the highest bidder. Calvin isn't in any condition to help."

Encizo looked at the man who had become more of a brother to him than even his own sibling. "No. It took a while to figure out the extent of his head trauma, but he's suffered memory loss and hallucinations. He also fought under blackout conditions. I'm making certain that he gets medical assistance. I'm still healthy."

Bolan was silent for a few moments. "Right now, I'm on my way back to the plane. We're going to go full-speed back to Nyala to pick you up. We can't let Bitturumba leave Al Uwaynat. We can't let anyone leave that base."

"It's that bad?" Encizo asked.

"There are four carriers for a variant of Ebola Thunder that makes the Darfur outbreak seem like a head cold," Bolan replied. "That's just the first step in a plot to spread catastrophe all across Africa."

Encizo heard the alarm in the Executioner's voice and regretted having lost James for the final, desperate run into Libya. With him gone, they'd just lost a third of their fighting force.

From the concern that Bolan demonstrated, they'd need every advantage that they could get.

CHAPTER TWENTY

30,000 feet over southern Europe

The Executioner was a terrifying image as he stood in the passenger cabin of the high-speed aircraft that rocketed through the skies at 642 miles per hour. Below, the European landscape rolled past in a blur. Alonzo Cruz and Colonel Mhousid Kaffriz were hunched in their seats, wrists and ankles bound by plastic cable ties. The two men were as cowed and restrained by terror as much as polymer restraints. Their eyes were locked in fear on the big, six-foot-three-inch killing machine who had torn through the Mobile Laboratory Research Center. He'd promised them death if they dared speak without being addressed. The two men knew that they were facing execution, but Bolan's words held the menace that their demise would not be swift, and it would be as painful as the tall wraith could summon.

Cruz finally spoke up. "You have no legal right to do this."

"As if you have the blessing of law to murder thousands of people and plan the deaths of millions more?" Bolan asked. "If not, then we're on the same moral ground."

"This is inhuman," Cruz pressed. "I'm important!"

"Sit back and relax," Bolan ordered. "Important? You're just another common murderer. You confessed to your part in the slaughter of thousands."

"I confessed to save my life," Cruz answered. He managed a laugh. "It'll never hold up in a court of law. Never."

Bolan allowed a chuckle to escape his lips. "Do you honestly think I'm worried about making a court case against you? Did you notice if I offered your mercenaries and all of his bodyguards a chance to surrender? Did you, in your delusions of self-importance, somehow hallucinate that I had a badge or some form of legal authority?"

Cruz's face paled.

"You are at my mercy." The Executioner picked up Cruz's satellite phone. "What's your brother's number?"

Cruz told him. "Why?"

Bolan dialed the portable phone. "I need a ticket to Libya, under his sponsorship."

"He won't give it to you. We've based our public-speaking careers on being vocal opponents," Cruz said.

"You're brothers. You're his money source, the one who gave him all the weapons and funding he needed to take over the top of the food chain among the Janja-weed militias. Without you, the Thunder Lions would still be using rusted-out, battered AK-47s that haven't been serviced since 1948," Bolan countered. "You've given him the means to be the top dog in a dog-eat-dog continent like Africa. He needs you, and so, you're my passport to Libya."

"Thor will chew you up and spit you out," Cruz warned.

He ignored Cruz and listened to the connection settle in on the phone. Bitturumba's familiar voice answered on the other end.

"Lonzo? Did you get him? Is that fucker Stone dead?" Bitturumba asked.

"That's funny. I'm here talking to your brother," Bolan replied.

There was a long silence on the other end. Finally, Bitturumba recovered his ability to speak. "What do you want? Is this Colonel Stone?"

"If that's what you want to call me," Bolan replied. "What I want is a face-to-face meeting. You and me. Together in Libya."

"What makes you think I will give you the time of day?" Bitturumba asked.

Bolan held the phone to Cruz.

"Thor. Thor, he wants to execute me. He's going to kill me without a fair trial. He's just going to do it in cold blood!"

Bolan brought the phone back to his ear. "You seem to care a little about Lonzo. You don't want me to kill him, and I'll have him with me when we have our meeting. Who knows, you might even have the chance to save him from me."

"And you're supposed to come to me? What makes you think that I can make this kind of a deal?" Bitturumba asked. "My land is the Sudan."

"You're there with General Ammuz. He should have enough pull in Al Uwaynat to allow me to land there. After all, he's got enough brass to arrange for the takeover of the whole country," Bolan informed the Janjaweed general. "Let Ammuz know that his lackey, Kaffriz, is here with me, too. I'm pretty certain his son-in-law has some worth to the general."

"Kaffriz is a soldier. He is expected to risk his life," Bitturumba responded. "He's not a soft-bellied spoiled brat like my brother."

"I'd like to hear that from Ammuz," Bolan said.

Moments later, Ammuz was on the phone. Bolan had it on speaker mode, so the prisoners could listen to both sides of the Executioner's conversation with the conspirators. "Colonel Stone, I presume. But I doubt that rank is real."

Bolan knew that the Libyan general was trying to prod his ego. Unfortunately for Ammuz, such tactics were wasted on the Executioner. Colonel Stone was a false shell, a hollow nonentity. The rank was just a means to bring him to positions where he could act.

"You're right, Aldreh. The rank is fake. The name is fake. But what *is* real is that I have your son-in-law in my custody. Well, custody is a bad term. It implies that I intend to put him in some form of jail."

"You're violating the Geneva conventions," Ammuz countered. "I know despite your false rank, you're still a soldier. And the rules of war apply to you."

"I used to be a soldier," Bolan admitted. "But real soldiers don't unleash plagues in their own cities, killing the citizens of the nations that they are sworn to defend. You and Kaffriz are just parasites. Cowards who would rather stand back and let something else fight for you. I have no compunctions about slicing Kaffriz's head off and mailing it to you."

Ammuz sputtered inarticulately. "Coward?"

"I'll be coming to Libya," Bolan said. "Save us a spot on an airfield for me."

"You'll be walking into a death trap, Stone," Ammuz growled. "I'll have every gun in my command aimed at you."

"Which is exactly what I want," Bolan answered. "That means I don't have to waste my time chasing down stragglers."

Ammuz choked on his rage. "You're insane."

"I'm familiar with the whole litany. I'm insane. I'll be killed. I'll never be able to stop you. I could map out the next ten things you'll say. You know why? Because I've taken down dozens of tin-pot, would-be conquerors like you. I know your thoughts down to the second," Bolan said. "You and Bitturumba are just two more notches on my gun belt. Two more losers who don't know that they're dead yet."

Bitturumba bellowed into the phone. "You son of a bitch! I'll cut out your liver and eat it!"

Bolan paused for a moment, letting the Sudanese warlord's words fade. "Usually it's the heart that they want to eat. You've got bonus points for originality."

Bitturumba let out a frustrated breath. "Well played, Stone. Well played. I want my brother. You want your shot at me. You want to see me at Al Uwaynat? Then come on down. I'll be expecting you."

"I'll call you when I'm on my way," Bolan promised. "This way you can bring up all the men you think you can use to bring me down. The more, the merrier."

"What trick do you have in mind, Stone?" Bitturumba asked. "What makes you think you'll stand a chance in hell against two armies who know that you're coming?"

"Wouldn't you like to know?" Bolan asked.

He hung up. The Executioner could almost hear the snarls of frustration.

Cruz shook his head in disbelief. "What are you going to do?"

"Stop off at Nyala and send Dr. Marshall back to her

duties of healing the sick and comforting the suffering. I'll pick up my partner, and all the guns we can carry. Then, I'll drag the two of you to Libya with us. Once I get there, I'll kill your brother, I'll kill General Ammuz, and cripple the Libyan coup and exterminate every single Thunder Lion I find."

"Two men, against thousands?" Cruz asked.

"You'll be chewed to pieces." Kaffriz spoke up for the first time in hours. He was pale, and in pain. His throat cracked with each word. The damage to his arm was wearing on him. "It's not like…"

"Like what?" Bolan asked. "Everything you've thrown at me has failed. What honestly makes you think that you have anything that can slow me down?"

Kaffriz went silent. Cruz stared in horror.

Outside, the Mediterranean flashed like a mirror as the Gulfstream jet accelerated over it.

Nyala, Sudan

CALVIN JAMES'S EYES were unfocused as Bolan and Marshall entered his hospital room. The look on James's face was one of self-recrimination, a scowl that had been etched as much in pain as distress. Marshall knelt next to him and gave his hand a squeeze. Bolan glanced to Rafael Encizo, an unspoken question.

"Cal has suffered a major concussion. The helmet protected him from any permanent brain damage, but he's not going to be running and gunning anytime soon," Encizo said. "Three weeks down, at least."

Bolan nodded and walked up to James. The Phoenix Force warrior's shoulder was in a sling.

"Sorry, Striker. I'm on a lotta painkillers," James

said, mush-mouthed. "Not exactly loving being out of my head."

"It's okay," Bolan said. "Just be a good patient."

James managed a weak smile in response to Bolan's admonition. "I'll try." He aimed a shaky finger at Marshall. "I have someone to help keep me behaving. I just wish I'd remembered to duck. Not saying I'd enjoy a trip to Libya, but I would hate to leave you without a full fighting force."

Bolan grinned. "Now I know that something got knocked loose. We're going on a crazy run."

"I'm all about crazy, man. Learned it from David, and practiced it in the canyon," James replied. "What are you going to do?"

"Simple misdirection," Bolan said. "Right now, Bitturumba and Ammuz are girding up for us to come at them guns blazing. I've got Jack watching over Cruz and Kaffriz at the moment."

James frowned. "You'll sneak in ahead of time and set things up in your favor. Not like me."

"You didn't have the time or the room to go in ahead and sabotage. As far as you knew, the whole column was getting away on the other side. Instead, you facilitated the destruction of a battalion of Janjaweed killers with almost minimal losses."

"You'd still need someone to cover for Jack, watching the prisoners while he flies them in," James muttered.

Colonel Asimo Murani, who had accompanied them to the hotel-room door, cleared his throat. "I volunteered."

Bolan nodded in appreciation of the Ethiopian officer's offer. "I'd still rather that you didn't risk your life."

"I let Major Farrow risk his to protect my men. It would be a dishonor to his courage and selflessness to not offer my services," Murani stated. "Frankly, I'd be happy to send up a few of our old MiGs with ground attack packages to flatten everything for you."

Bolan shook his head, dismissing that suggestion. "That might inspire Tripoli to go to war with Ethiopia. Khadaffi would be willing to stomp through everything you built back up in the Sudan."

"I still have some aircraft that could be useful," Murani offered. "Something to help. If not to shoot, then to give you some form of surprise."

Bolan nodded. "If you have transport craft and two parachutes, I'd like to get to Al Uwaynat a few hours before you and my pilot deliver the hostages."

Murani nodded. "Anything else?"

"Khaki uniforms. I've got Libyan military insignia on hand," Bolan replied.

Murani raised a quizzical eyebrow. "You've got some huge balls, Stone. A blue-eyed boy dressing up as a Libyan officer?"

"Color-changing contact lenses. Add in this tan, and I'm as olive as any Mediterranean native. Rafe looks even more Arabic."

Murani nodded. "Then I have to ride your jet to Al Uwaynat, just to see how the hell you'll pull this off."

Bolan held out his hand. "Welcome aboard. I'll do my best to bring you home safely."

"And if we don't make it back," Murani said, "at least it'll be one hell of a ride."

Al Uwaynat, Libya

GENERAL AMMUZ COULDN'T believe that one man had dared throw down such a challenge that he challenged not one but two different armies to be on hand to face him. As it was, Ammuz was restrained by caution. Somehow, Stone had to have realized that Al Uwaynat was not completely as secure as the base of operations for Ammuz's ploy for control of Libya. While Ammuz could work with Bitturumba due to Khadaffi's secretive imperative to promote the cause of Islamic revolution across Africa, care had to be taken that only handpicked guards even knew about the container dwelling and the four plague carriers inside.

Luckily, Bitturumba's Janjaweed and Thunder Lion supporters were trustworthy. Bringing in five hundred of them on a pair of transport aircraft was an easy way to bolster Ammuz's numbers without letting on to Tripoli that the Libyan general needed assistance protecting his headquarters. The missive from Daffier was simple. "Don't let the world know what you're training the Sudanese for."

It wasn't as if the world intelligence agencies couldn't guess that the Libyans and the Thunder Lion hard-liners would obviously be in collusion over dealing with their mutual opponent, the nation of Chad. Though the Sudan and Libya shared only arid wasteland as a border, they did occasionally share training of troops. The presence of one force in the other's country was common enough not to raise red flags, and considering the recent pounding that Bitturumba had suffered in Darfur, it seemed likely that the militia leader would want to bolster his forces with foreign intervention and training.

Ammuz grimaced, and took a sip of liquor. Trying to keep the machinations within machinations straight was a maddening process. It was a headache-filled mess of lies folded into each other, and that was why the coming of Colonel Stone was not just a blessing, but a relief. Even if the American brought an armored division into Al Uwaynat, it would be honest combat. Guns versus guns, and when the smoke cleared, all that remained would be corpses to push into a mass grave. With the shooting, Ammuz would be able to funnel his anxiety into activity, rather than worthless speculation.

Bitturumba knocked on his office door. "The transports are landing. My men are here."

"You seem ill at ease," Ammuz mentioned. "Come in, and let's talk."

Bitturumba looked into the hall, his lips pursed in grim contemplation. After a moment, he squeezed into the office and closed the door behind him. "I'm not a superstitious man, mind you."

Ammuz nodded. "Your skill and logic have vaulted you to the top of the East African food chain. Superstition would only be a hindrance."

Bitturumba smiled weakly. "In Darfur, Colonel Stone invaded one of my bases. European mercenaries and my own men mistook him for a black leopard. Apparently he had penetrated base security alongside a true black leopard. They completely took wary, prepared, professional soldiers off guard. I was expecting men, but was thrown off by the beasts of the jungle."

Ammuz tilted his head. "You'd received some form of prophecy about falling in battle to a leopard who walks like a man, or some such nonsense."

"No prophecy. It was a curse. My cousin was an animist witch. She was one of my first…lovers. As she died when I was through with her, she said that on the eve of my greatest dream, a man who is more black panther than human will steal my victory," Bitturumba said. "I cut the unholy bitch's throat. I thought no more of it until Stone made his move against the bioweapon lab."

"And suddenly, the insane jabberings of a dying witch seem to bear some weight through the power of coincidence," Ammuz said.

Bitturumba nodded. "Coincidence. That's exactly what I want to rationalize all of this as. Happenstance and psychology."

"You have the cream of Libya's Revolutionary Guard and hundreds of your hardened veterans on hand," Ammuz said. "How can one man who apparently turns into an oversize lap cat prove to be a threat to twenty-first century military equipment backed by thousands of soldiers?"

"Thank you," Bitturumba said. "I needed to have some logic and reason."

Ammuz's phone rang. He answered it. It was the radar section of his base's command. Al Uwaynat was part of a picket line of radio trip wires that covered the hotly contested border between Chad and Libya. Radar towers swept the airspace between the two nations, looking out for their southern neighbor's hostile aircraft.

"There was a brief sighting of a high-flying aircraft coming up from the Sudanese border," Ammuz said with a grin. "He's trying to sneak in. He's trying to get the drop on us."

Bitturumba perked up. "And he's given himself away."

"With our combined forces, backed up by Baldr's elite operations team, we're ready for anything. Everyone knows what to expect. We have three ready, highly prepared forces on hand," Ammuz commented. "Stone is as good as dead. I'll send out patrols to look for where he might have parachuted in."

Bitturumba nodded. "And we'll bolster security here."

"Once Stone is out of the picture, we'll start the operation. Your infected carriers will go to Tripoli," Ammuz said. "We'll have swept the desert of that interfering American thug, and nothing else could possibly stand in our way. Your accursed black leopard man doesn't have a chance in hell against us now. He's doomed."

Bitturumba took a deep breath, visibly relieved. No longer facing a mystical threat, but rather a highly trained man, he now had the chance to live, and grow old as one of East Africa's greatest monarchs.

However, expecting a tall, blue-eyed Caucasian wraith, Bitturumba, Ammuz and their combined hardened forces didn't notice a solitary dark-eyed and stocky man in a Libyan army uniform standing beneath Ammuz's window. The squat stranger's understanding of basic Arabic left him fighting to keep a smile off his lips. The enemy was so full of certainty that they had Bolan where they wanted him that they had no clue that Rafael Encizo had driven onto the base. He and Bolan had crossed the border on a low-flying transport plane, one that had skirted the tops of sand dunes, keeping off Libyan radar. The newly detected aircraft was a misdirection, a ruse to draw off enemy attention.

The Phoenix Force warrior appreciated the Executioner's finely laid trap.

"They think you're on the way," Encizo whispered so low only his hands-free com-link could pick it up.

"I see a convoy leaving the base," Bolan returned. "Let's shake their confidence."

CHAPTER TWENTY-ONE

Mack Bolan lowered his field glasses after watching the convoy of trucks and jeeps leave the base outside Al Uwaynat. He made a count of at least two hundred men in more than twenty vehicles. Bolan looked back to the Kawasaki off-road motorcycle that he had taken along with him. Sheathed in a scabbard on the side of the bike was a bolt-action Barrett XM500 .50-caliber antimaterial rifle.

The low-flying cargo plane that had dropped them off had brought a pair of such bikes, but Rafael Encizo had declined to bring his version of the antiarmor rifle. If some Libyan guard examined the vehicle and found the American weapon stowed on board, the forces at Al Uwaynat would know that they had a disguised enemy within their ranks.

All Encizo had was a concealed mini-Uzi machine pistol cradled in a special shoulder harness, balancing out his 9 mm Heckler & Koch USP concealed under his uniform tunic. A belt full of palm-size SLAM devices was hidden away under the tails of the uniform top, as well. The Cuban's mission was one of quiet stealth and sabotage.

Bolan was on hand to provide a wild-goose chase out here among the dunes. He climbed on the motorcycle and kicked it to life. The Kawasaki roared across the wavy desert terrain, carrying him along like a bullet toward the convoy of patrol vehicles before they spread out to explore the desert where Bolan could parachute to earth. Racing across the sands, protected from view by the rolling, uneven terrain, Bolan cut to within five hundred yards of the Libyans. He slid off the bike and drew the Barrett, ascending to the top of a dune.

He threw the bolt to chamber the top round off the first magazine. A single .50 Browning Machine Gun round, a 700-grain harbinger of doom, now rested under the cocked firing pin of the heavy-duty rifle. He scoped the lead jeep and adjusted for movement as he lay prone across the top of the dune. Bolan was fast getting into position, and in one trigger pull, he dropped a lethal tungsten-cored penetrator into the front right axle of the lead vehicle. Bolan's shot smashed the wheel of the jeep and shattered the suspension. The jeep load of men screamed in surprise as their ride plowed bumper-first into the hard-packed sand of the road. Metal crumpled as the wheels popped off the shattered front end. A following truck was too close to put on the brakes or swerve. Five thousand pounds of the juggernaut transport ground the lead jeep into a folded mass of flattened steel and ground human meat.

Bolan worked the bolt action and swung his aim toward the transport truck that had just pulped the remains of the crushed vehicle. He triggered four rapid rounds from the magazine into the truck bed. The cab and front axle of the big transport were snarled on the mash of blood-smeared steel. The four rounds lanced into the riflemen crammed into the back of the truck. They were still stunned, and Bolan's bullets tore through Libyan soldiers, blowing vital organs into pulpy stew. It was a cruel action, sending freight-train slugs tearing through fragile human flesh, reducing human beings into limp sacks of flesh and pulverized bone.

Chaos broke out from the rest of the convoy five hundred yards downrange. AK-47s crackled impotently, bullets struggling to reach the Executioner as he fired at them from the top of the sand dune. Gravity took hold of the hurtling rounds, dragging them into the sand before they could reach him. Meanwhile, Bolan was far more concerned about the jeep-mounted DShKs. Those 12.7 mm armor-smashers had more than enough reach to hit him, the difference between the Soviet cartridge and the Browning round that the Barrett fired being only a matter of nominal insignificance.

Bolan kept his cool as the heavy-duty jeep-mounted weapons roared at him. He sighted on each machine gunner with almost lazy disregard for their furious fusillades. A single round for each Libyan in the back of the jeeps, and their powerful DShK went silent. The .50 BMG rounds tore through each gunner as he hung on to his shaking weapon. Torsos detonated under the fearsome slash of the big bullets, launching ragged corpses into the road.

Bolan had burned off thirty-three shots in total, killing replacement gunners as they rose to take the reins of the jeep-mounted machine guns. Finally, the convoy had experienced enough of Bolan's firepower, and the Libyans threw down smoke grenades to cover their frantic retreat. Jeeps and trucks wound off down the road back to the base.

"Striker, more bad guys heading out the gate." Encizo's voice came over his radio network. "You better scramble."

"Confirmed," Bolan answered. He put the rifle back into its scabbard, then fired up the Kawasaki to race away.

The Libyans were routed by the Executioner's opening shots. Far off, still distant from the crippled, retreating soldiers, he saw the clouds of dust kicked up by reinforcement trucks. Ammuz and Bitturumba were undoubtedly aware of his presence right in their backyards.

The element of surprise had been lost, but Bolan had replaced it by producing confusion, throwing the defending hardmen off their game plan. They had been anticipating catching Bolan as he landed in the distance, alone and on foot. When the fresh troops showed up, they would find nothing but sand and shell casings. Bolan was going to let the reaction force exist without the blessing of his Barrett's life-ending precision fire.

He had other fears to instill in different protectors of Al Uwaynat.

Hit-and-run harassment was going to be the order for the next few desperate hours. Encizo was still among the enemy, planting charges where they could cause the greatest destruction and distraction. That kept Bolan from firing on the base itself, but the plan was to run the Libyan and Sudanese conspirators ragged as they chased after him.

The tactic was not going to last forever. Sooner or later, the enemy would get back to coordinated efficiency and organize to hammer him into oblivion. That was all right with the Executioner, because he had another ploy on the back burner, simmering to fruition as the Gulfstream G150 came closer. It was the next phase of distraction to throw at his foes.

One step at a time, though.

Right now, he circled Al Uwaynat at a hundred miles an hour like a raptor circling its prey.

RAFAEL ENCIZO LOOKED out over the perimeter fence, watching the oily smoke smear against the blue sky. The column of smoke marked the wreckage of the ambushed Libyan convoy. The little Cuban smiled, feeling the tug of spirit gum that held his prosthetic beard and mustache to his skin. While the desert heat made the artificial hair itchy and uncomfortable, it was still preferable to a face full of Libyan bullets.

Base security was distracted by the presence of one of the world's most dangerous human beings, and it gave the Cuban infiltrator free rein across the Al Uwaynat military base. As long as he wasn't pulled from his wanderings to be hurled out into the desert in pursuit of the Executioner, he would have a relatively easy time in the compound. The fact that he walked with a purpose, and was in a hurry to reach his destination in the compound, gave him a semblance of authority and responsibility. The clipboard he carried with him also provided an extra layer of disguise. To the other soldiers, he was on an important assignment and none of them wanted to be written up by an officer. The mini-Uzi and the 9 mm HK USP were well hidden, but he wasn't the only unarmed soldier, despite the full alert.

Encizo had planted SLAMs all across the base. He didn't expect the portable munitions to be a perfect weapon, but coupled with the fuel or ammunition supplies, the one-kilogram charges would shake the Libyans and their Thunder Lions out of their tactics. There was one planted on the base's central power transformer. Another was attached to the belly of a 5000-gallon gasoline tank. Two more had been lodged in the crates of RPG warheads in the munitions storehouse, and others were planted among crates of 12.7 mm and 14.5 mm incendiary ammunition at the armory. He headed for the airstrip now. The Cuban's route and stop-offs were random and circuitous, disguising his intent as he went about his work. The winding route also afforded him the ability to keep his eyes open for the possibility of a too-alert Libyan soldier trailing him. The fuel supply for the motor pool was already set to erupt spectacularly. Aviation fuel would burn even hotter with a proper spark.

Two pounds of concentrated, shaped RDX explosives would provide that proper spark.

Encizo paused in his path around the base. He glanced around again to see if any guards had grown suspicious of his movements, and was rewarded with the knowledge that he had avoided any enemy scrutiny. However, the presence of armed Europeans in front of a storage building caught his attention. The Cuban was aware that Heinz Baldr, Alonzo Cruz's chief of security, had a cadre of operatives with him on the base. He'd heard Ammuz mention Baldr's name. Encizo also recognized their uniforms from seeing them back in the Sudan through binoculars. This crew, however, didn't possess the same listless boredom as the men that Baldr had used to staff the African facility. These men were awake and ramrod-straight, alert sentries instead of bored riflemen.

Encizo altered his course to get closer to the building. The European mercenaries stiffened at his approach, but the Cuban posing as a Libyan passed them by without paying more than quizzical attention to the two men.

"Move along, mate," a British-accented thug warned. "No pissy pissy around here."

Encizo rolled his eyes, continuing on his way to the airstrip. He had been outwardly dismissive toward the racist Englishman. The fact that a European was so blatantly posted as a guard on a Libyan military base set his instincts on end, mind on full alert. The Phoenix Force infiltrator keyed his hands-free radio with a clearing of his throat. "Striker, suspicious activity on base. Grid square 19."

"Clarify," Bolan requested. From the racket in the background, Encizo knew that the warrior was racing at top speed across the sands on his motorcycle. By keeping to the dunes, the Executioner kept from being pinned down by Libyan pursuit squads that seemed to be continually passing through the gates.

"Cruz's security has a storehouse on full lockdown. Not even allowing Libyan soldiers to wander too close," Encizo explained.

"Bitturumba's gift to Ammuz," Bolan surmised. "How tight is security?"

"Farm tight," Encizo replied. "Seems our visit to the compound might have been a ruse. They wanted us to knock out production of the virus."

Bolan grumbled in concern on the other end. "Cannon fodder to make my penetration look good. Stay to your plan. Don't risk blowing your cover if you can help it."

"Absolutely," Encizo replied. He glanced over his

shoulder toward the rude Briton on guard duty. There'd be time enough to deal with Baldr's mercenaries when the balloon went up. Encizo merely had to remain patient and stealthy as he continued to lay on a foundation of sabotage against Ammuz's forces.

Right now, another SLAM was on an appointment with thousands of gallons of aviation fuel.

MACK BOLAN DISMOUNTED from the motorcycle and drew his Barrett again. The big rifle, as compact and handy as a .50 BMG caliber weapon could get without generating shoulder-shattering recoil, was laid to rest on its steel bipod legs. He scanned the base with the mounted high-power scope, confirming the location and identity of the mercenaries that Encizo had just reported. It wasn't lack of trust of the Cuban's intelligence gathering or analysis skills. Bolan merely wanted to get an in-depth, closer view of what was going on. The powerful scope would allow him an easier reconnaissance of the hired guns than Encizo could accomplish, thanks to his distance from the sentries.

Naturally, Encizo was right. The riflemen situated at the entrance rivaled the stillness and alertness of the sharp-eyed Royal Guard at Buckingham Palace. These men were professionals, keeping mentally alert while physically still, conserving their energy for a potential conflict that could come literally to their doorstep at any moment. Bolan briefly considered putting a .50-caliber rifle bullet into each sentry, but if they were guarding a portable laboratory container from Cruz and Bitturumba, then there was the possibility that one of his rounds could cause a containment failure, unleashing a new nightmare that his and Encizo's protective filters would prove useless against. Even if the Stony Man warriors were protected from contagion, thousands of Libyan civilians in the nearby city of Al Uwaynat would suffer and die gruesomely for Bolan's impatience. While the storehouse itself didn't have infection precaution vents or other apparent machinery, there was a loading dock on the side of the building where a shipping container the size of one of Cruz's mobile laboratories could easily be loaded through. The portable lab's modular setup would have been noticeable by all manner of spy plane or satellite imagery. Only the roof of the building could conceal its lethal intent.

Bolan knew from experience that the labs were vulnerable to antimaterial weapons, reinforcing his decision to hold his fire on the mercenaries. The Executioner would need some other tactic to crack the lethal egg and seek out the deadly bioweapons within. He glanced to one side, seeing a trail of sand rising in the sky.

The Libyans were on their way, having tracked him down. Bolan was about to mount the Kawasaki trail bike when Encizo's voice rose on his radio, carrying a warning. "Helicopters warming up for takeoff on the airstrip."

Bolan swiveled. The Libyan vehicles still had three-quarters of a mile to cross before they were in small-arms range. The two helicopters on the strip, however, would render the Executioner an easy to track target, even if they were unarmed. Two Kamovs, equipped with doorgunners, sat on the tarmac. It was a flight about to encounter a delay.

The Executioner was familiar with the Russian MIL Mi-8S. While it was hardly a dangerous hunter-killer aircraft akin to the Kamov gunship, it was capable of holding twenty-four troops in its substantial belly. The door panels were taken off, and Bolan could see that PKT heavy machine guns hung on flexible door mounts. The Kalashnikov machine guns had more than enough power for the helicopters to stay out of small-arms ground fire, and still rain death from a kilometer away. Two of the Mi-8Ss in the air would be far too much lethal opposition for even Bolan to survive.

He put the crosshairs of the Barrett on the cockpit windshield of one of the Mi-8Ss. The rifle jolted violently into Bolan's shoulder, the reaction of six tons of kinetic force being attached to a .50-caliber bullet sent downrange. The safety glass protecting the pilots buckled under the remaining kinetic energy that hadn't bled off in the 1500-meter flight from Barrett to airstrip. The helicopter shook violently as one of the two pilots jerked in traumatic death reflex reaction to being shot and the helicopter's nose lurched up about four or five feet. Too bad for the troops inside the transport that the tail boom didn't rise, but it rammed into the airfield. The stabilizing rotor was wrenched off its nut, driven into the ground by the hard impact, and the metal blades shattered as the rotor cartwheeled into the concrete. Shards of the broken blades scythed like shrapnel. Ground crews shrieked in unison with the tortured metal of the bending tail boom, crushed by the weight of the main body of the bird slamming into it.

The doorgunner in the helicopter next to the one that Bolan decommissioned suddenly opened. The man on the PKT had either been firing due to reflexive shock from a shard of tail blade stabbing into him, or venting uncontrolled rage in response to an injury. In either case, the 7.62 mm Russian rounds ripped a catastrophic gash across the cabin of the wounded helicopter. Libyan troops packed into the transport writhed inside the passenger compartment, bodies torn by heavy-caliber slugs that knifed through the metal and human skin alike.

The doorgunners in the flopping Mi-8S twisted in agony, as well, their bodies quivering under a storm burning them to pieces at a rate of 650 rounds per minute. The second Mi-8S rose, under full control, getting out of the way as the first craft toppled onto its side. The 70-foot-diameter rotor, all five blades, splintered as the twin 1500-horsepower turboshafts smashed them into the asphalt. A new wave of shredded aluminum blades slashed out, overwhelming scurrying ground crew members. Bloody corpses vomited floods of gore through foot-wide lacerations, turning the helipad into a sticky red swamp, writhing with freed entrails.

Bolan racked the bolt on the Barrett and tracked the rapidly climbing helicopter. He missed the airborne bird with his second and third shots, working the action as fast as he could. The Mi-8S pivoted to present its flank to Bolan, sliding sideways through the sky to get within a kilometer. This was to grant the uninjured doorgunner a full view of the Executioner in his position. The range was still a bit much for the PKT flesh-shredder, but the churning cloud of sand accelerated rapidly toward Bolan. The Executioner's fourth shot hit the doorgunner before the storm of lead rain had gotten too close. The 750-grains of armor-piercing slug was intended for the port side Klimov turboshaft, four feet to the doorgunner's left and above him, but when the Libyan's helmet exploded like a grenade due to the hydrostatic shock of the .50-caliber round's awesome energy, Bolan wasn't disappointed with his aim. The Mi-8S shot forward, making itself a harder target to hit, but for now, the aircraft had been mostly defanged as a threat. It still had over two-dozen heavily armed Libyan Revolutionary Guard troops inside.

The mechanized column of Libyan hunters had closed range. Small-arms fire crackled through the air over Bolan's head. He had no time to get on the Kawasaki and retreat, but that wasn't the soldier's way. He had a clear shot and turned, picking a length of dune ridge. He opened up on the approaching military vehicles. Since they were coming right down Bolan's throat, five hundred meters distant, he didn't have to adjust his aim drastically as he had to do for the distant, moving helicopter. He hammered off seven more shots. It was suppressive fire, but one jeep generated a volcanic eruption of shattered engine parts while another truck was stopped cold with its driver cored by 750-grains of AP ammo. The convoy ground to a halt, heavy machine guns given a more stable platform from which to engage Bolan.

The Executioner reloaded quickly. The first round tore the head from a machine gunner's shoulders. A second shot destroyed the thigh of another man, the wounded shooter clutching his 14.5 mm cannon for support. The big cannon swung toward the truck bed next to his jeep, and fat explosive rounds shredded the dozen men in the back of the transport, turning their flesh to ribbons. The explosive slugs smashed bodies in the cab of another truck with the ferocity of a mad god. The wounded man screamed in agony as his fellow Libyans turned on him, gunning him down before he killed any more of his own.

That was the break that Bolan needed, and he stuffed the Barrett back into its side-scabbard. With a twist of the throttle, he rocketed away as fast as the off-road bike could carry him. The Libyans, in disarray, took half a minute to get going again, four of their vehicles rendered useless, and dozens of their fighting force slain in just a brief exchange.

The chase was on, and now, the Libyans had a helicopter with twenty-four troops in the sky, giving them the ability to counter Bolan's mobility. The doomsday numbers were crashing down around the Executioner.

Outnumbered and surrounded, he needed a brand-new strategy, but he didn't want to commit yet to Encizo's hidden explosive charges. Not just yet.

It was time to start working on Bitturumba's nerves. He connected to Jack Grimaldi and Colonel Murani on board the incoming flight.

CHAPTER TWENTY-TWO

Thormun Bitturumba knew that the Executioner's plan wasn't merely to spend an afternoon sending sniper fire to throw the Libyan base into disarray. With his .50-caliber Desert Eagle locked in his fist, he kept close to cover, near walls and vehicles, rarely exposing himself for more than a few moments. He also utilized hand signals to direct the traffic of Thunder Lion militiamen, so as not to give himself away aurally.

The airfield was covered with bloody corpses and the mangled metal remains of a tipped-over, shot-up helicopter. He'd directed a couple of platoons of his Thunder Lions to assist the Libyans on the tarmac, while he kept the rest of his units in position to respond to any further assaults by the Executioner. They bolstered the Libyans in perceived weak points in security, while guard towers around the base bristled with eager, bloodthirsty gunmen.

Bitturumba's cell phone vibrated against his chest. He plucked it out.

"I might not be named for a god of thunder, Thor, but

how do you like my sky shaking?" Bolan taunted on the other end. The American sounded as if he were talking from the back of a motorcycle, the buzz of a motor drowned out by the harsh crack and flap of the wind.

"I thought you wanted a face-to-face meeting," Bitturumba countered. "Instead, you're sniveling behind hundreds of yards of sand. For someone named Stone, it seems as if your feet are mere clay."

"Ask Ammuz's men how soft my feet are," Bolan said. "My footprints are pretty firmly set in their faces. One could say that they're pretty shaken by our conversations of late."

Bitturumba leaned against a wall, phone to his ear. "So you're on the ground. What about Lonzo?"

"Let the man talk to his brother, Asimo," Bolan said.

Colonel Asimo Murani, Bitturumba assumed, but since neither his last name nor his rank were given, it would only be a wild guess.

"Absolutely," Murani replied on a third channel. "Talk, rich boy."

"I'm not a goddamned performing animal, you bastard!" Cruz protested. The panic in his brother's voice hit Bitturumba in the gut.

"Lonzo, what's wrong?" Bitturumba asked.

"These fuckers stuffed me into a vest full of C-4," Cruz complained. "C-4 and boxes of nails."

"A Palestinian special," Bolan interjected. "For a while, I thought you might have appreciated it. But then, your little weasel brother told me that you're only paying lip service to the Prophet. Either way, it will keep you from getting too anxious to grab him."

"Fucker!" Cruz and Bitturumba bellowed in unison, despite being separated by miles and a radio hookup.

"We have your range, Stone!" Bitturumba growled. "You didn't get to shoot down Ammuz's second helicopter. They'll hunt you down like the vermin you are and crush you without blinking twice. You'll never escape!"

"If Ammuz's men get too close to me, you'll be an only child, Thor," Bolan taunted.

"I know your type too well. You wouldn't risk the lives of your men by setting off that bomb," Bitturumba answered.

Murani chuckled. "I don't need a bomb to take your brother's head off, you murdering scum."

Bitturumba heard the sound of metal scraping on metal.

"C-4 is very stable," Murani continued. "It won't blow up even if I hack him into stew meat with this machete."

"Lonzo forgot to mention that the black man holding him hostage had a very large knife," Bolan added. "Shame on him."

"Granted, I'm going to get all kinds of brains and body parts all over the cabin of this airplane. But I'm certain Stone knows people who can hose entrails off the interior of a Lear jet," Murani said.

"Nah. We'll just burn it and buy a new one," Bolan replied. "After all, I had Thor's Cayman Island accounts hacked. He can afford it."

Bitturumba felt a tremor of rage roll through him. It was one thing to kill his cannon fodder left and right, but to steal his hard-earned money? He gritted his teeth and tried to keep the anger out of his voice, failing with each word. "What do you want?"

"Pull your men and the Libyans off the airstrip," Bolan said. "And ground that Mi-8 still flying."

"And if I don't, that crazy Ethiopian is going to chop my brother apart with a machete," Bitturumba concluded. "You're that willing to have the United States vilified by murdering a continental hero?"

"Why would the U.S. be implicated?" Bolan asked. "Colonel Stone is a fiction. A lie. He doesn't exist. Any record of my activities is expunged as soon as it shows up on the news wires. No one knows, except for you and Ammuz, that I kidnapped the owner and CEO of Crusade Pharmaceuticals. Even if the Libyan government claims that I took him hostage, I'm not here as a government operative. I'm a terrorist. In fact, I'm the scariest terrorist you ever saw, because it's my job to pour blind panic down your throat until you choke on it."

"A terrorist who terrorizes terrorists," Bitturumba said. "A predator sitting higher on the food chain."

"Quit stalling, or your brother will need to wear trash bags to keep his bowels from falling out," Bolan said. "Pull them back and land that chopper. You have five—"

"All right!" Bitturumba snapped. "All right."

Bitturumba got on the walkie-talkie to Ammuz, feeling his manhood shrinking by the moment.

MACK BOLAN BROUGHT the Kawasaki to a crawl and killed the engine. Grimaldi, in the air, sent him the signal that the Libyans were crawling back behind their fence, empty-handed. It was a minor victory, and the influx of tired, badgered troops would add some confusion to the ranks. Cruz's phone rang in Bolan's pocket, and he took it out.

"All right, Stone. You can stop running," Bitturumba said. "You have a safe run of the airstrip."

"Sure. Right into the sights of your snipers," Bolan said. "I may have been born at night, but I sure as hell wasn't born last night. I'll wait until my plane comes in. I want a nice luxurious cabin to sit in as I watch Al Uwaynat burn like your firebase."

"Fine!" Bitturumba snapped. "Whatever you want!"

The connection went dead, but Bolan's link to the Gulfstream jet was loud and clear.

"Sarge, shoot up," Grimaldi warned. "Rafe's going to start sowing doubts."

"Roger that," Bolan answered. He opened a compartment on the Kawasaki's saddlebag and removed an atropine injector from its protective case. The plot that he'd formed was a cruel stroke, even for his ruthlessly efficient tactics. As he squeezed the atropine into his bloodstream, the Executioner knew full well that against the united front of Bitturumba's Janjaweed extremists and the coup-hungry soldiers gathered by General Ammuz, he needed an ace in the hole. It would take something big to even the odds.

Nerve gas was not a weapon that Bolan, nor the rest of the Stony Man warriors, would ever use lightly. Unfortunately, against a threat that could exterminate entire populations across the African continent, Bolan had very little choice. The VX was a necessary evil.

Still, Bolan sent a silent prayer of luck to Rafael Encizo, who was operating at ground zero. If the Cuban's atropine had somehow gone stale, or the injector didn't deliver the right dose, then Encizo's infiltration would rapidly turn into a suicide mission. Even if the antidote protected the Cuban, there was the chance that responding Libyan or Thunder Lion troops might realize that he wasn't a corpse. It would all come down to Encizo's acting ability and his patient. The fact that he'd be among dozens of dead Libyans would provide him with another cushion of distraction.

It was a slim thread of hope for the Phoenix Force warrior, and Bolan wished that he could have taken the risk for his friend.

RAFAEL ENCIZO HADN'T BEEN more uncomfortable in his adult life, though his abuse in Castro's prisons as a young teen kept him from qualifying his discomfort in his entire life. The spot on his thigh where he'd taken his injection of atropine throbbed painfully. The false beard glued to his face by spirit gum itched in the desert heat and his perspiration so much that he mentally toyed with the idea of carving it off with the razor-sharp edge of his Cold Steel Recon Bowie knife. He was surrounded by hundreds of men who spoke Arabic far better than he ever would.

All of that discomfort paled in comparison to the inner turmoil spawned by the tiny sample of binary chemicals he carried in the pod. It was the most frightening object that he'd ever held, even more terrifying than the 1.5-kiloton atomic munitions he had carried on missions with Phoenix Force. With a squeeze of his fist around the smooth, metallic capsule, the two liquid ampules housed within the shell would break, their contents mixing to produce one of the most lethal concoctions ever devised by man.

VX nerve agent was a truly horrific weapon, one of the true weapons of mass destruction and a cruel, lethal poison that could seep through skin as easily as it could be inhaled. Colorless and odorless, its wake of destruction was all too easily noticed. Encizo had seen victims of VX firsthand, and the memories of convulsion-distorted corpses never faded, helpless victims twisted by out-of-control muscle spasms a prevalent, recurring

nightmare. The horrible weapon, however, was his and
Bolan's last, best chance to sow dissent between Ammuz and Bitturumba. Despite having killed countless
enemies in combat using everything from his bare hands
to atomic demolition charges, the insidious neurotoxin
left a bitter taste in his mouth, his ethics threatening re-
bellion against this plan of action.

The Libyans under Ammuz had been pulled back
from the airfield, but they remained in group formations.
Encizo was just another one in a sea of swarthy, bearded
faces, another man dressed in khaki fatigues. A sergeant had stuffed an AK-74 assault rifle into his hands
earlier, and the Cuban now hung it off his shoulder by
its strap. He had palmed the lethal capsule of VX binary
components, keeping it tucked out of sight, but ready
to release.

Hushed tones rippled through the massed crowd of
nervous soldiers, and Encizo's smattering of Arabic
helped him understand their fears. The American soldier was present, circling the base like a human vulture.
He had slain dozens of their fellow Revolutionary
Guardsmen. Fear gripped the knot of soldiers gathered
in the shadow of the storehouse where Baldr's guards
stood vigilant. The mercenaries tolerated the Libyans'
presence in the cover of their building, made nervous
by the swathe of destruction that Bolan had unleashed
upon the airstrip with only a few rounds of fire. Ammuz's orders were simple. Wait for his signal, then rush
the incoming jet en masse, rifles crackling. It was a
good plan. Not even the Executioner could hold off a
wave of humanity as big as the combined forces of the
Libyans and the Thunder Lions.

That was where the VX capsule came in. The nerve

agent was designed as an area denial weapon, and it was a common formula among even Third World countries. What was even more important to this plan was the history of a Sudanese pharmaceutical plant having allegedly processed the deadly chemical before the United States government launched a cruise missile to destroy it. With the ability of Bitturumba's country to produce stockpiles of the deadly, silent killer, suspicion would be thrown upon the Janjaweed general. Was the VX leak sloppiness on the part of Bitturumba's brother and Baldr? Or did the Thunder Lions' commander release it to even the odds, putting the Libyan army on the defensive and opening up a huge break in the country's southeastern border defenses?

Criminally minded military men could be driven to the wildest conspiracy theories easily, simply because they were involved in their own dark dealings. General Ammuz could be made to resent Bitturumba's chemical-weapons presence, either assuming malice or carelessness. With that resentment, a wedge would be driven between the unified conspirators.

Bitturumba and a large group of his Thunder Lions were situated away from the knot of Libyans that Encizo had blended in with. As the Cuban moved closer to the storehouse that Baldr's men were protecting, he gauged the distance and felt the wind on his face. Encizo's dispenser held only a small dose of the deadly chemical killer. It was a top-secret CIA design, meant for eliminating targets in a small area, such as an apartment building, without threatening a larger urban area. As distasteful as the thought was to Encizo, he was glad that the kill radius was relatively small, only about fifty cubic meters. Baldr's mercenary guards were upwind of the device's deadly little cloud, but the Cuban was able to position himself so as to minimize the exposure of the Sudanese militiamen across the gap between them and the Libyans.

All it would take now was one hard squeeze. The glass cylinders of chemicals would break, and the two halves of the binary compound would combine into the killer compound known as VX. A compressed air charge would fire once Encizo relaxed his grasp, exhaling the nerve agent in a wide spray, creating an invisible cloud that would sweep through the Libyan troops surrounding him.

Just one hard squeeze, he mentally repeated. Around him, men would begin falling over, their muscles contracting violently. Bones would snap, tongues would be bitten off and mouths would foam. Horrible death would strike down dozens of human beings.

Encizo fought to put away his ethical qualms. He had to. In the balance, he remembered what these men had combined to unleash. He had to mentally list all of the times Phoenix Force had gone to war with Libyan military and government agents to prevent an atrocity. He remembered that the soldiers on this base were chosen by General Ammuz to engage in a coup where the main ingredient for change was a viral outbreak that would kill millions of civilians in a manner that was as gruesome and agonizing as the effects of VX. He told himself that Ammuz's takeover was only the first step on a path where tyranny would ride into power across Africa, riding on the shoulders of more artificially produced epidemics designed to cause helpless men and women, children and elderly to wail in agony as their internal organs disintegrated, and blood hemorrhaged from every orifice. A handful of conspiratorial scum, twisting in agony, was all that was necessary to stop millions of innocent Africans from suffering similar demises.

Encizo clenched his fist, letting his anger at the conspirators give him the strength to commit the act. The glass ampules splintered. VX was born from the union of molecules. With the memory of Ebola Thunder–ravaged children fresh in his mind, sprawled in the gory morass of a mass grave, he released the capsule. On letting go, the compressed air canister sighed, blowing its lethal, invisible kiss into the air for conspirators to catch it.

A Libyan soldier heard the sound of the aerosol dispenser release. He looked at Encizo.

"Did you fart?" the soldier asked.

Encizo shrugged. It was a strange choice of last words. The inquisitor had only a few more moments of life in him. Already, the Libyan's face displayed a nervous tic. Encizo pocketed the empty nerve gas capsule, knowing that he was going to have to mimic the death throes of the men around him.

Men began to spasm, shoulders hunching up, folding at the waist. A couple vomited as abdominal muscles clenched so hard, their stomachs disgorged gouts of bile. Encizo let his legs and arms fold up as the VX clawed through the ranks of the crowd, triggering neurological misfires. Unable to fire off the signals to release the diaphragm in exhalation, lungs stopped sucking in fresh air. Hearts palpitated, their rhythms thrown off as neuroreceptors no longer regulated cardial compressions. Death started claiming souls around the Cuban. Blood stopped flowing under cardiac pressure. Lungs no longer supplied oxygen to the rest of the body.

Encizo kept his eyes clenched shut, but he couldn't

shut off his ears. The gurgling, choking sounds of strangling soldiers, others vomiting, the bile splashing on the ground, dying, nervous wails filling the air all combined to roll over Encizo like a steamroller. Hands slapped and nails scratched on concrete. Bodies twisted as muscles contracted violently. Encizo heard the first snaps and cracks of bones. It was as if a whole room of people began cracking their knuckles at once. The crunching sound ground on Encizo's eardrums, sending chills up and down his spine. Bile surged in the back of his throat, and he let it pour from his lips, the stinging vomit pooling on the ground. It was camouflage, and the Phoenix Force veteran let the contents of his stomach settle as he lay among the dead.

GENERAL AMMUZ WASN'T HAPPY to have been forced to call off his troops in their pursuit of the American soldier. Being put on the defensive and pulled back from a successful surrounding of the lone crusader grated on the general's nerves. Stone had killed dozens of Libyan soldiers so far, and Ammuz wanted his head on a silver platter. Unfortunately, Bitturumba had a point.

Let the man think that he had finally gained the upper hand. Once the American's airplane landed, he would drive his motorcycle down into the trap that both sides had put up.

Ammuz double-checked his war load. He had a pair of 9 mm stainless-steel Taurus handguns, one on each hip. The big pistols had plenty of room for his huge, muscular paws, and held more than enough shots with their 17-round magazines. However, Ammuz's primary weapon was his RPK-74. With a full 45-round magazine he could hammer out prolonged streams of deadly fire with it as if it were just a rifle.

Against the American's might, he'd need all of that firepower. And all of the men on hand.

"All units, report in," Ammuz said into his radio. Subcommanders began to rattle off their positions and the readiness of their squads.

"Sir! Sir!" a voice interrupted. It was Major Ossun. "Something's happening to Gamma Company! They're falling over, sick!"

"What?" Ammuz asked, panic filling him. He knew that Gamma Company was the one by the storehouse containing the living biological weapons from Alonzo Cruz.

"I saw fifty men suddenly seize up, vomiting and foaming at the mouth," Ossun said.

"But not vomiting blood?" Ammuz asked. "No signs of Ebola symptoms?"

"No. It looks more like…nerve gas," Ossun replied.

"Nerve gas!" Ammuz exclaimed. He looked around for where Bitturumba had his soldiers. "What about the mercenaries?"

"Unaffected," Ossun stated.

Ammuz's eyes narrowed. He grabbed up his binoculars and peered through them, scanning the base. Sure enough, there was a morass of corpses laid out beside the storehouse, though the mercenaries at the entrance, hidden behind a protective wall of sandbags, were unaware of the mass outbreak of death.

Ammuz briefly considered that it could have been a tactic on the part of the American, but he thought of Sudanese ownership of chemical weapons. The U.S. government had launched a cruise missile to obliterate a VX production facility in the nineties. Bitturumba could have brought the nerve gas as an ace in the hole against the American soldier, but why didn't the big Sudanese mention it? And why in the world didn't Baldr's mercenary force succumb to the release.

Would you settle for just the wasteland of Chad when you had the ability to open up an inroad to the Libyan coast? he asked himself.

Nausea rumbled in Ammuz's stomach. He clicked the Thunder Lions' communication channel.

"Thor, did you bring in any nerve gas?" he asked.

Nothing. No answer from Bitturumba, but in accented English, he heard the following phrase, "They're onto us. How did they know?"

While the words had truly come from Thunder Lion lips, the speaker himself was long dead, slain by the Executioner and Rafael Encizo in the Sudan. Aaron Kurtzman, however, had recorded the message when the Janjaweed ambush set for the pair had been countered by the Stony Man warriors' superior skills.

It sounded convincing enough, however, to set Ammuz's nerves on end.

"Thor!" Ammuz bellowed, but radio jamming from an NRO satellite made it all but impossible for the Libyan commander to get through to his Sudanese counterpart. Ammuz switched channels.

"The Thunder Lions are betraying us! Open fire on those traitors!"

Half a world away, Kurtzman heard Ammuz's panic and smiled in satisfaction at Bolan's ruse.

Autofire erupted in Al Uwaynat as the world-conquering coalition splintered and turned on itself.

CHAPTER TWENTY-THREE

Bitturumba had been expecting almost any ploy on the part of the American soldier, but when he heard Ammuz bellow over the radio, his stomach felt as if it had been filled with concrete.

"The Thunder Lions are betraying us! Open fire on those traitors!"

Bitturumba looked toward his men. Major Korunda's eyes were wide with confusion, not understanding the sudden switch in attitude among the Libyans.

"Return fire if shot at!" Bitturumba ordered over the radio, feeling that the command was more important than clarification of the situation. All around the base, FAMAS and AK-74 rifles chattered to violent life, spewing out high-velocity projectiles as Sudanese and Libyan suddenly found themselves ordered into combat.

"But—" Korunda began.

"Stow it, "Bitturumba said. "Ammuz is the only force that outnumbers us here. Stone knows that, and he somehow got that Libyan bastard to think that we made some kind of first strike. Kill everything that's in your way."

Bitturumba saw a squad of Libyan soldiers race around a corner, and to emphasize his point, he opened fire on them, his big Desert Eagle hammering out its death messengers toward the Revolutionary Guardsmen. Two men flopped onto their back, horrendous paths of destruction through their faces, other men jerking violently as they took peripheral hits from the big, powerful handgun.

"Shoot them!" Bitturumba bellowed.

FAMAS rifles chattered, 5.56 mm rounds spearing through the surprised enemy. On full-auto, the Janjaweed militiamen's high-velocity bullets slashed through flesh and bone like chainsaws, ripping apart the khaki-clad gunmen as they were scrambling for cover from Bitturumba's initial fusilade. The Sudanese general reloaded his handgun, then saw one of his soldiers lying, gasping his final breaths where a Libyan had gunned him down. Bitturumba took the dying man's FAMAS and tugged free the bandolier of magazines as he faded into a corpse.

Bitturumba put his radio to his lips. "Free fire zone. Anyone who's not wearing Thunder Lion black dies! Grenades are a must. Dig them the fuck out of this sand trap!"

Thunder rumbled across the base, and Bitturumba felt the adrenaline rush as once again, at his bidding, the skies shook with his power. It wasn't the sheer superpower of artillery, but it was enough for now. The African god of thunder was feeding on the rush.

He spotted another squad of Libyans who were rushing to blindside a group of his men. The general opened fire, leading the charge to shatter the ambush. Swinging in on the khaki-clad rifleman's blind spot, he and his militia wiped them out brutally. Muzzle-mounted rifle grenades broke the formation of Libyan troops apart, and the remains were swept away by a rainstorm of high-velocity autofire.

Hooking his team up with the besieged soldiers, Bitturumba had doubled the size of his force. The larger group of fighting men drew a lot more attention, as three platoons of Libyans tried flanking maneuvers. Hand-held fragmentation grenades and RPGs rippled off their vengeful bellows, blossoms of fire erupting in the midst of the assaulting groups. Severed limbs and shredded torsos flopped on the concrete. While it was slightly more difficult than taking on unarmed civilians, Bitturumba felt lucky that Ammuz's forces were not battle-hardened. They had training, but the Janjaweed had been in constant conflict over the past several years. Between internal conflicts in the Sudan and border skirmishes with Chad, as well as Ethiopia's intrusion all the way to Khartoum, the Thunder Lions were experienced. They might have had a healthy fear of coming under concentrated fire, but they knew to head for cover and shoot back.

Ammuz's Revolutionary Guardsmen were nowhere near as blooded as the Sudanese they'd allowed on the base. It was only a moment of hesitation that slowed the enemy, but Bitturumba's troops did a lot of damage in that brief lapse of reaction time. Bitturumba laughed as he made a Libyan soldier dance under the slashing force of his borrowed FAMAS.

"Well played, Stone!" Bitturumba shouted over the din of assault weapons and dying soldiers. "Well played, you son of a bitch!"

THE EXECUTIONER HAD BEEN certain that his divide-and-conquer tactics would work, but when Bitturumba started launching rockets and throwing grenades at Ammuz's soldiers without a concern for brokering some form of peace, Bolan was stunned. It was surprising how well the Sudanese general had bought into the "kill or be killed" brutality of the conflict he'd fanned. Then again, Bitturumba was not someone who suffered betrayal or failure lightly. The Executioner almost felt bad for the Libyans, having born the brunt of not only the Bolan's hit-and-run tactics but the Thunder Lions' coordinated and focused rage. Still, Bolan had needed a way to even the odds against the home team operating in their own complex. The men under Ammuz's command were receiving a thorough drubbing.

The duel between the former coconspirators had been bolstered by an electronic flash of misinformation, a recording made of the Thunder Lions' communications taped by Aaron Kurtzman, filtered and rebroadcast through the shared radio link the two armies were supposed to use for coordination. The recording, broadcast from Stony Man Farm, coupled with Rafael Encizo releasing a burst of nerve gas, worked well enough to fill the Libyans with the belief that Bitturumba and his Janjaweed fighters had intended to overwhelm General Ammuz's forces. The mind-set of the would-be ruler of Libya was such that he saw only deception and betrayal lurking beneath the skin of every man he met. It was a common paranoia among plotters that Bolan often exploited. When conspirators worked together, they almost always seemed to harbor doubts that their allies were out for something more than they had agreed to. Psychologically, it was easily explainable, each schemer projecting their own greed onto their partner. When Bolan lit the fuse on the explosion of doubt it often did far more damage than even his brutally efficient marks-manship.

In that regard, the Executioner was doing far more than simply observing the madness of the conflict through the 10x magnification of his Barrett's scope. Bolan pulled the trigger after lining up on another Thunder Lion wielding an RPG-7 rocket launcher. The .50-caliber slug tore a ragged, fist-size hole through the Sudanese militiaman's chest, and in his death throes, the man triggered the launcher. The rocket-propelled grenade speared skyward, riding atop a cottony column of churning smoke. The 110 mm shell soared thanks to its rocket motor's output until gravity won out over the dying thruster. Bolan turned his attention to another black-uniformed Sudanese, but the flash of the detonating shell as it crashed into the ground was hard to miss. Bodies flew from the heart of a close-quarters melee between the Janjaweed and the Revolutionary Guardsmen. The carnage had carved a swathe in the hell-bent brawl that Bolan had sparked. Dozens of soldiers died at ground zero of the detonation. In the meantime, Bitturumba's forces continued to rain autofire and grenades on the Libyan defenders, waves of lead and fire slashing away large chunks of the two masses of opposing troops.

The Thunder Lions had the advantage of skill and ruthlessness, enabling them to whittle down the superior numbers that they faced. Libyan soldiers in the perimeter towers had briefly wreaked havoc among the Janjaweed militiamen before RPG teams blew them off the stilted gunnery positions. The towers now smoldered, flames vomiting smoke that curled lazily into the sky. Bodies were strewed about, some of them falling across barbed wire atop the perimeter fence, but far beyond suffering pain from the flesh-rending slashing prongs on the wire. Twisted machine guns smoked on the concrete at the fence line. There were some members of the Libyan Revolutionary Guard who were capable combatants, but the vast majority of Ammuz's command were support personnel, not infantrymen or elite commando units. The trained soldiers would have been a vital equalizer in the conflict for Ammuz's side, but they had been depleted when they had pursued the Executioner, and he whittled their numbers. Now the expert fighting men were outnumbered by Bitturumba's hardened militia killers, and the Libyans were fading quickly.

"Rafe, you all right down there?" Bolan called.

"I've felt better," Encizo answered, his throat raw from the bile that had caught there. "Nobody seems to be paying attention to me or the corpses I'm with."

"What about Baldr's men?" Bolan asked.

"They pulled back into the storehouse," Encizo explained. "Want me to go in?"

"Be careful," Bolan said. "I have a little more house-cleaning to do before I catch up with you."

"Take your own advice, Striker," Encizo warned. "Those guys seem to be killing anything not wearing the same uniform."

Bolan fired the last round he had for the Barrett. The .50-caliber slug ripped the skull from the shoulders of another Sudanese militiaman. "That's the effect I've been going for."

Bolan discarded the empty cannon and hopped onto the back of the Kawasaki. From now on, all he had was the rifle slung across his back and his signature pistols.

But now, the odds had been slashed to a level where he would be able to do what he did best.

Rafael Encizo used a SLAM to knock a hole in the entrance at the storehouse's rolling, corrugated-steel dock doors. The blast of 2.2 pounds of RDX peeled open the heavy metal shutter, throwing a wave of shrapnel into the interior of the building. Heinz Baldr's men screamed as splinters of jagged steel stabbed into their flesh. Assault rifles opened up even as injured European mercenaries cried out in agony. The gaping hole in the dock doors became an inhospitable no-man's-land as bullets snapped through the air so thickly that a cone of death flowed outward for hundreds of yards through the entrance. Both Sudanese and Libyan forces fell under the indiscriminate fusillade that carved through the base.

Encizo wisely was nowhere near the entrance, just close enough to rebound a grenade off the dock and into the hole. He stayed out of range of the thunderous gunfire while six-and-a-half ounces of concentrated high explosives and twin fragmentary shells ignited in a flash of lightning. Gouts of smoke ripped out of the ragged gap in the wall. The Cuban commando knew that he'd pacified one entrance for only a brief moment, and had to take care of his back. He raced around to the sandbagged front door where he had been warned away by a rude British mercenary. The door swung open and guards popped into view.

Encizo was there, already anticipating their surprise maneuver. He emptied one AK-74 on full-auto, catching gunmen as they tumbled into the open. A hail of 5.45 mm bullets tore into the Europeans before they could check their forward momentum. Rather than wrestling to reload the now-empty rifle, Encizo tossed it aside and pulled a spare rifle from his shoulder. The flanking maneuver was blunted as Encizo continued his rain of doom with only a second of interruption. However, the Cuban realized that the mercenaries would have to try to take him from the shattered dock entrance.

"Cover me!" Encizo shouted in Arabic. Libyan soldiers, riflemen who were in no position to deal with the Thunder Lions, saw one of their own under siege from the foreigners that Ammuz said had betrayed them. White or black, the enemy was clear, and the infantrymen cut loose on the hole in the wall, firing into the shattered maw to give Encizo cover fire.

The Phoenix Force specialist was pleased that his disguise still worked. Libyan soldiers rushed to his aid and protection, risking their lives to help him out in his desperate task. The Cuban tried not to see the irony in their sacrifice for his sake. There was a jolt of guilt over having gassed their brethren still rattling around in his psyche, but he pushed that under, reminding himself of the factors that had given him the strength to release the VX cloud on the members of the coup.

AK-74 rifles chattered in counterpoint to the mercenaries' arms. Despite the ferocity of the Libyan counterattack, they were losing ground, being chewed to pieces by expert marksmanship. The European specialists had superior cover and tactics. The charging troops were out in the open, vulnerable to the well-aimed rifles of Baldr's mercenaries.

Encizo knew that the Libyans were dooming themselves, but they had bought him vital moments with their deaths. He reached the front door, perpendicular to the wrecked dock. He discarded the second empty

AK-74 and drew another one from across his broad back. He took a moment to replenish his arsenal with rifles belonging to the dead hired gunmen. Since the mercs had died without having fired a shot, the rifles were fully loaded and ready to rock. Encizo opened up, draining his borrowed AK in a series of rapid precision bursts, plunking 2- and 3-round salvos into the distracted European riflemen.

A large container was on the floor, situated away from the dock. It hadn't been damaged in the brutal firefight with the Libyans, and through bullet-pocked armored glass, Encizo could see four men arming up and donning body armor. They scrambled to get to an escape hatch, but the ventilators built into the top of the container were all the evidence that Encizo needed to know that those four men were a catastrophic biological threat. The Cuban took a step into the storehouse, SCAR rifle at the ready when one of the corpses near the door jerked to life. A leg kicked his feet out from under him and as Encizo sprawled on the ground, a fist rocketed down to crush his face.

"You bloody bastard!" a familiar voice bellowed. It was the British mercenary who'd insulted Encizo earlier. The knuckles of his fist lashed at the Cuban's face, but Encizo rolled and pulled his head out of the way of the plummeting blow. The merc only ended up splitting his knuckles by punching the concrete floor after he brushed Encizo's cheek. Had the blow landed firmly, making a solid connection, it would have broken Encizo's jaw. As it was, the Phoenix Force veteran was still reeling from being tripped.

The British mercenary swung again, hoping to land a better punch with his remaining good hand, but Encizo seized the man's wrist, easily stopped the man from pulling free of Encizo's grasp. With a hard twist, the Briton's forearm bones splintered, breaking thanks to Encizo's phenomenal strength. He shrugged, tossing the mercenary to the floor. Rather than bruise his knuckles, Encizo fired the SCAR at contact range, 7.62 mm bullets smashing a gory crater through the hired thug's chest.

Encizo looked up at the container and saw that the air lock had been opened. The four plague carriers stood outside, glaring at him from behind cover.

"Our blood is loaded with unstoppable death," one of the four death bringers said.

"Our breath is a wind of plague," another stated.

"You cannot hope to win!" the third exclaimed.

"Even now, our disease is closing in on you," the last stated.

Rafael Encizo's jaw set. The smashed wall would no longer be able to contain the four mass murderers. Once outside, they would unleash doom upon the world. He threw his rifles down, breathing deeply.

He prayed that the gambit he and Bolan had concocted to neutralize a potential biothreat would work. It sounded good on paper, but when Encizo was face-to-face with the harbingers of the apocalypse it was a whole different matter.

GENERAL ALDREH AMMUZ watched in dulled shock as Al Uwaynat was shaded under a thickening darkness, choking smoke blocking out the sun. The rattle of autoweapons and dying screams formed a grisly symphony that was the funeral dirge for him. There was no way in hell that Ammuz would be able to hide this bloody conflict from Khadaffi, and losing hundreds of troops to Thormun Bitturumba would brand the Libyan as a colossal failure, regardless of whether his coup ploy was ever found out. All he could hope to do now was to survive.

Demotion and humiliation was at least remaining alive. He'd twist some schemes together later. He picked up his radio and called out to his troops, all too aware that his numbers were dwindling.

"Sir," a lieutenant under his command called over the airwaves, "we have a situation. The building that you declared off-limits has been breached. Our people tried to hit it, but they were driven off by Cruz's mercenaries."

Ammuz looked over to the storehouse that Bitturumba had delivered a package of promised supreme power. "That was where the nerve gas leaked, correct?"

"Yes, but it appears that one of our soldiers took up the attack. He must have been separated from the rest of his squad," the lieutenant said. "The fighting has died down for now, but if we could rally and take the building, we might have a chance."

The plague carriers, Ammuz mused. With those four men, he'd at least be able to hold the nation hostage, keeping Khadaffi from bringing his full might down. Once he got that storehouse under his personal control, he'd be able to barter for immunity, perhaps an honorable discharge and passage to a hidden corner of South America. It was a slim chance, but Ammuz didn't have many options to walk away from this without incurring the wrath of the government he'd sought to usurp.

"With me, men," Ammuz ordered. "We fight for our freedom!"

The Libyans thought that their commander was engaging in hyperbole, but they clutched their rifles just a little tighter and followed him en masse.

That's when assault-rifle fire poured out of the barracks where Heinz Baldr and his cadre had been stationed. Ammuz watched his troops topple under precision marksmanship as he pressed onward with his charge. He strove to hang on to his last remaining thread of hope.

HEINZ BALDR WATCHED the Libyans regather their forces and make a second assault on the storehouse. The mercenary commander was certain that the insane Ammuz was making some form of play to end all life throughout the desert, letting loose the four pedestrians of Armageddon. It was a suicidal grandstand, but at least it was a way to avoid national and international scrutiny and hatred in the wake of a failed coup.

"Keep knocking them down!" Baldr commanded.

"We're running low on ammunition," one of his men said. "There are just too many of those psychopaths running around out there."

Baldr's lips tightened into a bloodless line of concern. He checked and he only had one and a half magazines remaining in his bandolier, and then he was down to the Walther on his hip. The storehouse was quiet now, seemingly empty of all life, but he knew of the cruel contagion seething inside its four walls. He also realized that there was plenty of spare ammunition in there with the remains of his lost soldiers.

"All right. We need to make our move," Baldr said. "Get to the storehouse, now!"

The depleted ranks of the mercenaries knew that their only chance was to get more ammunition. They girded themselves for the charge and raced into the open.

THE EXECUTIONER SPOTTED the twin forces swooping down on Encizo's location and knew that his friend was in desperate need of assistance. With a rev of the Kawasaki's throttle, he launched the motorbike off the top of a dune, soaring over the barbed-wire fence. He'd aimed at a clear section of concrete and braced himself for the landing. That didn't make the jolt that almost blew out the suspension any more gentle, but at least Bolan still had feeling in his legs.

Ammuz was unmistakable as a six-and-a-half-foot megalith leading his Libyans toward the storehouse. Bolan knew that his brakes wouldn't be able to stop the motorbike in time to avoid a collision with the throng of soldiers. He decided he didn't need to stop the Kawasaki and turned sharply, projecting the two wheels as the forward wedge of the rocketing missile. Ankles and shins shattered as Bolan and his 400-pound ride, well over a quarter ton of mass, plowed into the group. Bodies hurtled to the ground and Ammuz barely dived out of the path of the crashing bike. Bolan rolled clear of the Kawasaki. His khaki fatigues were shredded, but the blacksuit underneath protected him from a painful case of road rash.

The Libyan general gawked at the Executioner as he rose to his feet, going for the Desert Eagle on his hip. The big man swung his RPK-74 around, but since Bolan had crashed through the crowd of Libyans from behind, Ammuz's opening burst tore into his own men. Bolan moved like lightning, barely keeping ahead of Ammuz's aim as he raked the light machine gun. Dying screams filled the air as 5.45 mm rounds punched through soft tissue and viscera to plow into other bodies behind,

when they weren't stopped by solid bone. Too terrified
to dare open fire on their own boss, or the sleek, dodging Executioner as he raced for cover, lest they hit their
gigantic leader, the Libyan soldiers scrambled. Bolan
somersaulted, rolling across his shoulders to escape the
chasing line of full-auto lead that did the American's
work for him. He stiff-armed the Desert Eagle and triggered two .44 Magnum slugs that smashed into the chest
of the Libyan giant. Both bullets had broken ribs and
torn through lung tissue, but the powerful column of
gun-toting muscle before him snarled in impotent rage,
the 45-round magazine having drained from his auto-
weapon.

Incredibly, the massive Libyan's hands clawed at the
twin pistols on his hips. Bolan adjusted his aim and fired
the .44 Magnum again. This time, however, there was
no toughing out a slowly lethal mortal wound. The wide-
mouthed hollowpoint round sheared through Ammuz's
forehead, popping the dome of his skull up like the lid
of a trash receptacle. Brains geysered out of their suddenly opened bone casing, churned into froth by the
passage of 240-grains of lead at 1500 feet per second.

The Libyan general's hands slipped from the handles
of his Taurus handguns, and rubbery, lifeless legs folded.
It was like watching a redwood crash in a forest.

Wounded and dismayed Libyans, looking at their
murdered brethren, stared in shock at the tall wraith
who tore off his tattered uniform shirt. Icy cold eyes
stabbed at them.

"Flee, and live," Bolan gritted, a well-memorized
phrase from his quiver of learned Arabic threats.

Leaderless, the Libyans chose life over valor.

Now, all the Executioner had to do was to stop

Baldr's forces from overwhelming Encizo before he could deal with the biohazard in the storehouse.

Unslinging his VEPR, Bolan triggered the attached 40 mm grenade launcher, lancing a thunderbolt of high explosives and shrapnel into the charging mercenaries. That was a good enough opening argument, flattening a dozen of the Europeans, but he would have to work for the rest of the hired guns. There was still the menace of Bitturumba to deal with, as well.

Here, among the smoke-hazed carnage of Al Uwaynat, the Executioner had his work cut out for him.

CHAPTER TWENTY-FOUR

Rafael Encizo looked at the four plague carriers, his dark eyes narrowed in concentration, his lips pressed firmly shut. Instinctively, he knew that the vaccine he and the others had taken would not be affected by the atropine, but there was still a doubt. Encizo was glad that Alonzo Cruz did not dare go anywhere without protection from his own artificially evolved plagues. Following a little intimidation from the Executioner, Cruz gave up the vaccine syringes for the whole line of lethal microbes that he intended to release. Encizo, Bolan, Murani and Grimaldi were all vaccinated against the Tripoli Ebola variant, the virus that seethed within the bloodstream of the four armed killers hiding behind cover. The Phoenix Force veteran had discarded his rifles in an effort to get the quartet of the apocalypse to believe that he was giving up the fight.

"Ever seen someone suffer from Ebola?" the first plague carrier asked. "Seen them suffer and writhe as their blood boils, turning to an acid that destroys their arteries and veins and capillaries?"

"Too often to let the four of you go unabated," Encizo answered. He peeled out of his uniform tunic and rolled down his blacksuit sleeves. With a tug, he loosened the mini-Uzi machine pistol from where it hung on his shoulder harness. The leather envelope that the Israeli chopper had been stored in flipped the folding wire stock out as it was drawn. A flick of the thumb, and the compact chatterbox was live and ready to thunder out its death song at a rate of 950 rounds per minute.

"We are destined," the second of the plague carriers said. "We have been selected by the god of thunder, the new lord of the future."

"You mean Bitturumba?" Encizo asked. "He's a god now?"

"Always has been," the third answered. "He brings the thunder to the plains, he rains blood upon the unbelieving."

"I bet his farts smell like roses, too," Encizo grumbled. Through the hole in the wall, he heard the rumble of an explosion.

"Bad guys coming down on you," Bolan's voice interrupted. "What did you say?"

"I'm talking with the four footmen of the apocalypse," Encizo replied. "Delightful group if you enjoy psychosis."

"You're out of grenades?" Bolan asked.

"Trying to determine if a blood spill will produce too much of a contagion leak," Encizo whispered.

"Saying your prayers?" the fourth plague carrier asked.

"Bear said that there's a ninety-eight-percent chance that blood won't spread the disease as significantly as respiration," Bolan told him.

"Yeah, I'm getting bored with these freaks anyway.

We can always burn the bodies," Encizo said. He popped up and fired the mini-Uzi from his shoulder. The Phoenix Force veteran's stance and aim, forged in countless battles, enabled him to target the head of one of the plague-spreading Thunder Lions and deliver a 5-round burst through his face. Facial bones imploded, the disease carrier's features collapsing in on themselves. He flopped onto his back, assault rifle raking the roof as his death grip tripped the trigger.

The other three gawked at their lifeless ally, giving Encizo a second free shot. This time he tapped two 9 mm rounds through the ear and temple of a second death bringer. Brains gushed out the other side of the man's skull. The two remaining Ebola-riddled Thunder Lions opened up with their FAMAS assault rifles, 5.56 mm rounds chattering as they sought to bring down the Cuban dynamo, but Encizo had dived below a line of crates that absorbed the lightweight, hypervelocity projectiles. With powerful chest strokes, he scurried along the smooth concrete floor, moving away from the spot where the two pedestrians of Armageddon focused their rifle fire.

Rising to his knees, Encizo shouldered the mini-Uzi and pumped a prolonged burst into the chest of the third of the riflemen. Disease-carrying blood spurted from half a dozen wounds, and the Phoenix Force warrior tried not to imagine microbes taking to flight on the droplets, using them like they were the decks of aircraft carriers to launch. Besides, the Phoenix Force pro had more pressing matters as the last of the Thunder Lions swung down on him, FAMAS chattering vehemently. The Cuban was down behind cover once again, flinching as 5.56 mm projectiles ricocheted off the crates.

The far wall sparked, puffs of dust filling the air where the copper-jacketed lead disintegrated on hypervelocity impact. Encizo plucked a grenade and lobbed it over his cover, feeling a FAMAS bullet sear millimeters from the back of his hand. The heat of the passing projectile let him know how close he was to certain death, but when he brought the wrist back down, he saw nothing had touched him. The grenade's fuse went through its countdown, and Encizo ticked off the final seconds of the bomb's life.

When Encizo counted to six, seven, eight, he knew that something was wrong. The cotter pin was still wrapped around his thumb, so in the heat of the moment, he hadn't forgotten to prime the bomb. There was no detonation. He did hear, however, the clatter of a fallen rifle and the scuffle of boots desperately running on concrete. He got up, seeing the last of the plague carriers bolt out of the hole. The Cuban tracked him with the mini-Uzi, but the fear factor of the unexploded grenade had given the deadly diseased man wings on his feet. Even at over 1200 feet per second, the 9 mm slugs he fired at the Thunder Lion were too slow to catch the man. The machine pistol locked empty, but the Phoenix Force vet ripped out the spent magazine, feeding it a fresh one.

Encizo rushed toward the destroyed docks, but heard autofire blazing outside. He paused at the edge of the shattered doors and peered around carefully, looking at the fleeing plague carrier bleeding all over the ground. Heinz Baldr had opened up on him, and looked at the leaking corpse at his feet. The Cuban shouldered his mini-Uzi and targeted Baldr. The mercenary realized that he'd been exposed to Cruz's Ebola Tripoli variant, and let his rifle drop to the ground, accepting Encizo's storm of 9 mm slugs. Being machine-gunned to death was far preferable to the fate of internal organs exploding and leaking out of his eyes, ears and nose. The burst tore him from sternum to throat, shattering the Austrian's heart and blowing chunks out of his neck.

Baldr looked almost thankfully to Encizo, then toppled lifeless across the corpse of Cruz and Bitturumba's final contagion agent. The Executioner jogged into view, feeding his spent VEPR. The ground around the storehouse was littered with slaughtered mercenaries, the hired guns having proved inferior to Bolan's superior fighting skills. The one-man army sized up Encizo as he peeled the spirit gum–affixed beard from his jaw.

"Filthy, disgusting stuff." The Cuban spit.

"This the last of them?" Bolan asked.

Encizo nodded. "Baldr did my job for me, and I treated him to a merciful death."

Bolan looked at the lifeless Austrian. "It would have been a fitting end for his kind, suffering the kind of death he intended for millions of others."

In the distance, down by the airstrip, the two Stony Man warriors saw Grimaldi bringing in the Gulfstream G150. The ace pilot landed the sleek aircraft and taxied it to a halt.

Alonzo Cruz's satellite phone, the umbilical between Bolan and Thormun Bitturumba, warbled, signaling that the big Sudanese commander wanted to talk again. Bolan answered it.

"Is my brother on that plane?" Bitturumba asked.

"What do you think?" Bolan asked, cocking his brow. The big soldier smirked as he heard the growl of frustration on Bitturumba's end.

"Well, thanks to you, he's not around to pay for it. Give me my brother, and you can fly out of here," Bitturumba snarled.

"I'm a little doubtful," Bolan answered. "After all, you no longer have a valid reason to be in Libya."

"Neither do you, Stone," Bitturumba returned. "But the thing is, I have hundreds of men left. And you have a hostage. Our positions are relatively equal, because my people are exhausted from tearing apart the Libyans."

"You also lost Baldr and his forces," Bolan added.

There was silence on the other end. "He was just the hired help. Honestly, Stone. I'm tired of this."

"I'm pretty worn out, too," Bolan said. "But not so tired that I can't see a half-dozen ways that you can screw me."

"And you have my brother wrapped up like he's got a mad on for Tel Aviv," Bitturumba said. "How do I know you won't press the trigger on him when you're flying away?"

"That little bit of doubt keeps both of us honest, don't you think?" Bolan asked.

"I'd like some more reassurance," Bitturumba said.

"Let's do this, then. My partner will board the plane, and then send out your brother and Kaffriz," Bolan explained. "You send your men outside the perimeter. The jet takes off and I walk Cruz to you, no vest of explosives."

Bitturumba grumbled. "Fine. I'll pull my men back to the entrance. And you, no rifles. I'll have sharpshooters watching you."

Encizo, listening to the satellite phone as it was in speaker mode, looked questioningly toward Bolan, but the look on the soldier's face was one of confidence, despite the tremor of nervousness he feigned in response.

"Sure, whatever you say," Bolan replied.

"And I don't give a shit about Kaffriz," Bitturumba said. "You can keep him, or you can just dump him off. It doesn't matter to me."

"Absolutely," Bolan answered. "Just put your men in the desert, away from any gates."

"They'll be at the gate," Bitturumba rumbled, asserting himself. "I'm not letting my people wander into some kind of minefield. I'm not stupid, either, Stone."

Bolan's smile helped Encizo to remember the saddlebags on the Kawasaki. Each of the four compartments hanging on the bike was loaded with fifteen pounds of C-4, and stored next to 500-unit boxes of roofing nails. High explosives and the deadly little points would combine to produce an area-denial weapon of stupendous power. The shrapnel of such a concoction was more than enough to kill dozens of soldiers instantly, and wound hundreds. It was a surefire method to take the fight out of the Thunder Lions, and by insisting on sending the men to the safety of the desert, Bitturumba had condemned his forces to excruciating death. Encizo's Kawasaki was situated at the gate where Bitturumba was stationing his men.

"All right," Bolan said, acting badgered by the big general.

"You've got ten minutes," Bitturumba warned, then hung up.

"Striker, I'm so glad you don't use your powers for evil," Encizo mentioned.

"Let's get to Jack and the others," Bolan said.

THORMUN BITTURUMBA HAD overstated the exhaustion of his men, but not by much. The Janjaweed soldiers had used up most of their ammunition, but even with only one clip remaining on average, it was still more than sufficient firepower to scour the big American from the face of the Earth. He had two SVD-armed snipers ready, the scopes on their rifles and the long reach of their 7.62 mm Russian cartridges enabling them to reach out and tag Bolan easily at the agreed-upon meeting location.

Bitturumba left his rifle with them, but the massive Desert Eagle was on his hip. He only had a magazine left for the big hand cannon, but he felt that if he couldn't kill one man with eight bone smashers, then he might as well give up the ghost.

"Anything funky goes up, you pour every bullet you have into that bastard Stone," Bitturumba ordered.

"And what if he's hiding behind your brother?" one of the snipers asked.

"If you scratch him, roll over on your rifle and blow your own head off," Bitturumba warned. "Suicide will be kinder than anything I'll do if I get my hands on you."

The two Thunder Lion sharpshooters nodded, nervous.

Bitturumba began his long walk. The Libya situation had been blown to smithereens, and Crusade Pharmaceuticals would undoubtedly be investigated by people with the authority to freeze his brother's assets. It was a devastating blow, but the Sudanese general knew that he had skilled pilots who could take Ammuz's transport planes and deliver them back to the safe arms of Darfur. Surrounded by Janjaweed allies armed to the teeth, he'd be untouchable.

There was still the bombshell that the American had hackers rip apart his Cayman Island banking accounts. The supposedly impenetrable and off-the-books stores of money that Bitturumba had saved up were gone, millions of dollars that he'd funded his militia with missing and in the pockets of some U.S. government agency. Bitturumba had other stashes, but nothing in comparison to the wads of cash he'd had on hand in those private bank accounts.

The Thunder Lions wouldn't starve, however. And they still had stockpiles of firepower, even with the loss of the firebase. He still had the support and blessing of other jihad leaders, warriors who thought he was one of their own. With their assistance, he would be able to regain his former position. Still, the dream of being a kingmaker in Africa was dashed beyond all hope of recovery.

Bitturumba saw Bolan walking with his beautiful little brother. He remembered when they first met at prep school in England. Their father had arranged for them to be roommates, knowing that he had sired two extraordinary young men. Cruz was a brilliant mathematician who had the ability to balance record books to hide the most blatant violations of law, and Bitturumba was a giant among his people, with brilliance and charisma that matched his powerful frame. Both young men had felt alone and incomplete in the world, but at school, they'd found a common bond that went deeper than genetics.

Cruz looked battered and weary, his cheeks covered with bruises, his dark eyes red-rimmed. Bitturumba kept himself from giving in to rage over the only person who was ever worthy of the thunder god's devotion. Women and other men had all disappointed the Sudanese giant, with Alonzo being his sole soothing relief from spiritual numbness. That Bolan had mishandled his brother threatened to drive Bitturumba into a blind rage. He clenched his fists, seeking control.

Gods were patient in their vengeance. He would go after the American again, and this time, he would assemble the world's greatest army of killers. With them at Bitturumba's direction, the man calling himself Colonel Brandon Stone would be hunted down and exterminated. American cities would burn, screams of horror and agony splitting the air as the skies reddened to the color of blood. It would be a magnificent clash, the Thunder God of Africa against the American Crusader. The death toll would be horrendous, and against such a brigade of murderers, Stone would fail.

Bitturumba smiled. Cruz looked at him, tears wetting his cheeks.

"Here's your boy," Bolan said.

Bitturumba saw Cruz stumble as the big American gave his shoulder a hard shove. The Sudanese general reached out, catching the small Spaniard in the crook of his arm. He cradled his brother gently.

"Are you all right, Lonzo?" Bitturumba asked.

"I'll live," Cruz said, shaken.

"Did he harm you?" Bitturumba pressed.

"He didn't touch me. He also told me that there was no crazy Ethiopian with a machete," Cruz added.

Bitturumba looked up.

"You'd be amazed what people will believe when they hear it on the radio," Bolan taunted. "So, you satisfied?"

Bitturumba nodded. "Walk away. When we meet again, we'll battle as equals. But this time, instead of Africa, it will be America that is shaken to the core."

"You mean like this?" Bolan asked, thumbing the firing stud on a remote detonator.

Behind him, the crack of doom resounded, and the general looked back at the gate. A blast crater vomited debris and dust into the sky, and the Thunder Lions who had been ready to rush to his aid, as well as his two snipers, had been replaced by a moaning and wailing assemblage of dying humans. Limbs had been shorn by the blast, nails embedded in torsos and faces. Bitturumba whirled, glaring at Bolan.

"I'm not about to let those murderers walk away scot-free," Bolan stated. "Any survivors will remember why they spend life with a nail lodged in one of their bones, or why they can't walk."

"You sadistic maniac," Bitturumba growled. He let go of Cruz, stepping between the Spaniard and the American.

"Right," Bolan said, stretching out the word until the tenor of the answer relayed the Executioner's disbelief of the pot calling the kettle black. "With your history of rape and murder, I'm the sadistic maniac."

Bitturumba's hand dropped to his Desert Eagle, and Bolan's did likewise. Neither man drew his sidearm, but their eyes locked.

"Going to make your move, big man?" Bolan asked.

"Don't do it, he's a demon," Cruz whispered.

"And I'm a god," Bitturumba snarled. He unbuckled his holster and tossed it aside. "Come now, Stone. You and me. You don't want to wait for my revenge?"

"I'd rather not let innocents get caught in the cross fire," Bolan replied. He let his own Desert Eagle land on the ground next to him. He drew his Beretta 93-R and dropped it beside the Magnum gun. "This way, we're still equals, roughly."

"You've been hunted by Ammuz's people on motorcycle. The desert heat has taken its toll on you, not to mention all the battles you've engaged in over the past few days. I've lead my men against the Libyans, but I didn't exert myself as fully as you have," Bitturumba boasted. "This is hardly the fair fight, the battle of titans I expected to go down between us."

Bolan shrugged. "You're the one who wanted to go primitive."

With a speed that he was certain would dazzle the big American, the general lashed out, a ham-size fist barely missing the lithe, blacksuited warrior as Bolan jerked out of the way. A powerful palm-stroke slammed into Bitturumba's sternum, knocking the wind out of him and throwing him back. The big Sudanese general realized that the intensity of the blow had been magnified by his own forward momentum, driving him into the outstretched heel of Bolan's hand. Bitturumba knew that even though his opponent was not as fresh a combatant as he was, Bolan was no fool when it came to hand-to-hand combat.

The two men circled each other, eyes locked in a stare as they tried to read each other's motives and intentions. One misstep and the winner would be able to deliver a crippling blow.

The sound of a handgun being pulled out of leather broke the pair's concentration, and the Executioner dived to the concrete. Bitturumba's Desert Eagle thundered, a fat slug sizzling into the air wild and wide of Bolan. Cruz struggled to control the monstrous handgun's recoil and take another shot at Bolan, but the big American had reached his Beretta 93-R.

"Damn it, Lonzo! Stay out!" Bitturumba bellowed. The Sudanese general dropped to the ground, tugging up the leg of his pants, revealing an ankle-holstered .45-caliber autoloader.

Bolan had two armed targets now, but since Cruz actually had his gun in hand, the Spaniard was the initial option for the warrior. The Beretta, in 3-round-burst mode, chattered, spraying a line of bloody blossoms that crawled along the middle of Cruz's face.

Bitturumba had his tiny 1911 almost in hand when he saw Cruz jerk under the brain-smashing impacts of Bolan's Beretta. *"No!"*

Bolan turned the Beretta toward the Thunder Lion general, but rage had turned the man into a living thunderbolt. Three hundred pounds of muscle ran over the Executioner like a freight train, knocking the Beretta out of Bolan's grasp. Bitturumba completely ignored the presence of the .45 Detonics Combatmaster on the ground. Bolan had managed a 3-round burst even as the general had charged, but the bullets didn't get the giant's attention. A hammering fist barely missed crushing Bolan's dodging face into paste, smashing instead into the concrete next to his head. Bitturumba lifted the ham-size paw, ignoring the jolt of agony as Bolan speared his knee into Bitturumba's testicles.

Bolan barely got his head out of the way of the second crashing fist. He clawed his knife out of his harness and jammed it up into Bitturumba's ribs, but the berserk giant grabbed the soldier by the throat and squeezed brutally. The Executioner twisted the blade in his opponent's breastbone, prying ribs apart and grinding the slashing point through the Sudanese's aorta. If the angry titan didn't die soon, the power of his massive fingers would pop Bolan's head from his shoulders.

A wrenching turn and Bolan speared the knife into Bitturumba's heart. Feral eyes glared, full of hate for the Executioner. Prying with all of his might, Bolan wrenched the 9-inch blade free from Bitturumba's rib cage, heart and lungs flopping out as if the Executioner had opened a trapdoor in Bitturumba's torso. Finally the monster pressure that threatened to tear off Bolan's head disappeared, and three hundred pounds of lifeless weight flopped on top of him.

Bolan pushed aside the corpse of the would-be tyrant, coughing to get his breath back.

He struggled to his feet and looked down at the dead conspirators. The half brothers lay side by side. It seemed fitting that the pair finally came to rest together.

Clearing his throat, he keyed his communicator.

"Jack, come pick me up. I don't want to be here holding the bag when the rest of the Libyan army comes calling."

In the desert heat, with only dead bodies around, the microbes released at Al Uwaynat would find very little to survive on. Their lifespan away from a human host was measured in minutes. By the time survivors and re-sponse teams arrived, Cruz's deadly plague would be long dead. A far more insidious infection, the conspiracy headed by Cruz and Bitturumba, had also been cleansed. It hadn't been easy, and victory had come at a cost.

But for now, the world could rest a little easier.

The Thunder Lions and their puppet masters would no longer prey upon Africa.

ROGUE ANGEL™

POLAR QUEST
by AleX Archer

When archaeologist Annja Creed agrees to help an old colleague on a dig in Antarctica, she wonders what he's gotten her into. Her former associate has found a necklace made of an unknown metal. He claims it's over 40,000 years old—and that it might not have earthly origins. As the pair conduct their research, Annja soon realizes she has more to worry about than being caught in snowslides. With no one to trust and someone out to kill her, Annja has nowhere to turn—and everything to lose.

Available January wherever books are sold.

ROGUE ANGEL™
AleX Archer
POLAR QUEST

Antarctica.
The land of snowslides,
alien artifacts and espionage

GOLD EAGLE®